As another London season commences, it's time to make note of any hushed whispers, swirling rumors and scurrilous gossip from the ballroom shadows as together we name the 1813

Society's Most Scandalous

The winner of the *ton*'s most dishonorable accolade will be published on the morning after the final ball of the season. With the infamous Fitzroys' twin daughters and niece making their long-awaited debuts, we can't wait to discover what scandal awaits!

Read Hattie Fitzroy's story in
How to Woo a Wallflower by Virginia Heath

And look for Kitty's and Annie's stories in
How to Cheat the Marriage Mart by Millie Adams
How to Survive a Scandal by Christine Merrill
Coming soon

Author Note

Who doesn't love a bit of juicy gossip? We might pretend to be above such things, but even if we would never spread a salacious rumor, we humans cannot help but listen to one with interest. Especially if it is about someone famous.

Nowadays, gossip is instant and swirls down Wi-Fi cables much faster than any newspaper could tell it, but during the Regency, print ruled. Thanks to the technological and transport changes of the industrial revolution during the eighteenth and nineteenth centuries, newspapers became mainstream, spreading all sorts of information far and wide in days rather than weeks or months as people were used to. The populace devoured them! They had never been so informed before! That is why it was the first era where gossip was king, and newspapers and scandal sheets flourished.

The Society's Most Scandalous series pays homage to that time, and I am delighted to be writing the first installment of the trilogy. I am delighted because I get to introduce you to the powerful and aristocratic Fitzroy and Claremont families, rivals from time immemorial and uneasy neighbors in Mayfair's swanky Berkeley Square. I am also delighted because I got to collaborate with two of my favorite Harlequin Historical authors—Millie Adams, who is writing the second book, and Christine Merrill, who has the final story.

We hope you enjoy our little foray into gossip and scandal...

VIRGINIA HEATH

How to Woo a Wallflower

Special thanks and acknowledgment are given to
Virginia Heath for her contribution to the
Society's Most Scandalous collection.

ISBN-13: 978-1-335-72335-2

Recycling programs
for this product may
not exist in your area.

How to Woo a Wallflower

Harlequin Enterprises ULC
22 Adelaide St. West, 41st Floor
Toronto, Ontario M5H 4E3, Canada
www.Harlequin.com

Printed in U.S.A.

When **Virginia Heath** was a little girl, it took her ages to fall asleep, so she made up stories in her head to help pass the time while she was staring at the ceiling. As she got older, the stories became more complicated—sometimes taking weeks to get to their happy ending. One day she decided to embrace her insomnia and start writing them down. Virginia lives in Essex, UK, with her wonderful husband and two teenagers. It still takes her forever to fall asleep...

Books by Virginia Heath

Harlequin Historical

His Mistletoe Wager
Redeeming the Reclusive Earl
The Scoundrel's Bartered Bride
Christmas Cinderellas
"Invitation to the Duke's Ball"

Society's Most Scandalous

How to Woo a Wallflower

A Very Village Scandal

The Earl's Inconvenient Houseguest

The Talk of the Beau Monde

The Viscount's Unconventional Lady
The Marquess Next Door
How Not to Chaperon a Lady

Secrets of a Victorian Household

Lilian and the Irresistible Duke

Visit the Author Profile page
at Harlequin.com for more titles.

For Amy Fisher.

Thank you for everything you do,
but most especially for organizing me
and being the bad cop in my stead.

Prologue

26th April 1813

My dear Lords, Ladies and Gentlemen of the ton,
    As another London Season commences it's time to make a note of any hushed whispers, swirling rumours and scurrilous gossip from the ballroom shadows as together we name the 1813 Society's Most Scandalous.
    Have your nominations delivered before the Season's closing party to The Times, *Fleet Street, London.*
    The name of the winner of the ton's most dishonourable accolade will be published, as always, on the morning after the final ball of the Season.
    This year that will be hosted by the Duke and Duchess of Avondale whose son, Lord Frederick Fitzroy, ironically won the honour last year, when he eloped to Gretna Green with Lady Dorothea Claremont, the eldest daughter of the Avondale's arch-rivals the Duke and Duchess

*of Warminster! At her betrothal ball, no less—
to another man!*

*Can this Season top that? We certainly hope so!
Yours ever in scandal,*
The Times *Society Editors*

Chapter One

Berkeley Square—May 1813

'Doing something for others is so rewarding, isn't it?'

Lady Harriet Fitzroy's mother, the Duchess of Avondale, held up her knitting to the room as if it were a thing of beauty rather than a holey, misshapen disaster. 'What a splendid idea this is! I am so glad Dr Cribbs suggested it. It is the perfect distraction to keep our nerves off the Queen's ball tomorrow night.'

A ball Hattie was quietly dreading, although she kept that to herself because she really only had herself to blame for no longer being able to dance. While all the other debutantes were twirled around the floor by dashing partners, she would have to sit on the periphery pretending she was entirely comfortable to be there. All thanks to a reckless gallop across the same fields she had ridden over her entire life.

'Launching three girls all at once is so stressful.' Her mother attempted, momentarily, to appear frazzled by it all but could not hide her delight at the prospect, as there was nothing she enjoyed more than the whirlwind of the

London social Season. Thanks to Hattie, she had missed two in a row, so she was determined the entire Fitzroy clan would make a statement this year, one which reclaimed her position as the undisputed doyenne of the glamorous elite. Nobody attended a party or threw one like the Duchess of Avondale. Everybody said so. Hattie's mother had a knack for sprinkling sparkle wherever she went and the charm to make her guests leave feeling as though they had had the most magnificent time. 'And now that all the preparations are finally done, a quiet afternoon spent with a few select friends is just the tonic to help settle my nerves before tomorrow.'

A few friends! There was an ocean of difference between her mother's definition of *a few* and Hattie's. 'Only you could turn making socks into a social occasion, Mama.'

There was nothing that rallied the ladies of the *ton* more than a good cause, and her mother was always the most enthusiastic of them all when it came to taking up the call to arms. There were baskets of wool everywhere, all freshly delivered from the expensive haberdashers in Bond Street which the Duchess favoured, and twice as many Wedgwood cups and saucers than usual lined up on the sideboard waiting for her gaggle of guests to turn up. At the last count she had officially invited twenty ladies but as there were at least thirty cups—and the poor kitchen staff were running around like headless chickens preparing what promised to be an afternoon tea for an army—it was obvious twenty was a very conservative estimate. 'Wouldn't it have been easier to simply donate all the money you have spent on this little gathering to the hospital instead?'

Doctor Cribbs, the eminent Harley Street physician

who had worked miracles to heal Hattie, had set up his charitable Ragamuffin Infirmary in Covent Garden with some of his altruistic colleagues several years ago. The infirmary helped provide medical care to the capital's many sick or injured children who could otherwise not afford it. No sooner had they helped a child and waved them goodbye, another two came through the door. It was, she now knew, a never-ending struggle which constantly needed funds, able volunteers and equipment. Hattie had become involved shortly after returning to town a month ago, when Dr Cribbs had asked her to visit so that she could inspire some of the patients in the same way as he had inspired her to recover. As she would be for ever in the good doctor's debt, she had agreed, and four weeks on the infirmary was now her second home. Partly because she enjoyed having a purpose again, but also because she knew from first-hand experience how devastating and frightening a life-changing accident could be on both the body and the mind.

'Of course it would have been simpler to donate—but where is the fun in that?' To be fair to her parents, they had parted with huge sums already for the cause, and with no fanfare at all. But then, her father preferred to keep his philanthropy private, so it was never mentioned outside of their walls.

'Besides, it kills two birds with one stone, dear.' Her mother took no offence at Hattie's comment nor made any apology for the reason for it. 'Because it gives us all the perfect opportunity to subtly catch up on all the gossip before tomorrow *and* do something good for the needy at the same time.' She admired her knitting again, clearly pleased with herself for her cleverness as well as her benevolence. 'It wouldn't do for me to turn up at the palace tomorrow uninformed when everyone expects me to always be in the know.'

Hattie rolled her eyes at her twin Annie and then at her sister-in-law Dorothea. Both were wrestling with their needles and yarn trying to master the dark art of the sock while their cousin Kitty's hands moved in a blur as they effortlessly turned a heel. She was the expert who had spent the last four days teaching them all to knit in readiness for the Duchess's impromptu Keep a Ragamuffin Warm in Winter tea party.

'Heaven forbid you relinquish your title as the Oracle of all Scandal.' Hattie stretched out her bad leg and flexed her foot. Nowadays it tended to atrophy if she stayed still too long, proving Dr Cribbs's favourite mantra that you had to work a weak limb or it would wither. Thanks to him, she had exercised her right leg so hard in the last year it worked half as well as it had before the accident—albeit with the dratted ungainly limp, which she had to accept no amount of exercise was likely to eradicate. But it was what it was and she refused to dwell on it. Walking with a limp was better than not walking, or worse, not being alive at all when she very nearly hadn't been, so she was grateful.

Her mother grinned unrepentantly, taking the comment as a compliment. 'As I keep telling you all, a woman is nothing without her reputation.'

'Your Grace.' Their butler poked his head around the door. 'The Countess of Boreham's carriage has just pulled up outside.'

Annie screwed up her face in disgust as she glared at their mother. 'Please tell me you didn't invite Lady Boreham!' Hattie glared too, in solidarity. 'Especially after her dreadful son sent Hattie that bouquet yesterday! As if my sister would ever consider that odious man as a suitor.' Both twins shuddered theatrically at the thought.

'While I sympathise and could think of nothing worse than entertaining him as a son-in-law, I had to invite her, dears. She thinks that she is one of my oldest friends.' Their mother shrugged an apology then smoothed her skirts ready to receive her first guest.

'But she's as dull as dishwater and drones on and on about her awful son ad nauseam, trying to convince one of us to marry him!' Annie was incensed now and Hattie couldn't blame her. An afternoon with either of the Borehams was a fate worse than death, but at least Lord Boreham still considered Annie out of his league. Thanks to Hattie's dratted limp, the pompous fool now thought he had a chance with her. That she would scrape the barrel and settle for him because no other man would consider her now that she was far from perfect. The gall of the man made her blood boil, even though, deep down, she also worried that he might be right.

'She does, Annie, I cannot deny, but she's harmless and, in her defence, has always been very handy with a needle so I could not, in all good conscience, exclude her. Her tapestries are exquisite so I dare say she will excel at socks too. Those who are good with their hands can usually turn them to anything.' There was no point arguing with Mother's warped logic because she had always been a law unto herself. 'And it could be worse, we could have been blessed with *his* dire company too, but I spared us all that ordeal by stating plainly in the invitation that this was a gentlemen-free occasion.' She wafted her hand in the air, smiling smugly as if they should all thank her for that small mercy. 'You are welcome, girls.'

'What is wrong with her son?' After growing up in the country, Kitty was new to society and knew practically no one yet.

'What's right with him would be a more appropriate question.' Dorothea lowered her voice in case it carried beyond the drawing room. 'Behind his back we all call him Lord Boredom.'

'Or, as I prefer to call him, Dribbling Cyril Who Talks Nothing but Drivel,' said Annie in an unsubtle whisper. 'Whatever you do, Kitty, never get trapped with him at a function. Or you'll surely perish from the sheer tedium before he allows you to escape. That is unless you don't drown in his spittle first.' Hattie's twin mimicked dodging the spray which always came from the uninspiring gentleman's mouth in abundance. 'He's been on the hunt for a bride for so many years now it's gone beyond a joke, yet he still persists and is so puffed up and so thick-skinned, he is oblivious of the reasons why he remains single. If he corners you, he will woo you with a list of all the uninspiring reasons why you would be lucky to have him. His mother is cut from the same cloth as her awful son as far as her conversation is concerned, but at least she doesn't spit.'

The sound of Lady Boreham's monotone drifted from the direction of the front door as she was relieved of her coat. 'And there is my cue to leave.' Hattie stood, wincing slightly as her right leg complained at the sudden movement, but she ignored it and forced it to fall into step behind the left. 'As much as I would love to discuss the romantic enticements of Lord Boredom with his tedious mother, I am due at the infirmary in half an hour. Doctor Cribbs has a new patient he wants me to work with.'

'How convenient.' Her mother was still put out that Hattie had chosen the infirmary over her knitting party. 'But if you must, you must.'

'I must.' Wild horses wouldn't keep her here. Aside from the dull Lady Boreham and the looming presence of her son's bouquet on the mantel, her mother had also invited their neighbours—the pious and disapproving Duchess of Warminster and her annoying daughter Lady Felicity Claremont.

The Claremonts had always quietly looked down their noses at the Fitzroys, which had been bad enough when both families had worked hard to avoid one another. Now that Hattie's brother Freddie was married to the Duke and Duchess of Warminster's eldest daughter Dorothea, politeness dictated they had to pretend to get on. 'Even if I didn't want to go, which I very much do now that I know Dribbling Cyril's mother is here, after he saved my life I owe it to Dr Cribbs to assist in whatever way I can.' Even her mother could not argue with that.

She also did not need to listen to another patronising diatribe from either the prim Felicity or her judgemental mother on how inadvisable it was for a young lady of her stature and breeding to frequent the insalubrious area of Covent Garden—even for charitable purposes. According to them, propriety dictated Hattie should better serve 'the great unwashed' from a distance as befitted her status. The Duchess of Warminster would certainly never allow one of her daughters to risk their precious reputations or their potential marriageability doing such a menial task, even properly chaperoned. Never mind that Dorothea Fitzroy née Claremont had blown her own reputation to smithereens when she had fled the last ball of last Season to run away entirely unchaperoned with Hattie's brother! An outrageous double standard the Duchess of Warminster chose to ignore.

As if she'd read her mind and knew exactly why Hattie refused to change a perfectly changeable appointment, her twin shot her a pleading glance. 'Please take me with you!' Annie dropped to her knees in prayer then shuffled on them until she grabbed Hattie's skirts. 'We are sisters! We shared a womb! Please don't leave me here and make me listen to another lecture from Dorothea's mother!'

'Well, I suppose...'

'Out of the question!' Their mother glared at Annie. 'Hattie has an excuse, albeit a flimsy one.' She narrowed her eyes at her eldest by just a few minutes because the Duchess of Avondale was not easily fooled. '*You* do not! And if you continue to protest, young lady, I shall be sure to tell Lord Boredom you were disappointed not to receive his flowers too and then insist he pencils his name on your dance card tomorrow as compensation!'

Hattie laughed as she waved them all a cheery goodbye and slipped out of the servants' door at precisely the same moment Lady Boreham stepped into the drawing room, and at the exact same time as the disapproving Duchess of Warminster's voice could be heard at the front door.

St Martin's Lane was blocked at its junction with Long Acre, and by the sounds of the raised voices up ahead and the line of stationary carriages both in front and behind his, it was likely to remain so for quite some time. Jasper, the Earl of Beaufort suspected that it would be quicker to walk the short distance which remained to Covent Garden rather than sit in his carriage and waste more time twiddling his thumbs waiting. After two solid days on the road, he was sick of the sight of these confining four walls, and sicker still of sitting down. Not for the first time, he lamented taking the blasted Battlesbridge carriage in the first place when he knew it would have been faster on horseback and he wished he had ignored his mother's pleas over the dangers of travelling all that way alone as he usually did. However, because he had once again failed to rebuild the bridges between him and his estranged father despite a long month of trying, he had caved in and agreed to the mind-numbing safety of the Duke's much slower carriage for the sake of a quiet life.

One whole wasted month! His longest annual visit home yet in seven years and, typically, a pointless waste of his time. It made no difference that without Jasper's ever-increasing financial contributions the estate would have long ago gone bankrupt, his ailing but still resolutely curmudgeonly sire would still never forgive him for bringing the ancient and noble house of Battlesbridge into disrepute. Although how making a generous living from owning a gentlemen's club was more disreputable than mouldering away in a debtor's prison was beyond Jasper. However, for some inexplicable reason, the more successful The Reprobates' Club became, the more the Duke took issue with it. Which was ironic when one considered that without it, by now, there would likely be no food on his father's table and an exceedingly leaky roof over his stubborn old head.

Yet, despite much biting of his tongue and more diplomacy than he had believed himself capable of, Jasper still managed to leave under a cloud. Instead of building bridges in the two extra weeks his poor mother had begged him to remain for, the only thing he had achieved was widening the chasm between him and his father further. Bitter experience had already told him it would be pointless.

As always, he should have listened to his head and come home sooner. It would have saved him the effort of having his offers to help with the management of the estate thrown back in his face and hearing the tired old diatribe that the only way Jasper would get his greedy hands on any of the Battlesbridge lands or accounts was when he prised them out of the Duke's cold dead fingers.

As if Jasper needed the money! Nowadays, thanks to a lot of hard work and his canny talent for business, he was positively swimming in the stuff—but to the Duke he would always be a useless wastrel who had quit Oxford to start a shameful gaming hell where he could sin with impunity. It made no difference that The Reprobates' was an honest and above board establishment which fell well shy of despicable, that Jasper worked, not sinned, there for at least eight solid hours every single day and that if he hadn't quit university to start the business in the first place, then his ungrateful father would be living under a bridge.

More annoyed with his father's entrenched short-sightedness than the stationary carriage, Jasper lowered the window as a disgruntled pie seller marched past muttering under his breath. 'What's happened?'

'A drover's cart has lost its load and there are broken barrels of bleedin' ale everywhere.'

An answer which confirmed all Jasper's worst suspicions. If he didn't walk, he'd be trapped here for goodness knew how long, so he grabbed the door handle and alighted.

'As soon as you can turn around, take my luggage to the house.' Covent Garden was only ever meant to be a brief stop while he checked everything was as all right at The Reprobates' Club as his business partner had assured him in his letters. Then he fully intended to wend his weary way home to his fancy new house in Russell Square and the hot bath he had been fantasising about for hours.

'Let my housekeeper know that I shan't be long. I will walk back.'

The coachman nodded and then briskly forgot about him to assess the road behind trying to decide the best route out of the chaos, clearly relieved to have escaped the chore. Jasper couldn't blame him. After his torturous and volatile extended stay at the ancestral estate, he craved the ordered peace of home.

Jasper watched his father's carriage set off and decided to let all his anger go back to Battlesbridge with it. He took a few moments to scan the road ahead of himself, before setting off, wondering if it might make more sense to cut through New Street and the back alleys to shave off a few minutes if the most direct route turned out to be impassable to pedestrians too. He had barely marched thirty feet when a feminine voice stopped him in his tracks.

'Jasper?' He hadn't noticed the Avondale crest when he had passed the carriage, so the sight of one of his best friend's baby sisters smiling at him through the open window came as a surprise. More surprising was that, for some inexplicable reason, the smile he could never remember noticing before today, suddenly took his breath away.

Chapter Two

'Hattie? Good heavens above!' He hadn't seen her in what must have been close to two years. Not since the Easter before she had had her accident. 'Fancy seeing you here?' Genteel ladies only usually ventured into the colourful environs of Covent Garden at night to visit the theatre, and then they did so with a battalion of chaperons rather than the solitary maid who was seated dutifully beside her.

'I was about to ask the same thing but seeing as we are a stone's throw away from it, I assume you are bound for your scandalous club?' He could not recall ever really having a substantial conversation with Hattie, so hearing her ask him a direct question, her confident gaze unwavering, was odd when she had always blinked at him like a startled deer in the past.

'I am indeed.' He found himself drawn to her carriage window. Found himself suddenly intrigued by the stark changes in her and willing to linger. 'I have a month's worth of dreary accounts to catch up on. But what brings you to this neck of the woods?'

'I have been volunteering at the infirmary.'

'The Ragamuffin Infirmary on King Street?'

'The very one.' Hattie beamed, and that transformed her face from pretty to downright beautiful. When had that happened? 'Within spitting distance of the daily debauchery of your club, which propriety dictates I shouldn't find entertaining—but which of course I do. The Reprobates' Club always lives up to its shocking name.'

Which was also the secret to its huge popular appeal. Where Brooks's was staid and White's erred on the side of the traditional, and the depravity of the hells was too much for most, Jasper's club filled the gap in between. It was naughty and frivolous rather than sordid. A place for fun, gambling and raucousness which allowed its wealthy patrons to blow off harmless steam in the lap of luxury they were accustomed to.

'Doctor Cribbs is a saint. One who lives piously among us sinners and puts us all to shame with his benevolence.' He never apologised to anyone for owning The Reprobates' or its outrageous reputation. Why would he when that establishment had saved him and so many others from poverty?

She nodded, obvious affection in her expression for the man. 'And Dr Cribbs is a genius. The miracles he works on those children are quite astounding.'

And talking of miracles…

'How are you keeping…nowadays?' His eyes flicked to her legs without thinking and he winced, wondering if he should have asked. Her brother Freddie had kept him informed of her progress throughout her extended convalescence at the family estate, so he knew Lady Harriet Fitzroy was no longer what she was. Hardly a surprise when the riding accident had been horrific, crippling one leg as well as breaking a wrist and two ribs. One of which had punctured a lung. For weeks afterwards she had fought for her life, battling an infection, and then defying all the odds. Hell, she'd even been given the last rites twice, so it really was a miracle she was sat in this carriage at all. Yet here she was, back in town, out and about independently and volunteering no less—no mean feat when one considered the mountain she had had to climb.

'I am in very good health, thank you for asking.' She smiled but did not elaborate further, clearly reluctant to bring up her struggles even to an old family friend. 'It has been for ever since we last collided, hasn't it, Jasper?' A decisive change of subject if ever there was one, so he happily took the bait. He was a great believer in pride, even if it did often come before a fall. Pride did not only save face. It kept you going no matter what. Gave you the determination to succeed against all the odds. It put steel in your spine. Forced you to stand and fight when all you wanted to do was curl into a ball in defeat.

'Indeed. Yes. If memory serves it has to be at least two springs ago.' A time during which he had, in the main, lived his life to the fullest how he pleased while she had fought tooth and nail to get hers back. He had no idea why he suddenly felt guilty at that distinction, but he did. Probably because he had a tendency to feel guilty about everything. 'I believe the last time we collided was at Avondale Hall for your mother's house party. She had invited everyone on the planet, as I recall, certainly all the soon-to-be eager debutantes of the 1811 Season.' What was the matter with him! The 1811 Season was supposed to have been her Season too—until the accident had scuppered things within days of that party.

She had been eager then too, he remembered, although not quite as excited about her debut as her more vivacious twin who was chomping at the bit to take society by storm. But then again, she and Annie had never been anything alike in either looks or character. Up against Annie, Hattie had always faded into the background. The other Fitzroy daughter had always been the prettier of the two with her dark hair and perfectly proportioned features. Everyone could see from an early age that Annie was destined to be a great beauty. Even when the twins were twelve, when Jasper had first met Freddie's family, that had been patently obvious.

Whereas Hattie had been almost as awkward as an eighteen-year-old prospective debutante as she had been at twelve, more comfortable in the great outdoors racing her horse across her father's country estate or climbing the hills which surrounded it. Happier shooting targets with her brother than she had ever been discussing the more genteel feminine pursuits among her peers. A skinny, gangly girl with unremarkable dark blonde hair who was yet to grow into her features.

Looking at her face and what he could see of her figure now through the window—and all credit to Mother Nature—she had done that magnificently since he had last seen her. The adolescent, gawky angles had rounded in the most delightful and womanly way. The mouth which had seemed too large was plump and ripe; the shy, often startled, big blue eyes now held his with unmistakable intelligence and a new confidence which hadn't been there before. A confidence which surprised him in view of her circumstances.

'Those girls were quite brazen in their pursuit of the eligible bachelors in attendance as I remember it, despite their tender years. I was staggered at the unashamed boldness of a few of them.' She chuckled at the recollection. 'Their mothers weren't much better.'

'Oh, they were the worst! Be in no doubt. The lengths some of those matrons went to in their attempts to make me their son-in-law that weekend beggared belief!'

Hattie threw her head back and laughed at that. Not the customary, repressed tinkling laugh he was used to hearing from gently bred young ladies who were careful to always look demure and pretty, but the genuine, unabashed and unselfconscious sort. 'What did you expect? Three single, wealthy and titled gentlemen all trapped under one roof in the middle of nowhere for four whole days was all their wildest dreams come true. You were a captive audience.'

'We were sitting ducks.'

'You were.' The flash of sympathy dissolved into another earthy chuckle. 'They really wouldn't leave you or Freddie or George Claremont alone.' She leaned on the window frame grinning. It made her eyes sparkle in the most addictive fashion. 'I found that irony so hilarious I might have encouraged them a tiny bit to be more intrepid.' She held her index finger and thumb an inch apart. 'Perhaps a little more than that.'

'You encouraged them!' Jasper made an unconvincing effort to look offended. 'I never realised you had such a mean streak.'

Probably because Hattie, like the rest of those determined debutantes, had seemed so young back then. Beneath his notice. Slips of girls. Silly children with silly lives which he couldn't be bothered with because he had more important things on his mind—like earning a crust and building his business while behaving, at least on the surface, like the reprobate his club had been named after.

'The three of you used to lock yourselves in the billiards room for fear of being caught in a compromising position. Even then you all had such shocking reputations and were already confirmed scandalous reprobates, yet there you all were, quaking in your boots and gripping your billiard cues like weapons, in genuine fear of being ruined.'

'Until they found us in the billiards room and laid siege, thanks to your evil sister giving them the housekeeper's keys.'

She laughed again and he heard it like a man, enjoying the silky way it caressed his nerve endings. 'As confession is supposed to be good for the soul, I should probably tell you that it actually had nothing to do with Annie.'

'It was you!'

'What can I say? Lydia Rycart offered me five shillings for the keys.'

'You sold me and your own brother down the river for five paltry shillings?' Jasper liked this hitherto unseen but mischievous side of Hattie. A side which clearly had always been there beneath the shyness.

'I am all for gripping life by the lapels, and when a ripe opportunity presents itself, only a fool wouldn't seize it.'

'But you gripped those lapels for five measly shillings, Hattie, when I would have paid you ten to keep them away. I still have nightmares about that weekend.' He shuddered for effect, enjoying the way amusement made her bright blue eyes dance. 'And about debutantes in general, for that matter.'

'I cannot say I blame you for that as most have fluff for brains and those that don't are, by and large, a mercenary lot. All chasing after the eligible gentlemen like hunters after a fox. All prepared to do anything to claim the kill.'

That was a fitting analogy. 'Which is why this fox tries to avoid them like the plague nowadays—except when I get a royal summons from the Duchess of Avondale herself, of course. Demanding my attendance to the first ball of the Season and riding roughshod over all my excuses because she was launching *her* girls. *Her girls* was underlined in all four of her letters, so I didn't dare argue. But I should like it noted that I wanted to. No contented bachelor should have to be subjected to the Season. At least not if he wants to remain a contented bachelor. If I end up caught in the parson's trap on the back of it, it will be your mother's fault and there will be hell to pay.'

'I am sure you will find ample ways to avoid it, Jasper, as you always do. Your shocking reputation alone should go some way to protecting you.'

'Because that worked so well for your brother last year, didn't it?'

'Freddie threw himself willingly into the parson's trap, as well you know. He and Dorothea are sickeningly happy.' She screwed up her face as if she found that happiness a puzzle. 'Worse, it's made my mother more determined to see the rest of her brood happily married off with all haste, hence she is so obsessed with our debuts and cannot fathom why I am not as excited by it as she is.'

'Your mother is a romantic.' Everyone knew the Duchess had married her Duke for love. 'One who views the marriage mart through rose-tinted spectacles.'

Hattie scoffed at that. 'The lenses in mine are blessedly clear and I have low expectations of finding a soul mate in the stuffy ballrooms of Mayfair. But as Annie has longed for her first Season, I am trying to pretend I am looking forward to it too—for her sake. It is the least I can do after I ruined her first Season.'

'How has the experience been this second time around?' Something told Jasper he should find a way to address her accident specifically rather than keep skirting around it while it lingered unsaid in the air between them, but he couldn't quite find the right words to address it politely when she seemed so determined to avoid it.

'Much the same as the first—only worse because my mother is on a mission to do it bigger, better and grander than she had originally planned.'

'It sounds exhausting.'

She wafted a hand in front of her face for comic effect, and he liked that she did not take herself too seriously. 'I am quite worn out, but my mother is in her element.'

'If I know your mother, she is loving every second of it.' The Duchess of Avondale was a legendary hostess and society guest. Effervescent, charming and fun. He could imagine her plotting, planning and scheming behind the scenes in preparation because he had witnessed it in action the first time around. Everything would have to be just so. Everyone committed to the cause. Absolutely everyone would have to be in attendance to witness the triumph too—hence he had been summoned with specific instructions to flirt with all three of her girls shamelessly and fill up their dance cards to make all the other young bucks jealous. All part of her carefully constructed master plan to ensure the Fitzroy girls were the undisputed diamonds of the Season—even if they were much older gems than tradition dictated.

Hattie shook her head in exasperation. 'Since our return to town the last few weeks have been a never-ending maelstrom of nonsense, and the last few days little better than organised chaos. It is a relief to have an excuse to escape for the afternoon—although I seem to have inadvertently discovered more chaos in the process.' She frowned as she gestured down the road towards the blockage where tempers were audibly becoming frayed. 'I have been deliberating whether or not it would be quicker to walk to the hospital.'

He wanted to ask if she was capable of a five-minute walk, but didn't, respecting her pride by assuming she wouldn't have brought it up if she couldn't. 'As I have abandoned my own conveyance in favour of Shanks's pony, I would be delighted to escort you seeing as we are headed the same way. That is if you do not fear what being seen with a scandalous reprobate like me will do to your reputation?'

She laughed that away and allowed him to help her out of her carriage. Because it felt appropriate given her injuries, he offered her his arm and pretended not to notice how heavily Hattie leaned on it while her concerned maid lingered a short distance behind. The first few steps were obviously difficult for her. The limp more pronounced than he had been prepared for, but she covered her pain with breezy small talk about her dreaded debut, making his heart simultaneously bleed for her for all she had lost and swell with pride at her resilience and tenacity. The intensely physical and competitive sportswoman he knew of old might be gone, yet there appeared to be no trace of bitterness in her character nor self-pity in her manner.

'If I never have to visit the modiste's again, it will be too soon.' After a few minutes her gait was more assured and the pressure of her hand in the crook of his elbow lessened. Even the taut pull of stress had disappeared from her features as her muscles warmed to the task.

'You never know, you might enjoy it all once it starts.'

She blinked at him as if he were mad. 'It is difficult to feel enthused about taking up my place among the wallflowers.' Her expression was wistful. Accepting, and that bothered him.

Jasper stopped and stared at her in mock outrage that she would suggest such a thing. 'You shan't be a wallflower, Hattie.' The mere thought was inconceivable. 'Your dance card will be so full I doubt there would be space for me to scratch my name on it. In fact, I shall invoke our long connection to insist you reserve me a dance in advance. I want the first waltz.' An impertinent request which tumbled out before he could stop it.

'That is very decent of you to offer—even if it was done out of obligation—but I am afraid I shall have to politely decline.'

'It wasn't done out of obligation.' The truth, although he couldn't even explain to himself why. 'I asked because I would be honoured if you would dance with me.' Another new and unexpected truth he could not quite believe he was admitting to, so he made a joke out of it in case she noticed. 'That I would also be making all your suitors green with envy has only the smallest bearing on the request.' It was his turn to hold his finger and thumb an inch apart. 'Everyone knows that Jasper Beaufort always snags the most perfect partners wherever he goes and that makes my rivals furious.'

Her smile this time did not touch her eyes. 'And yet still I must politely decline.'

The disappointment was instant. 'Because you *do* fear for your reputation after all or because you have already promised the waltz to someone else?' The flash of jealousy came out of nowhere, but he managed to cover it with a conspiratorial wink.

'Because I can't, Jasper.'

For the briefest moment, her light seemed to dull, before she banished it with a matter-of-fact shrug.

'I physically can't.'

Chapter Three

He was embarrassed by her admission, she could tell, and Hattie hated that she had managed to turn a perfectly pleasant conversation into stilted awkwardness when that had certainly not been her intention. Especially as it was the first proper conversation she and Jasper had ever had.

Growing up, she had always been intimidated by her brother's handsome and charming friend. As well as more than a little enamoured by him too. Enough that she hadn't been able to hide her girlish crush from her more confident but intuitive twin, who had teased her mercilessly about her attraction for years. Consequently, whenever their paths had collided, she had been a tongue-tied, stuttering, blushing mess. Not helped by the baffled looks of sheer bewilderment he had always regarded her with whenever she had tripped over her own words on the rare occasions he'd attempted to converse with her.

She wasn't that bumbling girl any longer. After everything she had been through, those cringing interactions with him now seemed like a lifetime away. Two lifetimes in fact. That things were back to being awkward was more the fault of her own misplaced vanity than his thoughtlessness, and all because she had wanted him to see the confident and feisty incarnation of herself she had always been—with everyone except him.

Such awkwardness was pointless now, especially as she no longer regarded Lord Beaufort as if the sun rose and set with him. She was long over that silly crush and even if she was still a little enamoured of his chiselled good looks and likeable nature, she knew too much about him to want to know him any better than as an entertaining acquaintance. Especially as Jasper was the *most* gossiped about person of her acquaintance. The swirling rumours of his exploits, affairs and scandals were legendary, casting her brother's questionable past into the shade, and he was unapologetic and open about all of it.

Even if Hattie was on the lookout for a husband, which she very much wasn't for obvious reasons, only an idiot would set her cap at such a scoundrel and she had never been daft. She needed a man who adored her for what she was and considered looks unimportant, not one with a famously wandering eye. Not that Jasper's discerning eye was likely to wander her way lustfully anyway. As he had rightly just pointed out, he always snagged the most perfect partners wherever he went, and with the minimum effort too, as they threw themselves at him—and she wasn't perfect any more. Therefore, it was ridiculous to try to maintain the vain façade that she was.

'I am so sorry Hattie...that was thoughtless of me... I...um...should have realised before I...well...put my big, fat foot in it.'

'Please do not feel sorry for me, Jasper Beaufort, don't you dare!' She stared towards where they were headed rather than witness the pity in his unusual green eyes. 'For I can assure you that I am at peace with it.' Which she was—up to a point. There were some aspects, like the hideous state of her leg, which she would likely never come to terms with, but she had accepted what was and had worked hard to carve out a new existence which made her happy.

Hattie loathed all the pity more than she loathed the jagged scars on her shin.

So much had been sent her way since the family had returned to town for the Season, she was suffocated by it. Offended by it. The assumptions, the judgements, the well-meant condolences as if her life were over and all she could expect between now and meeting her maker was to march empty time on the outskirts. Poor, limping Lady Harriet. All her dreams crushed, and her prospects shrivelled. For who would want her now if she wasn't the daughter of a duke? At least she still had that, thank goodness, so perhaps something would turn up.

Although to his credit, Jasper had just talked to her as if she were normal, and that had seduced her into wanting to appear normal in return. That she wasn't, was hardly his fault. 'Earlier, you asked how I was doing...' As much as she hated thinking about her dratted leg, let alone talking about it, she owed him an honest answer. 'As you can see, thanks to Dr Cribb's timely and miraculous intervention, I can now walk well enough, albeit at a snail's pace. But because the bone initially healed badly that has left its mark, so I fear dancing will always be beyond me.' She risked glancing at him and hated the way his dark brows furrowed in sympathy.

'I am so sorry, Hattie.'

'I am not.' She straightened her shoulders as she stuck out her chin, quickening her pace to prove she wasn't the least bit broken by her situation. 'For it turns out having one leg several inches shorter is decidedly more preferable than pushing up the daisies, and that was my alternative. I would choose being a wonky wallflower over a corpse any day.'

He was silent as they turned on to King Street, searching for the right words when there weren't any, but she appreciated that he tried to find them to make her feel better. In the absence of any herself, Hattie decided to deflect in the only way she knew how.

With humour.

'If I were you, I would take a moment to appreciate the irony of my situation. Wrongdoers should always get their comeuppance and fate has dealt me, and by default you, the most beautiful hand as revenge for those five shillings.'

Confusion played across his perfectly proportioned features. Confusion and outrage that she thought he was that shallow. When those emotions went to war with his ingrained politeness, and he gaped like a fish scrambling for a suitable response, she had to laugh.

'Don't you see? Now I am the sitting duck. I might be a wonky wallflower, but I am still a wealthy duke's daughter who cannot use the next dance as a valid excuse to escape the crush of fortune hunters and dead losses who will be swarming around me like flies. One who might well have to borrow your billiards cue tomorrow night to fight them all off because I have already been receiving bouquets from the most determined.' She clutched her cheeks in mock horror. 'And one of them was from Lord Boredom!'

'Oh, dear.' Cautious amusement crinkled the corners of his eyes at the mention of the single most tedious bachelor of the *ton*. 'Poor you.'

'Poor me indeed as I am not even fast enough to dart away if he spies me! I shall be trapped. Cornered. A captive audience. And likely the only woman in the room who has no choice but to talk to him while everyone else is being twirled on the dance floor. It is almost a fate worse than death.' She gripped his arm, trying to ignore how solid it felt beneath her fingers and stared up at him pleading. 'I know I have a cheek asking this, after I betrayed you for five measly shillings, but if you are inclined to feel some pity for me for all the trials and tribulations I have recently suffered...' She batted her eyelashes far too rapidly to seduce a soul. 'In lieu of that dance you asked for but I cannot grant you, I would very much appreciate being saved from him tomorrow at the ball, Jasper.'

'I don't know...' His teasing tone was back, thank goodness, and the expression of pity gone as they paused in the middle of the road between the infirmary and his club. 'After your hideous treachery, I am not sure that a Judas like you deserves such charity—'

'Jasper? Lord Beaufort?' A dour, grey-haired man in a tall hat seemed to appear out of nowhere at her escort's elbow. When Jasper nodded the fellow inclined his head. 'I am Mr Leonard Pitt from the law firm of Mayhew, Reynolds and Pitt of Cookham.'

'It is nice to finally meet you Mr Pitt.' Her companion held out his hand, smiling at the introduction as if he was aware of the company, at least. But when the smile wasn't returned as the gentleman shook his with an expression of foreboding, it slipped from Jasper's handsome face in instant concern.

'I only wish it was under more pleasant circumstances, my lord. As you will know from my letter of last week…'

'I am afraid you have me at a disadvantage, sir, as I have been out of town for some weeks and have only just returned.'

'Ah…well. That makes things more awkward.' The solicitor pulled a thick envelope from his leather satchel and passed it to Jasper. 'It is my grave but solemn duty to pass over to you these deeds and documents as instructed in the last will and testament of Cora Marlow—' All the colour seemed to bleach out of Jasper's face at this news.

'Cora's dead?'

'I am afraid so, my lord.' Suddenly even more uncomfortable, the solicitor's complexion also paled as he shuffled from foot to foot. 'And as instructed by the deceased, it is also my duty to ensure the safe delivery of an…um…' his eyes flicked to Hattie and he winced '…of one of your belongings.' He jerked his thumb towards the carriage parked outside the club. 'But as this is a conversation of the most delicate nature, perhaps…' The curtains in the carriage twitched then and a small, ashen face appeared between them.

Whoever the little girl was Jasper dashed towards her. The moment he pulled open the carriage door, she stretched out her hands and he took her, cuddling her close with the air of a man used to dealing with a child. 'Oh, Izzy…' He kissed the child's dark curls with obvious affection. 'My poor darling.'

'Strangers keep telling me that Mama has gone to the angels.' The little girl burrowed into his coat and Hattie's heart broke for her. She couldn't be more than four or five. Not that there was ever a right age to lose a mother, that was tragically young. 'When is she coming back?'

'She isn't, poppet...' He stroked her dark hair, almost the exact shade as his, his voice choked. 'But you still have me.' He cocooned her as she wept, and as if in a trance turned away from everyone without another word to carry the child into his club. Mr Pitt scurried to follow, and the heavy door closed with a decisive thud behind them.

Chapter Four

Jasper stared at the missive in his hand in disbelief. Not only because it appeared that Cora—the indomitable, maddening and vivacious woman he had known for most of his life—was gone, but because her last request was that he honour his promise to bring up little Izzy in her absence.

They had briefly discussed this awful eventuality once.

Just once, in passing, during a morbid and philosophical late-night discussion on the transience of life after one of the doormen at The Reprobates' Club had unexpectedly keeled over and died. He had been a well-liked and robust fellow in his prime, and the death a shock to all of them in the early days of the club's existence when every employee had felt like family. Cora had been expecting Isabel at the time, was due any day, so perhaps had felt the fear of her own mortality more keenly than he had.

He recalled that she had been so distressed at the thought of not always being there for the child inside her that he had happily given his word to step up if the need arose. Of course he would. Because that was the honourable and decent thing to do, especially after he had let her down so grievously before.

At the time, and quite aside from the guilt he carried that she was with child in the first place, it had been an easy promise to make. He and Cora were both young, fit and filled with health and vitality, so he had no reason to think he would ever have to come good on it.

As neither had ever mentioned it again, and she and Izzy had settled comfortably in the life he'd provided for them in the country, that promise became one of those things which naturally went to the back of his mind. Something hazy and improbable, so not really worth any serious deliberation in the grand scheme of things. But there was no getting away from the fact that he had to deliberate on it seriously now, because there was a woman in the ground holding him to account and a grieving little girl finally sleeping beside him on the sofa who didn't have another soul on the planet she could count on bar him. The rest of her family were long gone and his family…well, there wasn't a cat's chance in hell his father would take her in no matter how much common decency dictated that he should.

Which meant he either shipped Izzy off to paid strangers to take care of her out of sight—a cowardly but neat option that made him feel queasy for more reasons than breaking his promise—or he carried out Cora's final wishes, exactly as she had laid out in her letter. No matter what the scandal or the consequences.

As it had at least a hundred times since he had first read it, his gaze focussed on just two sentences. The spidery, shakily written words piercing his heart and stabbing at his conscience.

*You once swore on your life that you would never
let me down again, Jasper, so I am begging you
not to do so this time. Keep our precious cherub
with you always as you promised so that I may
rest in peace.*

He knew already neither his conscience nor his heart
could do otherwise. Aside from the fact that he *had*
sworn on his life to never let Cora down again, he had
adored little Izzy since the moment she had been born.
The second he had held her as a squalling infant and
her limpid big green eyes had locked with his, he had
known he would do anything for her—even this.

Even this.

'I've made up a pallet in the room next to yours.' His
housekeeper Mrs Mimms spoke in a whisper as she entered the drawing room so as not to wake the child, her
eyes flicking to Izzy with both sympathy and undisguised interest because he had yet to explain her. 'Of
course, I'd have made up a bed if you'd bothered to get
some furniture for all those spare rooms you have upstairs—as I keep saying.'

'Well now you have an excuse to buy a bed and whatever furniture you think fit for a little girl's bedroom.'

'She's staying then?'

Jasper nodded.

'For how long?'

'For ever.' He swallowed at the gravitas of that answer. The implications. The huge responsibility which
he was nowhere near ready for and ill equipped to deal
with. The impending scandal which genuinely did not
bear thinking about when he and her mother had been
a huge scandal once before.

His housekeeper was silent for several moments before she inhaled, no-nonsense yet sympathetic despite her predictable disapproval. 'Then if I might be so bold, you are going to be needing more than a bit more than furniture to raise your daughter properly.' Because obviously she had been listening at the keyhole as the solicitor had read Cora's will. 'But I suppose a proper bed is a start for now.'

'Have you ever heard of somebody called Cora Marlow?' Hattie's nonchalant question over the dinner table had quite a profound effect on her brother Freddie, who almost choked on a boiled potato.

He coughed into his napkin then frowned. 'She isn't someone you should concern yourself with.' His eyes flicked to their father's in one of those unspoken messages which men shared whenever they felt a topic was unsuitable for the ladies present. Then he shot a different sort of look at their mother. 'This, Mama, is exactly why I disapprove of Hattie going to Covent Garden every day. Didn't I warn you that she was bound to see and hear things which an innocent young lady shouldn't?'

Hattie and Annie huffed in unison at his well-intentioned overprotectiveness—an annoying trait their big brother had always had but which had become unbearable ever since Hattie's accident. For reasons best known to himself, Freddie blamed himself for not being there to stop it, which was ludicrous when she had been galloping across their father's fields in Surrey alone almost since the day she had learned to ride. His *neglect* had never bothered him—until the day she failed to return—and no amount of rational argument now seemed to convince him that she wasn't made of glass.

'Oh, pish, dear,' said her mother with a regal flick of her wrist and a supportive smile towards Hattie. At least she understood that her daughter was keen to put what had happened behind her. 'The legendary but infamous Cora Marlow is still the subject of society gossip all these years on so Hattie could just as easily have heard it in the middle of Mayfair as she could have in Covent Garden. In fact, now that your sisters and Kitty are coming out, I suspect they'll hear all manner of salacious gossip whispered behind fans.' She beamed at her girls. 'The gossip is one of the best parts of coming out. It runs rife through the debutantes like a forest fire in a hot summer. Just be sure to share it with me if it is particularly titillating. You know how much I love to be in the know.'

With Freddie's concerns suitably defused, Hattie pushed some more, mindful that if she blurted out everything she had witnessed earlier, Freddie would likely overreact. While Jasper was his friend, he still had an atrocious reputation, and her brother was almost as obsessed with his sisters' reputations as he was with their safety. To him, every gentleman below the age of forty was a potential despoiler and he had taken to watching them all like hawks when they were around his family as if he expected trouble.

That aside, something told her to play her cards close to her chest not just for her own sanity's sake—but for Jasper's. He had been nothing but kind to her earlier, treating her like a normal person rather than an object of pity, so it did not feel right to use what was undoubtedly a tragedy of some sort for him as fodder for gossip. And if it was juicy gossip, she would much rather someone else be the one to spread it as that didn't sit right with her either. Especially as she herself was now at the sharp end of it, albeit for entirely different reasons.

'As that door swings both ways Mama, will you kindly tell me what was so scandalous about Cora that my idiot big brother's eyes are now bulging?' Just because Freddie was an overprotective prude now that he was married, did not mean that Hattie would allow her question to go unanswered. She had been worried sick about Jasper all afternoon. Worried sick and beyond curious. 'Only I overheard while doing my daily exercise in Hyde Park earlier—' she glared pointedly at her brother as she told the lie simply to prove him wrong '—that she had died.'

'*No!*' As Freddie's eyes widened in shock, her mother's filled with sympathy. 'Dead? Really? How tragic. She was so young, too, around your brother's age I believe. Isn't that right, Freddie?'

'I believe so.' At least he conceded that titbit. Verbally at least. His expression told her more because the initial shock was replaced by concern for his friend. As if he knew Cora had meant something significant to Jasper. 'I was in my last year at Oxford, so cannot say that I knew her as anything more than a passing acquaintance.' He sounded cordial and accommodating but was staring intently at his plate, chasing around a pea, a sure sign that he knew much more than he was prepared to let on.

'I never met her as we moved in *very* different circles.' Her mother frowned briefly as she wafted her fork. 'Although I did see her once. Fleetingly through the carriage window one evening as your father and I were leaving the opera. She was as beautiful as all the rumours suggested, so it is hardly a surprise she had such a profound effect on the male of the species. In fact, it was your father who pointed her out, with uncustomary awe and wonder as I recall, so I suspect she also affected him.' She winked at him across the table and her husband chuckled.

'You know I have only ever had eyes for you, Eleanor.'

'Maybe so—but those eyes still work, darling, and you'd have had to be blind not to notice how striking she was.'

Hattie's papa acknowledged that comment with a nod. 'True. She was stunning.' Then he winked at his wife. 'Not as stunning as you, my dear, of course.'

Their mother blew him a kiss, not the least bit offended. 'She also apparently had a charming way about her too, which I suppose only added to her appeal. Along with that air of mystery because none of us knew where she came from, so those were three irresistible things in her favour. Few men can resist a mysterious and seductive siren.'

'All very interesting, Mama, but I am still none the wiser as to who Cora Marlow actually was.'

'A courtesan.' Annie's matter-of-fact response earned her a disapproving stare from Freddie. 'Oh, for goodness sake, Freddie, if you think Hattie, Kitty and I do not know what a courtesan is then you are thicker than I thought. If Mama is prepared to acknowledge Papa has *eyes*, then you should acknowledge that your *delicate* womenfolk all have perfectly working ears. And Mama is right, the gossip I have been privy to in the last few weeks has been fascinating.'

She turned to Hattie conspiratorially then, ignoring their brother completely. 'According to Lydia Rycart, back in the murky days of yore—and by that I mean when our stick-in-the-mud brother was our age—Cora Marlow was the most lauded courtesan in the capital. She worked as a hostess at The Reprobates' Club and apparently all the men wanted her.'

'She worked for Jasper?' That explained the connection. Sort of. But not the obvious grief she had seen in his expression when he had heard the bad news, any more than it explained who the little girl was and why he had such a palpable bond with her. But vocalising that would mean admitting that she had strolled to Covent Garden today on Jasper's arm. An admission which, in his current irrational mood, would send her brother into a rage and get her banned from visiting the infirmary ever again without an armed guard.

'Not just worked for him, if you catch my drift.' Annie tapped her nose while Freddie looked about ready to combust. 'She and he were…you know…' She wiggled her dark eyebrows suggestively.

'Lovers?'

Freddie lost his temper at Hattie's comment, his cutlery clattering against the table as he slammed it down. 'That most definitely is not appropriate conversation for the dinner table!'

'Knowing what the word means and experiencing it with the same level of enthusiasm as you did at their age are two very different things, Freddie, I can assure you.' Amused at her husband's prudish reaction, Dorothea laughed. 'So do sit down and stop spouting steam at the recounting of a bit of old gossip. It makes you a hypocrite when we all know you used to be the source of so much of it.'

'Hear, hear,' said Annie toasting their sister-in-law with her water glass. 'Kitty has been living with us for months and despite all my best efforts, I still haven't managed to tell her the half of it.'

'We're still only up to his university days,' offered Kitty with a mischievous smile, 'and that has been bad enough. I cannot wait to hear about his misspent bachelorhood at the Albany.'

'There was one time at Almack's…' Before Annie launched into a story which veered the dinner conversation on a different path, Hattie held up her hand.

'Can we return to the shameful escapades of our sainted big brother after we've exhausted the topic of Cora Marlow? I am still none the wiser as to why she was infamous beyond the fact that she had an affair with Jasper.'

'Oh, it was so much more than an affair, dear. As I understand it,' the Duchess of Avondale continued the story without skipping a beat, 'Jasper was so besotted with her, he would hit the roof if any other man dared flirt with her. In fact, there were rumours of the threat of pistols at dawn when one randy buck chanced his arm with her. Jasper was as overprotective of Cora as poor Freddie is of all his womenfolk. Their liaison caused quite the scandal at the time, for we were all convinced he was going to break with tradition and marry her irrespective of society's and his own family's outright disapproval.

'A courtesan had never married a duke in their family before and he never once denied any of the speculation about their impending nuptials in the papers. That was what earned him the 1808 accolade of "Society's Most Scandalous" in *The Times*. That and the rapid rise of his outrageous club after his father had publicly cut him off. That particular year, you couldn't read a scandal sheet without Jasper's name front and centre.

She was his mistress for a good year or so before she disappeared.'

'Disappeared?'

'Indeed. Poof...' Her mother mimed an explosion. 'Mysterious to the last. One day she was the talk of the *ton* and the next she was gone. Disappeared as quickly as she arrived, never to be heard from again. But then such is the precarious existence of a courtesan. Once her benefactor loses interest, she has to find another or starve.'

'You think Jasper cast her out?' Because that didn't feel right to Hattie. He was undoubtedly a lot of things, but did not seem the sort to be so cruel and callous. The way he had held that child was all compassion and, to Hattie's eyes at least, love. Whoever the little girl was, she was in no doubt he adored her.

'Who knows?' Her mother shrugged. 'Mistresses come and go, and many by choice. Jasper wasn't as successful then as he is now so there is every chance she found a wealthier man to keep her. We all assumed they had both moved on to pastures new as Jasper certainly cut a romantic swathe through the willing ladies after Cora left, and she certainly always had plenty of willing volunteers to warm her sheets. Do you know what happened to her, Freddie?'

'I refuse to be drawn into this inappropriate conversation.' Her brother speared a French bean with more force than was necessary. 'Especially in front of the girls.' Never mind that Kitty was eighteen and she and Annie were twenty and not two.

'That means he doesn't know,' said his wife, giggling. 'Or if he does, discussing it breaches some sort of rakes' code that he agreed to when he used to be one.'

'Honour among thieves,' said Annie to get a rise out of him. 'What a hypocrite you truly are nowadays, Freddie. Anyway—' She turned back to Kitty with an evil glint in her eye. 'Back to Almack's and Freddie's tryst with a lusty widow who was older than Mama…'

Chapter Five

As debuts went, Hattie's had, unsurprisingly, been rather awful. While some of that was down to her own strange mood—she had alternately pondered and worried about Jasper incessantly since yesterday and could not seem to get the image of him tenderly cradling that little girl out of her mind no matter how much she tried. However, as that conundrum still hovered in the background, the sheer unmitigated misery of Queen Charlotte's Annual Debutantes Ball now dominated the foreground.

The patronising pity had been just as copious as she had expected, the subtle whispers and open stares were exactly as she had predicted. But what she hadn't anticipated was how vulnerable that all left her feeling, how envious she was of Annie and Kitty dancing, or quite how excluded she felt at not to be able to join them.

Her well-meaning family must have spread the word of her unfortunate limitations beforehand—or more likely her well-meaning brother who was the worst of the lot because he was convinced she was so fragile— as not a single gentleman had asked her to dance. Instead, several of his bachelor friends took the time to stand by her chair to talk to her, but by their discomfort and furtive, longing glances towards the dance floor as they awaited their next partner, it was apparent most were only doing so on sufferance. An awkward set of circumstances which served to make her more self-conscious about her situation than she would have been if they had left her to her own devices with the rest of the wallflowers.

The only saving grace of having press-ganged gentleman after gentleman chat about the weather out of duty was that it did help keep some of the fortune hunters at bay, but an hour in and the wolves were circulating. All waiting for the opportune moment to approach and plight their mercenary troth. And what a disparate bunch of suitors they were, all eyeing her like the hapless prey in possession of a large dowry that they assumed she was hoping would attract someone. All convinced she was prepared to lower her standards enough to consider them now that her limp had made her less of a catch, and all of them of the firm belief that she would be grateful for whatever crumbs she was offered simply because she must be desperate for a husband.

Well the joke was on them, because huge dowry and limp aside, she wouldn't entertain any of them and was not averse to telling them so if they made pests of themselves. For now, the constant stream of press-ganged gentlemen and the daggers she kept shooting the rest were enough to keep most at bay.

'I am afraid, duty calls me again to the dance.' The handsome baronet who had stood with her for the entire cotillion bowed, his apologetic expression not quite covering his relief that his current duty was done. 'Would you like me to fetch your mother or your brother to keep you company?' He managed to say this with such condescension that she was sure if she'd had an invalid's blanket around her knees he would have tucked it in.

Hattie wanted to growl at him for making her feel like such a chore but settled for an equally insincere smile. 'I am quite capable of fetching them myself should I need them, thank you very much.'

At a loss as to how he should respond to such a waspish comment, he bowed again and scurried away as if his breeches were on fire, leaving her properly alone for the first time all evening without a press-ganged decent gentleman or convenient family member in sight.

Just in time for the first waltz of the Season.

The one dance that every debutante dreamed of dancing.

The one dance so guaranteed to make or break a girl's reputation that even the dustiest wallflowers had all miraculously found partners, as the mothers and fathers of the *ton* called in favours to ensure their daughter was not one of the hopeless lost causes sitting it out.

Which left Hattie sticking out like a solitary sore thumb in the seats reserved for them because not even her meddling, overprotective brother had managed to secure her any company for this dance.

As the musicians played the opening bars, she caught sight of Lord Boredom out of the corner of her eye walking towards her with two cups of punch in his hands and decided she was all done with being a sitting duck and an object of pity.

She ignored the shriek of pain from her atrophied right leg and forced it to move at pace into the crowd headed towards the dance floor, then used those convenient bodies as camouflage to slip out of the ballroom altogether. Assuming she must be headed to the retiring room, one of the palace footmen pointed down a hallway. 'Tis the first door off the atrium, my lady, to the right of the main entrance.'

She thanked him and set off, wondering if she could feasibly hide for the next hour in the retiring room without being dragged back by her mother or if she should simply march out of the front door and keep going until she reached Mayfair. The former smacked of cowardice, the latter became more tempting the closer she got to the exit and the prospect of blessed escape.

She could plead a sudden headache, she supposed.

Or use her dratted leg as a more believable excuse, which nobody would dare argue with because they all walked on eggshells wherever that was concerned. She could send a note via one of the footmen to her mother the second the carriage departed, claiming she was in too much pain so had decided to take herself home to rest her leg rather than ruin their fun. Hope against hope that such a cruel lie wouldn't spoil the evening for the rest of her family, or worse, wrench Annie or Kitty away from the ball on a false pretence because her entire family tended to wrap her in so much cotton wool nowadays it was suffocating...

'I am an invited guest, damn it!' The shouting snapped her out of her futile pondering. 'I have an official invitation!' She would have recognised Jasper's deep, irate tone anywhere and as it seemed to be coming from up ahead she hastened towards it. 'I demand to be let in!'

Whatever the doorman answered was too muffled to

hear but the sounds of some sort of a scuffle were unmistakable. Curious and concerned after what she had witnessed yesterday, Hattie ventured towards them and then stopped, stunned at the sight of a dishevelled Jasper being manhandled towards the front door by two burly footmen.

The second he spotted her he put up more of a fight. 'Hattie! Tell these idiots I have an invitation!' He waved the crumpled card in the air. 'Tell them I solemnly promised your mother I would come and that I promised to save you from Lord Boredom!' Something was off about his diction. Every word with an 's' in it came out a little slurred. 'Tell them that I might not be good for much, might unintentionally let people down in their hour of need, but Jasper Beaufort always keeps his sworn promises no matter what!'

Thankfully, the noise from the ballroom drowned out his shouting before the honourable guests inside heard but it wouldn't be long before he made a complete spectacle of himself.

'This man is drunk, my lady,' said one of the liveried footmen trying to hold him back as she approached. 'A filthy drunkard in no fit state to attend this ball.'

Drunk he might be but filthy he wasn't. Even in a state of dishabille Jasper looked better than most of the gentlemen here. His cravat might be undone, and his shirt untucked but otherwise he was dressed appropriately. Although it appeared, by the incorrectly buttoned waistcoat, he might well have started drinking before he changed for the ball. Although why he was here at all after his bad news yesterday was a complete mystery to her.

'This man is the Earl of Beaufort, heir to the Duke of

Battlesbridge and a good friend to my father, the Duke of Avondale.' She skewered the footmen with her most imperious glare. 'You will unhand him immediately.'

At the mention of his title, the footmen wavered and loosened their grips, but didn't let go. 'Lord or no, he is in no fit state to meet Her Majesty.'

'That I will concede, gentlemen.' For Jasper's own good, Hattie could not allow him to stumble roaring drunk into the ballroom of St James's Palace. She offered his captors her mother's most charming smile, the one which always got the canny Duchess of Avondale exactly what she wanted without ruffling any feathers. 'But I suspect it is nothing some strong coffee and some fresh air will not fix.'

Hattie regarded Jasper with amused pity. The sort her parents had often used on her brother Freddie when he used to come home the worse for wear. 'So, if you will allow me to take charge of him, I shall personally see to it that my brother escorts him home.' Freddie was better equipped to deal with this than she and he knew him better. Was certainly privy to the whole situation rather than the snippets she had been trying to piece together, and it was hardly proper for her to escort a drunken bachelor home alone.

'I am not going home!' Two large feet braced themselves on the floor while his big body swayed between the footmen who seemed to be the only things keeping him upright. 'I promised both you and your mother I would be here, so here I am!' He made an ineffectual break for freedom and was once again restrained by the palace staff while two elderly matrons chose that moment to investigate the commotion and stood openly staring in outright disapproval. 'I've come to save you from all the fortune hunters!'

Hattie strode forward to claim Jasper's arm before more onlookers decided to gather. 'Which room would be best for us to retire to while I convince him to see reason?' She wafted her free hand away from the crowded ballroom. 'As I dare say the last thing we all want is Lord Beaufort causing more of a scene at the most auspicious ball of the social Season than he has already. I sincerely doubt Her Majesty would be impressed to read about an altercation involving a peer of the realm and her staff in tomorrow's papers either. It would royally spoil her birthday and neither of you deserve to be blamed for that.' Such an eventuality wasn't in any way their fault, but she figured it wouldn't hurt to sow some seeds of doubt to expedite matters. 'Or worse, if this incident attracts any more attention than it has already...' she flicked her gaze to the two staring women, then back to the men imploringly '...then Her Majesty's whole night will be ruined too.'

As the footmen wavered and relinquished their grip, she dragged Jasper to follow her, and miraculously nobody argued. Instead, one of the men scurried ahead and opened a door to a small receiving room and together they manoeuvred the suddenly limp lord on to a spindly sofa which barely seemed capable of taking his weight. With her new charge now slumped but thankfully subdued, she beamed at the servant as if he were her best friend in the world. 'Thank you so much. You have been most helpful, Mr...'

'It's Prescott, my lady. We don't bother with the mister.'

'Thank you, Prescott. Could you quietly summon the

Avondale carriage and ask it to wait around the corner rather than directly outside? The fewer people who see His Lordship in this state, the better for all of us on a night like tonight.'

The footman nodded, clearly worried about the potential repercussions she had hinted at and that caused her a pang of guilt. 'No doubt once His Lordship here is feeling better, he will reward you and your colleague for both your kindness and discretion tonight. I know that I shall personally mention how sensible you have both been to the Master of the Household after I have dealt with the problem at hand.' She rummaged in her evening bag for the guinea her father always insisted his girls carry everywhere in case of an emergency and pressed it into the footman's gloved palm. 'In the meantime, let's keep all this between us, shall we?'

'Of course, my lady. Nobody else needs to know.' The young man tapped the side of his nose conspiratorially, making Hattie thank her lucky stars that her mama had always instilled in her offspring the importance of keeping the servants on side and treating them with the utmost respect. 'Once the carriage is in place, I shall escort you out through the back by route of the servants' corridor so none of the guests see him.' She also thanked her wise papa for that emergency guinea too as that had doubtless been just as useful. 'But it might be a while as the mews is very busy.'

Of course it was. On a night like tonight, every carriage in Mayfair was probably cluttering the palace yard. 'While we wait, can I impose on you to procure us a big pot of coffee, Prescott, if it is not too much trouble?' There was no point dragging her brother away from the ball and his new wife until the carriage was

ready. Meanwhile she could assist in some small way
by sobering Jasper up, and pretend she wasn't relieved
to have the perfect excuse to avoid the ballroom in the
process. 'Order it as strong as possible—as I suspect
Lord Beaufort will need every drop of it to make it to
the carriage when it arrives.'

Prescott left them, and in case anyone else stumbled upon them, had the foresight to hand Hattie a key
so that she could lock the door behind him. When she
turned back towards Jasper, he was hunched forward
as if the entire weight of the world rested on his broad
shoulders. Without thinking, and in the absence of any
clue as to what to say to him to make him feel better,
she placed a soothing hand on his shoulder and rubbed.

'Oh, Jasper, what on earth were you thinking to come
here tonight after you lost Cora?' There seemed little
point in skirting around it now that she knew the woman
had been his mistress.

'Clearly I wasn't thinking, was I?' He groaned and
massaged his temples as his solid body deflated beneath her palms.

'Brandy will do that.' At least she assumed the alcohol on his breath was brandy. It smelled exactly like
the expensive cognac her father poured on special occasions. 'Did you drink the entire bottle?'

He shrugged, looking befuddled then returned his
head gratefully to his hands as if it weighed too much
for his neck. 'Mrs Mimms brought it after I put Izzy
to bed. It takes her for ever to fall asleep. Izzy that is.
Not Mrs Mimms. I have no idea how long it takes that
nagging harridan to nod off and not sure that I care to
picture it.'

Hattie could think of no response to that so rubbed his shoulder some more.

'Why is it, Hattie, when something bad happens, people always offer you a stiff brandy?'

He was talking to his shoes, his agitated fingers making a mess of his already rumpled hair. 'Had a fright—have a brandy. Had a shock—what you need is a brandy. Feeling upset, confused, riddled with guilt, had your entire world turned upside down in a single moment—have a brandy. As if a damned brandy can numb the pain of losing someone you loved or can miraculously turn you into a father when you have no clue how, when I can assure you it damn well doesn't.'

Father!

So Izzy was his?

She hadn't been expecting that, but then again, now that she knew it, she wasn't that surprised. The little girl had his colouring. Certainly the same dark, tousled hair. And he and the mysterious Cora Marlow were once romantically linked.

He slumped further forward, his voice thick with emotion as he rubbed his eyes with the heels of his hands. 'What on earth was Cora thinking to leave poor Izzy to me? What the blazes do I know about parenting?'

'Perhaps she knew that the pair of you adore one another?' That had been glaringly obvious even from the few moments Hattie had witnessed. 'That seems to me to be one of the most fundamental things when it comes to children.'

'Maybe so but that's hardly enough, is it?' He began to furiously pat down his coat then produced a crumpled piece of paper. 'The shopping list alone that Mrs

Mimms gave me is enough to give a man palpitations.' He thrust the list at her as if most of what was on it baffled him. 'Who knew little girls wore chemises and stockings too? And what is an under petticoat? Is that the same as a normal petticoat or is it something different? And where the blazes do I buy it all from as I doubt my usual tailor in Jermyn Street makes it?'

Hattie resisted the urge to envelop him in a hug and settled for sitting beside him instead so she could rub his back. 'I am sure you can procure it all from Bond Street.'

'Because I am sure a big hairy man is most welcome in an establishment which sells female unmentionables.'

Hattie supposed he made a valid point. Such shopping was a mother's job, not a father's. 'Did Izzy not come with any luggage?'

'Of course she did—the bare essentials.' That word with its triple Ss caused his tongue a bit of trouble. 'I have to fetch the rest when I close up Cora's house. But those things won't last long.' He stared solemnly into her eyes as if about to impart some great wisdom. 'Children grow. According to Mrs Mimms they grow exponentially at Izzy's age.' He expanded the gap between his palms in the air and stared at it in both wonder and disgust.

'And she's going to need governesses and tutors for all the feminine pursuits which I cannot teach her. What do I know about embroidery and music and deportment?' He clutched her hand, sending ripples of awareness ricocheting through her fingers and up her arm. 'At least you used to be a little girl so you have some grounding in the subject. I have nothing—beyond the knowledge of the female of the species I absolutely do not want her to have.' He frowned again, looking every bit as outraged by that as Freddie was that his baby sister dared to go to Covent Garden without a body-guard by her side. 'Oh, God! Now that's another thing to worry about!'

'Not for a goodly few years, Jasper. Izzy is what? Five?'

'Almost five.' He held up five fingers in case she couldn't count. Or he couldn't. Judging by the way he was squinting at them, thanks to the brandy he could likely see ten. 'It is a big responsibility bringing up a child—but an even bigger one to bring up a daughter. Especially one who is going to need as much protect-ing as Izzy is.' He pointed in the direction of the music drifting faintly from the ballroom as if it was the enemy. 'Because they all know where she came from and not one of them is going to ever let her forget it.'

Another valid point. As the illegitimate daughter of a courtesan, the prim and proper Duchess of Warminsters of the *ton* who esteemed bloodlines over everything else would never accept her no matter who her father was.

'At least you are destined to be a duke one day…that should make things easier.' A useless platitude if ever there was one, but all Hattie had in her arsenal. 'And at least you can afford a decent dowry for her when the time comes.'

'So that the fortune hunters can swarm over her like flies as they are you? That will hardly help poor Cora rest in peace when she is counting on me to make amends.'

'For what?'

'Letting her down before. Not being there when she needed me. My ignorance. My youthful idiocy. My many shellfish…' He screwed up his face at that wrong word. 'I mean selfish failings.' He threw up his hands then collapsed backwards this time like a sack of potatoes tossed into a cart. 'All of the above.'

'That is the brandy talking.' She touched the back of his hand. 'You are so pickled in it you really aren't thinking straight.' She quashed the urge to brush the hair from his face. 'It will take some time for your mind to fully comprehend things—but you will work it out.' As one who had had the ground ripped from beneath her feet and her world destroyed in a split second, she understood what it felt like to be flung into the void. 'I sincerely doubt a daughter will prove to be that much of a challenge to a man who can build a successful business from scratch on little but his own wits.'

'I hope you are right, Hattie.' His hand twisted and his fingers laced with hers, an innocent gesture which somehow felt profound. He tugged her closer and stared deep into her eyes as if the depths held all the answers. 'But what if I do it all wrong?'

She gave in to the urge to touch his face. 'You won't.'

His gaze bored into hers while his fingers gripped her hand for all he was worth, as if she alone were the only thing that felt stable in his world. 'How can you be so sure?'

'Because I believe in you.' She succumbed to the overwhelming need to wrap her free arm around his shoulders and was powerless to do anything other than cuddle him close. 'And I promise that you will have my help. As you say, at least I used to be a little girl, so how hard can it be?'

Chapter Six

'You still should have fetched me!' Freddie paced the breakfast room like a furious and stern father while her actual parents sat calmly eating their toast. 'Have you any idea what would have happened to your reputation if anyone had learnt that you had taken Jasper Beaufort home alone unchaperoned?'

Because he had heard several versions of the same answer already and because he was in no mood to listen, Hattie did not bother replying. Instead, she rolled her eyes at her mother who had accepted her edited explanation of events with the calm reason her brother seemed incapable of. In solidarity, her mother rolled hers back then nudged her father to intervene when it was obvious Papa would much rather read his newspaper than involve himself in the fray. With a resigned sigh he finally tried to pour oil on troubled waters.

'Your sister did what she thought was most prudent and, under the circumstances, I believe that while her decision was flawed, it was done with Jasper's best interests at heart. Fetching you would have only drawn more attention to his predicament and thankfully nobody saw her either leave or return to the ball. In fact, none of us even noticed she was gone and would likely still be none the wiser if she hadn't appraised us of her adventure on the carriage ride home.'

'She was gone less than an hour, dear,' added her mother, still oblivious that Hattie had been gone at least two, 'and she was technically chaperoned at all times— first of all by that nice palace footman who assisted her and then our very own coachman on the short drive to Jasper's house. She did not even alight the carriage, did you, dear?'

'Of course, I didn't,' said Hattie, while praying she was as convincing a liar as she hoped she was. 'I deposited him in the capable hands of his housekeeper and returned to the palace.' Which was the truth, albeit with much omission, because she had left him with his housekeeper after they had both helped him up the stairs to his bed, and all while the Avondale coachman waited outside thanks to the guinea she had promised him if he kept his silence.

'And what about all the minutes you spent alone with Jasper inside the carriage?' Freddie's eyes were bulging now.

'What about them?' Hattie glared back defiantly. 'Are you suggesting that a man who was so inebriated on the back of his grief that he could barely stand had the wherewithal to ravish me on the short drive from St James's to Russell Square? Are you suggesting that one of your *oldest* and *dearest* friends would do such an awful thing to your own sister? Because if you are, it begs the question as to why you would stay friends with such a monster!'

While her brother glared back, searching for an answer which justified his irrationality, Annie decided that was the opportune moment to enter the conversation. 'I would love to see the state of poor Jasper if he *had* chanced his arm with Hattie, for she has a ferocious right hook, as you well know, Freddie.'

Then, in case the newcomers to the family did not know the history, she leaned towards Kitty and Dorothea, grinning. 'Hattie almost broke Freddie's nose once after he hid in her closet one Christmas Eve and jumped out when she was sleeping, covered in a sheet pretending to be a ghost. He sported two black eyes for a fortnight afterwards and had to suffer everyone laughing at him in church the next morning for being pummelled by a girl six years his junior.'

'If he carries on, I might have to give him another pasting.' Hattie clenched her fist and slapped it into her palm then jabbed her finger at her brother. 'Nobody saw. My precious reputation is intact, you are my brother and not my father, and I saved *your* friend from an unjust evisceration from the press in his hour of need and that is the end of it!' She stood, ignoring her brother to address the rest of the breakfast table. 'Now if you will excuse me, I am due at the infirmary in an hour.' Which was another lie because she was due there in two, but she couldn't very well go about her day without checking on Jasper first.

'Take Evangeline with you, dear,' said her mother with a pointed glare at her son, 'for propriety's sake.'

'No need.' Hattie crossed her fingers behind her back and willed the Almighty not to smite her for yet another falsehood. 'I am meeting Mrs Cribbs, Lady Trenchard and the vicar's wife there.' At least she would be in two hours, as they had agreed. 'And surely three married chaperons are quite enough to protect one flawless reputation from nothing?'

Jasper had no clue exactly how he'd got home last night or quite how he came to wake on his own spinning bed fully clothed this morning. Lurking in the midst of the headache from hell and the worst hangover of his life were vague memories of being force-fed coffee, of the bitter beverage disagreeing with him and making a sudden reappearance and of falling face first into a carriage before being dragged up some stairs.

Yet for all his brandy-soaked fuzziness and the worrying gaps in his memory, he remembered Hattie had been there throughout. Her hand in his. Her arms around him. Her breath caressing his ear as she comforted him. Her fingers brushing his hair as she tucked him into bed and told him to sleep it off. Her promise that she would help him with Izzy and that she would always be there if he needed her.

Always.

Like a safe port in a storm, she had been his rock at his lowest ebb. There was also no doubt he owed her for coming to his aid before he managed to make a total fool of himself in front of the entire *ton* and the Royal Family because, while he had dealt with every other blow of the worst twenty-four hours of his life, a silly shopping list had sent him over the edge.

When he'd felt well enough to sit up, struggle gingerly into some clothes and slowly make his way downstairs, he had found no trace of his shameful behaviour in any of the morning papers at all. Thanks entirely to Lady Harriet Fitzroy, no one had any clue he had lost his mind as well as the entire contents of his stomach at the Queen's birthday ball.

It hadn't been his finest hour.

In fact, he was mortified to have to acknowledge it had been one of his worst and he was thoroughly ashamed of himself for his weakness when he should have been strong for Izzy's sake. Instead, it had been Hattie who had been the strong one, the sensible one, and he had no earthly clue how to repay her for her kindness.

Just as soon as the blasted room stopped spinning and his stomach stopped lurching he would start by writing her a grovelling letter of apology, and because a letter wasn't sufficient in itself, he would follow it up with a personal apology the very next time he saw her.

'Uncle Jasper...' Izzy poked her head around the study door, her big eyes wide and her bottom lip trembling, clutching her favourite doll. 'Mrs Mimms said I wasn't to disturb you because you are sick.' She edged inside, still a little unsure and intimidated by the unfamiliar surroundings of his house. 'But I am worried, and I need to know...' She chewed her lip, blinking back tears.

'What do you need to know, sweetheart?'

'Are you going to die on me too, Uncle Jasper?'

'Of course not!' He held out his arms and did his best to ignore the wave of nausea as she flung herself into them. Instantly hating himself for scaring her, especially as Mrs Mimms had told him, with one of her scolding looks, that Izzy had had another nightmare last night and instead of being there for her as he should have been, he had drowned his sorrows instead.

'My sickness was temporary and self-inflicted but I

am all better now—see?' He held her out so she could
see for herself and forced a reassuring smile praying
he did not appear too green around the gills. 'I am hale
and hearty and not going anywhere.'

Two little hands cupped his cheeks. 'Do you promise?'

He drew an X on his chest with his finger. 'Cross
my heart. You are stuck with me.' God help them both.
'I promise.'

He tugged Izzy on to his lap, wondering if distraction might ease some of her anxiousness even if it did
little to ease the pain and confusion of suddenly losing
her mother. 'I've had a brilliant idea. Why don't we go
shopping today?' It was a temporary solution at best,
but some fresh air and some new things might put a
smile on her face for a moment at least.

'What are we shopping for?'

'Nice things for your new room. Pretty things. Frivolous things. Things to play with. Books to read. Puz-
zles, games, ice cream. Whatever you want.' He would
worry about the unmentionables another day.

'I can have anything?'

'Anything they sell on High Holborn, you can have.'
His father would caution him not to spare the rod and
spoil the child, but as his sire was no role model Jasper
was keen to emulate, he figured if his father had never
done it, then that was a good enough reason for him to.
'What does your heart desire?'

Izzy pondered it for a while, her four-and-a-half-
year-old's mind giving the pleasant conundrum all the
consideration of a treaty negotiation after a prolonged
war. Eventually, she tilted her head, a gesture which so

reminded him of her mother it brought a lump to his throat. 'Can I have a kitten and a brother?'

He ruffled her dark curls smiling. 'Yes to the kitten—but I don't know any merchants in Holborn who sell brothers. Although why you'd want a brother anyway is beyond me when boys are such horrid, dirty, mischievous things and girls are so much nicer.'

She considered that and shrugged. 'Maybe—but I still want one. I've always wanted a brother, Uncle Jasper.'

Uncle Jasper.

A hollow title for someone who now needed to be so much more.

'I've had another brilliant idea...' One he knew would likely bite him once it leaked out, but would protect her in the future seeing as he was destined to be a duke. 'Seeing as you are stuck with me, maybe we should both change our names to mark the occasion. Make things official.'

Her face fell and that emotive lip quivered again. 'But I like the name Izzy.'

'So do I.' Parenting was like navigating a sheer cliff edge in the dark. 'And I certainly wasn't suggesting we should change that—or even the Marlow which follows it—I was more thinking you should add Beaufort to the end because that is my surname. That way, everyone knows that you belong to me and I belong to you.'

She considered that for a moment then nodded. 'I quite like the name Beaufort.'

'Splendid. Isabel Marlow-Beaufort it is then.' The room spun a little faster, no doubt more because of the enormous implications of acknowledging her than the residual alcohol in his system, so he sucked in a calming breath and willed it to stop. He had never put much stock in becoming a duke, but he supposed, now that it mattered, being one had advantages which went beyond his money. As a Marlow, Izzy was nothing. As a Beaufort, as long as the English aristocracy persevered, she would always be something and certainly never a victim at the mercy of the world like her mother had been for so long. After he wrote a grovelling letter of apology to Hattie he should probably also write to his solicitor to make things properly official. He could not wipe the smear of scandal off Izzy simply by sharing his surname, but it was a start.

'Will you be a Marlow-Beaufort too, Uncle Jasper?'

He swallowed. Suddenly overcome with emotion at the gravitas of what he was about to propose. 'I rather fancy a different name actually.' *Please let this be the right thing to do for her!* 'Instead of calling me Uncle Jasper, I was wondering if you would consider calling me…Papa?' It was ridiculous that his heart was racing. Ridiculous because he knew how much it would hurt if she said no.

In typical Izzy fashion she stared at him, brows knitted as she worried her bottom lip again with her teeth. Making him feel as if he could never possibly ever measure up to the challenge of that title. On bated breath he waited for what seemed an eternity until she finally nodded, then tested the word on her tongue. 'Papa.'

'Thank you.' Overwhelmed and more terrified by the responsibility than he wanted to acknowledge, Jasper enveloped her in a hug which would have likely lasted all day if Mrs Mimms hadn't interrupted.

'You have a caller, my lord.'

'I told you I am not home to any callers for at least

a week.' He hadn't even been able to cope with seeing Freddie yesterday when he had turned up at his door concerned. What was he supposed to say to him when he barely knew which way was up? How on earth was he supposed to explain away Izzy?

His housekeeper smiled. 'Even though this one is pretty, crept through the servants' entrance unchaperoned and certainly saved your pickled bacon last night?'

'Hattie is here?' Perhaps he was home after all—for her alone. He owed her both his gratitude and an apology. But why was he relieved now as well? Relieved and something else he couldn't quite put his finger on. Nervous? Awkward? Humbled?

Expectant?

The flesh of his palm awoke, the nerve endings dancing and reminding him of how her hand had felt in his. Until he remembered all the horrors he had committed in her presence and cringed. 'Oh, dear.'

'Oh, dear, indeed.' Mrs Mimms chuckled at his mortification and spun on her heel. 'I'll fetch some tea. It should be brewed to perfection after your lengthy apology. I just hope it doesn't stew too long while you beg for her forgiveness.'

Chapter Seven

Hattie had rehearsed several suitable speeches to explain her sudden, uninvited appearance at his house in the middle of the morning. All of which made her visit sound like an impromptu, fleeting courtesy call while on another errand than a decisive plan. Something which sounded more matter of fact than the overwhelming desire to see him simply because she needed to. All of those casual excuses evaporated like steam the second she stepped into his study and saw how pale Jasper was while his daughter sat swaddled content in his lap.

The little girl stared at her intrigued, so she offered them both an awkward smile.

'I just wanted to check that you were all right.'

He nodded, visibly uncomfortable, managing to still look boyish and handsome despite his grey pallor. 'Just about.' He offered her a weak smile, then squeezed the child in his arms. 'Izzy, this is Lady Harriet Fitzroy. Lady Harriet, this little cherub is Isabel Marlow-Beaufort.'

The little girl hid shyly behind her doll but still stared at Hattie suspiciously with latent fear in her eyes. Hardly a surprise after all she had been through. The poor thing was probably terrified of everything right now and she was a stranger. 'Hello, Izzy.' She beamed at her as she edged closer. 'My friends call me Hattie, so should you. Who's this?' She lightly touched the head of the doll wrapped in her arms.

Izzy arms tightened around her toy. 'Mabel.'

'Then I am pleased to meet you too, Mabel.' Hattie shook the doll's small porcelain hand as she smiled at Izzy. Up close she could see the child not only shared her father's dark, wayward hair but also had the same piercing eyes despite hers being more hazel than his unusual shade of green. 'And she is such a beautiful doll too. I wish I had owned a doll so lovely when I was a girl.'

Izzy turned to smile at her father. 'He bought her for me when I was born.'

The thought of such a big, strapping man's man like Jasper shopping for such an exquisite and obviously expensive doll to please his little girl touched her. 'Then she really is extra special. No wonder you treasure her.' Hattie's eyes met his over his daughter's head and obviously uncomfortable, he lifted the little girl from his lap.

'Izzy, why don't you go ask Mrs Mimms for some cake or some biscuits for the three of us?'

The child's eyes lit up at the mention of cake and she dropped her doll as she dashed to the door eager to please him, but skidded to a stop on the threshold to smile at him shyly. 'Would you prefer cake or biscuits...*Papa*?'

For some reason, that simple question seemed to completely flummox him until he shrugged and turned to Hattie in the hope she knew the answer because he plainly didn't. With both of them now staring at her,

Hattie shrugged too. 'As a general rule I never say no to either, Izzy—but cake is always my favourite.'

'Ask for both,' said Jasper, standing. 'And wait with Mrs Mimms so that you can help her carry our feast in.'

The second they were alone he winced. 'I am *so* sorry about last night. My behaviour was inexcusable.' He raked a hand through his thick hair sending it awry. 'Contrary to what you might think, I am not accustomed to…um…such reckless hedonism nowadays…it was an uncharacteristic lapse in judgement borne out of…' He gesticulated wildly, then noticing his hands flying about, clamped them tight behind his back to wince again. 'There is no excuse. I am mortified.'

'Of course there is.' Hattie couldn't help smiling at his embarrassment. An awkward, stuttering, blushing Jasper was not an incarnation of him she had ever seen before. 'There is no need to apologise for being human—especially not to someone like me who knows that grief goes through many phases. Shock, anger and self-pity are always the first to manifest themselves and, because they are the least restrained emotions, usually cause us to behave in a manner which isn't the slightest bit dignified or becoming.'

'You have lost someone close too?' His gaze searched hers so intently it unnerved her, as if he wanted to find her truth. 'Someone you loved?'

'Not in the same way but in a manner of speaking… yes.' Hattie wasn't usually one for baring her soul but to him, in this precise moment, honesty found its way out before she could stop it. 'I lost myself.' She patted her leg, shaking her head because it felt selfish to compare her accident in any way to the bereavement he had recently suffered. 'Or at least the me that I used to be, and I initially coped with it badly.'

He sighed in understanding rather than pity, then sat in the captain's chair behind his desk and motioned for her to do the same in one of the wingbacks in front of it. 'I suspect you coped with more decorum than I did. Only a complete halfwit downs three-quarters of a bottle of brandy on an empty stomach then rolls up roaring drunk at the palace.'

'Oh, I don't know. Laudanum is as potent a poison and arguably does a much better job of confusing the brain.' Admitting that aloud was humbling. Referencing that short but hideous time at all was unsettling when it had long been brushed under the carpet by everyone, including herself. An unpleasant pile of dirt which she tried to forget lurked and which her dear family had never once mentioned, ever, since it had happened. 'It certainly helped take me to a very dark place and turned me into someone I loathed. Thankfully, I hated myself so much I couldn't stand it and that encouraged me to fight rather than feel sorry for myself—which was a much better use of my time.' As that sounded like a condescending criticism of his misstep Hattie sighed.

'I am making myself sound so noble and wise, aren't I, but I can assure you that I spent months wallowing in self-pity before I sorted myself out. And I didn't manage that until my father found Dr Cribbs and the good doctor tore me off a strip and reminded me that things could have been worse, so please do not be hard on yourself for yesterday. Sometimes we all need to surrender to the self-indulgent futility of the moment because if we don't it festers.' Now she was waxing lyrical like a wise old sage when she was ill equipped to offer him advice, and as an acquaintance had no right to. 'But what do I know about being in love? Or losing it.'

'Cora and I weren't...' He paused to sigh and rake an agitated hand through his hair. 'Our relationship was...complicated.' He was choosing his words carefully. Probably trying to protect her delicate sensibilities exactly like her brother. 'In the last few years, we were...'

Hattie shook her head, brushing it all away. As her mother had speculated, Cora and he had both clearly moved on, but at least he had maintained a close relationship with his daughter. That spoke volumes about his character.

'You owe me no explanations for your past, Jasper. I am here to help not judge. As one who is now judged constantly, I would never dream of being so condescending to another. Besides—' she smiled and meant it '—I am a firm believer in the past staying there as it is redundant when only the present and future really matter.' Her eyes wandered to the pretty doll abandoned on the floor. 'For what it's worth, and regardless of what the strictures of society dictate that I *should* think, I find it reassuringly noble that you intend to raise Izzy here with you.' After only a month in the infirmary she now understood how hard life could be for so many children. Harder still if a parent abdicated all responsibility for them. A travesty which seemed to occur with more frequency than all decency surely demanded it should. 'If people do not like it, they should mind their own business.'

It was his turn to smile, or half-smile as that seemed to be all he could stoically manage. 'Is that another reason why I didn't see my name splashed all over the papers yesterday and today when I was expecting every column to be filled with speculation about Isabel?'

'It wasn't my secret to tell. The least I could do was give you a short reprieve, as once the news leaks, and it will, it is bound to be horrendous for you both. The gossip will be vicious. The behaviour of some unconscionable. I want no part of that on my conscience.'

'Thank you for giving me something else to worry about.'

'I am simply being honest. As you slurred yourself in your inebriated haze last night, they all know where Izzy came from and not one of them is going to ever let her forget it. Or would you prefer I offered trite, empty and dishonest platitudes instead? In the short term, for the sake of your own sanity, I suggest you give Izzy and yourself time to get used to your abrupt change of circumstances before you make those circumstances public.'

He huffed as he nodded. 'That is the conclusion I have come to, too. It wouldn't be practical or fair to her to hide her from the world for ever, but for now, you are correct. The fewer people who know of her existence, the better. At least for the next couple of months while she finds her feet. Izzy has no idea she is a scandal and it is hardly her fault that she is.'

'Nobody will hear of her from me and I think a couple of months is wise.' Hattie shrugged, sheepish. 'Although I must confess, I did mention Cora's passing to my family.'

'That explains why Freddie called yesterday evening—I wasn't ready to see him. I chose to take comfort in that brandy instead.' He winced again, clearly embarrassed. 'Not my finest hour.'

'Perhaps not but...' the best course of action was to make him feel better '...apart from me, my coachman, your housekeeper and Prescott the palace footman—who you definitely need to remunerate for his timely assistance—nobody saw you in that state. So all's well that ends well. For now at least.' Her heart bled for all the trials and tribulations he had ahead.

'Not quite.' His dark brows furrowed with guilt. 'I still thoroughly ruined your debut. Robbed you of that once-in-a-lifetime experience by selfishly forcing you into being my nursemaid as well as my rescuer.'

If ever guilt was misplaced! 'You really didn't ruin it. In truth, your predicament gave me the perfect excuse to escape one of the ghastliest evenings of my life.'

'Ghastly?' Those intuitive green eyes again searched hers. 'That bad?'

Hattie pulled a face to disguise how vulnerable and exposed last night had made her feel. 'Exactly as I predicted, it was so awful, I was resigned to hiding for the duration in the retiring room and was halfway there when I heard you in the hallway. Believe me, by then I was only too pleased to offer my full assistance in whichever way I could.'

'What were you hiding from?' Trust him to home in on that one pertinent and telling word.

'Lord Boredom.' Hattie huffed at that pathetic half-truth. 'And the abject humiliation of being the only debutante present who wasn't dancing the first waltz of the Season, as well as being the only lady left forgotten on the wallflower chairs.' She smiled to cover how miserable that had been and how pathetic it sounded against what he had to be going through.

'My lack of desire to return to that seat and the

steady stream of press-ganged conversation partners my overprotective brother kept foisting my way may have influenced my decision to forget to ask Freddie to take you home as I should have, and to take on that *onerous* task myself. That it took two hours was the icing on the cake and saved me from the circling vultures like Lord Boredom or the pitying looks of all and sundry.' A brutally honest summation of her motives which ignored the fact that she had also felt the need to see him home.

Jasper had been so lost, so sad and so vulnerable she couldn't abandon him because she knew how that felt. And because he had held her hand and bared his soul and that had felt significant. 'So you see, while I am not denying that I saved you from making a spectacle of yourself, Jasper, in your own, unintentional drunken way you also saved me from being one.'

'Every cloud...' He stared down at his toes, lost again. Or perhaps hideously uncomfortable in her presence.

'Yes...indeed.' Now what?

Hattie wanted to offer practical help. Ask how he was faring. What he was feeling. Be his shoulder to cry on because she suspected he needed one, but instead, as awkwardness descended like a veil between them, she waffled to fill the void. 'One ghastly, humiliating ball down, only another fifteen or so to go this month. But the first of everything is always the most awful, isn't it, so I am hopeful that by ball seven or eight I will have developed a more reliable tactic for surviving the ordeal than hiding in the retiring room...'

Oh, good heavens, stop, Hattie!

'Unless you feel a charitable urge to take to the

brandy again and give me another convenient excuse to escape.' Now she was waffling like the wind because she had apparently lost the power to control her jaws. 'If you do, then might I be so bold as to suggest this Friday might be a good night to imbibe as that is Lady Bulphan's do, which I know for a fact Lord Boredom is attending. I know because he sent me a note to that effect this morning.' Which had been the cause of much hilarity in the Fitzroy household until her overbearing and overprotective brother had spoiled the mood with his lecture. 'It was buried among a limp bouquet of red tulips which Annie claims are a definitive declaration of his interest in me.'

'Limp tulips are a declaration?' Jasper wasn't following and who could blame him when she was spewing out inane nonsense he couldn't possibly care about given his current circumstances.

'Crimson tulips are apparently a declaration of romantic intent.' That they were limp was a whole different sort of insult. 'Not that I needed any tulips to know that when he made a point of declaring that unsavoury interest to my cousin Kitty last night when all his attempts to locate me had failed. And be still my beating heart, he even told her I was a candidate with connections of such a high calibre he was prepared to overlook my unfortunate limp. As if I should be grateful for that...'

Stop! For the love of God, stop, Hattie!

'As much as I would love nothing more than to rescue you from Lord Boredom—because heaven knows nobody deserves his attentions and I owe you that and more for rescuing me last night...' Jasper managed the ghost of a smile within his frown. 'If you don't mind,

I think I am done with the brandy. I am certainly done with the consequences. There is a blacksmith inside my head using my skull as his anvil and the mere thought of food is disagreeing with me. But I can still rescue you sober.'

Hattie wanted to groan aloud. Thanks to her nervous, verbal outpouring, he now clearly felt indebted to her, which was the last thing she wanted. 'I wasn't actually…um…suggesting you save me as I honestly don't need saving, I was merely…um…' Marvellous! One minute she couldn't stop herself from talking and now she had no words.

'What I mean is, I was trying to be entertaining rather than make you feel in any way beholden to me and now I am mortified that you clearly *do* feel beholden to me when I loathe that. Believe me, there will be more than enough press-ganged and beholden conversation partners foisted my way by my well-meaning brother, that I will be able to avoid both Lord Boredom and hiding in the retiring room.' Her toes were curling so tightly inside her walking boots she was in grave danger of giving herself a leg cramp.

Thankfully, the housekeeper returned then. 'Cake and biscuits as requested, my lord.' Beside her, his daughter beamed proudly.

'I chose the cake, Papa. Because chocolate is your favourite.'

Jasper baulked at the tiered chocolate and cream confection on the overloaded tray. 'Splendid choice.' Then he swallowed hard as the housekeeper deposited it directly in front of him on his desk. 'Splendid.' The mere sight of it seemed to turn him green.

Fearing such close proximity to food might be his

undoing again, and glad to be off the cringeworthy topic of her depressing but sole ardent suitor and all her brother's well-intentioned attempts at matchmaking, Hattie leapt to the rescue. 'Perhaps it might be better if we had this in the drawing room?' Where she hoped there might be a handy sideboard strategically placed a safe distance from the queasy master of the house's chair. Taking control, but conscious her wonky gait would make her spill most of it if she attempted to carry the whole tray, she grabbed the offending cake stand and the plate of biscuits and whisked them out from under his nose. 'Can you show me the way, Izzy?'

The little girl hugged her precious doll tighter before she nodded and tentatively took the lead. Hattie followed, and by the rattle of teacups, she could tell that the housekeeper wasn't far behind.

Further down the hallway, Izzy opened the door to a light and airy room which had obviously been furnished with comfort in mind. Hattie had no idea what she had expected beyond a decidedly dark and masculine space, but it certainly wasn't this. Two large pale green damask sofas took centre stage, flanking an attractive Persian rug, while the unfussy lace covering the bank of open windows billowed softly in the breeze.

Instead of the dark wood panelling favoured by her father and his male peers, it had been painted ivory and only ran a third up the walls from the skirting board. Above that was either silk or expensive wallpaper which resembled it in a lighter duck-egg shade than the upholstery. All the wood, from the polished parquet to the side tables, was in a subtle light oak, and apart from a plethora of lamps and one bold clock sat on the enormous cream fireplace, there was a distinct absence of the usual clutter of *objets d'art* which most of the *ton* favoured.

It was a modern space but a surprisingly homely one, and not at all what one would expect from such a gossiped-about libertine. Not that he seemed much of a libertine any longer despite his recent foray into the bottom of a brandy bottle.

'It is a new house,' said the housekeeper, as if she'd read Hattie's mind while unpacking the tea tray on the sideboard. 'His Lordship bought it last year before it was finished, so the interior was made to his exact specification. Most of the rooms are still a work in progress, but the majority of the downstairs is done. Almost all of upstairs is as spartan as a monastery still and there is no rushing him into changing that.' As Jasper was yet to follow, no doubt because he was in the midst of trying to compose himself before facing the cake again, the older woman dropped her voice conspiratorially. 'He likes things just so and isn't one for hasty decisions, so I dare say all those empty bedchambers will remain barren for the foreseeable future.'

'Mrs Mimms believes in furniture everywhere.' Jasper said this, unoffended as he wandered in. 'Even if nobody is going to use it, she refuses to concede that I have all that I need in all the rooms that I use.'

'Why buy a house with eight bedrooms if you only need the two of them? Not that the second bedroom has any furniture in it either. Or even curtains. Or all the many, many things a little girl is going to need. I've made him a list but I dare say I shall have to nag him narrow before he gets around to purchasing all of it.' Mrs Mimms rolled her eyes at Hattie and then stomped out muttering, and he watched her retreat with affection.

'I think the least said about that *dreaded list* this morning the better.' He offered her a sheepish expression as they both knew that had been the catalyst for last night. 'Although I suppose she makes a valid point about the size of the house but something about this place called to me.'

'It is a lovely house.' At least everything she had seen of it so far was.

'It is.' He appeared pleased at her compliment. Proud of the home he had created here. 'It is also within walking distance to The Reprobates' one way and some unspoilt greenery the other, and blissfully too unfashionable and far enough away from the prying and judgemental eyes of the Mayfair set that I can forget society exists most of the time.'

'That must be sheer heaven.' She had always found Mayfair society cloying, precisely because they were every bit as prying and judgemental as he had said, but that sense of otherness had quadrupled since her return to town. As if she no longer fitted within its strict bounds and certainly no longer measured up to their ideal.

'It is a pleasant walk too.' Hattie admitted that before she thought about it. 'Quiet and peaceful once you've left Covent Garden behind and hit Bloomsbury. All the garden squares along the way are lovely, empty oases, especially now that the early flowers are in bloom. They are the perfect places to wander aimlessly. I found a particularly pretty one with a duck pond.'

He quirked one dark brow as he lowered himself into a sofa. 'And you discovered all that from the comfort of your carriage?'

'I might have alighted the carriage outside the infirmary where I am expected later and made my own way here on foot.'

Those intelligent eyes narrowed. 'With a maid, I presume?'

Before he gave her a lecture on propriety like her nagging brother, she sidestepped. 'Doctor Cribbs says that walking is good for my leg and I'll have you know I walk a good mile a day—sometimes two.'

He wasn't fooled for a moment by that diversion. 'Now it makes perfect sense why you came in via the servants' entrance at the back. You came alone, didn't you?'

As the housekeeper wasn't here to do it, Hattie turned her back on him to pour the tea. 'Well, I could hardly march unchaperoned up the front steps, as bold as brass, to check on you, any more than I could instruct the Avondale coachman to drive me here instead of the infirmary. The prying and judgemental eyes of society are less forgiving of us ladies than they are of you men. You can still swan around within their ranks even with the most shocking reputations whereas we are shunned if ruined. It's horrendously unfair—especially when all I am guilty of is being a good Samaritan.'

'By that robust and quick defence, I must also presume that your family have no clue as to your present whereabouts.'

'What they do not know cannot hurt them. And unless you have a burning desire to face an irrational and incensed Freddie on the duelling field, I suggest you keep this to yourself as well.' Hattie thrust a cup at him, keen to change the subject when she knew she was technically in the wrong. 'You still take your tea like treacle, I presume, with milk and two heaped sugars?'

He took it smiling, if a tad bewildered, and she sensed his eyes on her, studying her, as she limped back to the sideboard to fetch the other two cups. It was most disconcerting, but she covered it with bravado because, for reasons she did not understand, she wasn't ready to leave yet no matter how inappropriate this visit.

'Here you are, Izzy.' She passed one down to the little girl sat in the middle of the carpet, then in case he took issue with her feeding his child an adult beverage, she smiled at him unrepentant. 'It's nine parts milk, in case you were wondering, so perfectly acceptable for a little girl and I would hate for her to feel left out.'

After working in the infirmary, Hattie was of the firm opinion that the worst thing you could do to a child was alienate them by patronising them or excluding them. 'And it will help wash the cake down.' With that, she spun on her heel again to cut some cake, feeling bossy and intrusive but desperate to do something to help regardless.

Chapter Eight

It took Hattie less than half an hour to have Izzy eating out of her hand and now she was holding it as all three of them were sat in the privacy of his carriage on the way to Covent Garden. His guest had protested in every possible manner that he did not need to escort her back to the infirmary, stating she was quite capable of getting there on her own and that she had 'inconvenienced him long enough' with her impromptu visit.

But when she stood and strode to the door at such speed and with such determination that he almost missed the flinch of pain which briefly marred her features, and the way her step faltered as she forced her damaged limb to work, Jasper had put his foot down. It was odd, but in the three days of their short reacquaintance, he already understood enough about her to know that her fierce pride made her mask those things to the detriment of all else. Things which she saw as weaknesses even though those things were also testament to her phenomenal strength. He knew too that she did not want to be pitied and would swat away any perceived offers of help just as ruthlessly as she would an annoying fly. He had also just discovered that she talked incessantly when she was nervous, and he found that rather charming.

'There is every need.' Although common sense told him that the feisty Hattie would require it to be justified in a more acceptable way than his overwhelming need to see her safe. Or eke out more time with her. Or more likely both. 'I might not be much of one, but the code of the gentleman dictates that he has to escort a lady to where she needs to be or be marked a cad. Besides,' he allowed his own mask to slip enough so that every bit of his hangover showed, 'thanks to my unfortunate liaison with the brandy I am in grave need of some fresh air myself and as I promised to take Izzy shopping in Holborn it also kills two birds with one stone as your destination is en route.'

Only a tiny part of his insistence was to ensure her safety on this bright spring Tuesday when the risks to her person were minimal; the rest was entirely selfish. He wanted to be with her. Wanted to distract himself with her delightful company a little longer.

Her concern had touched him immensely too, and there was no doubting she was concerned for him as she had fussed over them both all morning. She might not have asked outright with words how he was feeling or coping—she was too sensitive to intrude on his grief—but her deep and sincere compassion for his situation was plain to see in her eyes which were refreshingly useless at hiding the truth.

He liked that about her. Where so many would be judgemental, Hattie had been nothing but kind. Especially to Izzy, who through no fault of her own was a scandal waiting to happen. Yet irrespective of the smudge such an acquaintance would make on her own reputation, Hattie had waded in and in her own unique and sometimes babbling, sometimes no-nonsense way.

'Two trips to the infirmary in three days.' In tacit agreement they had avoided conversation about his situation in front of Izzy. 'I had no idea Dr Cribbs was such a hard taskmaster. Are you always there so frequently?'

She smiled at him over Izzy's head. 'Usually, I try to volunteer a couple of times a week, but Dr Cribbs has a new patient of particular concern whom he has asked me to work with. A boy called Jim who isn't doing so well.' She patted her leg again by way of explanation. 'He broke both his legs when a cart overturned...' There was that compassion again, written as plain as day on her pretty face, announcing, unbeknownst to her that her desire to help others was an intrinsic part of who she was rather than the odd piece of benevolence she did when the mood struck her.

'Like me, the bones were initially set badly and one leg in particular isn't healing correctly. And exactly like me, he will likely not be able to use it unless the damage is corrected. But unlike me, he doesn't have anyone supporting him or even prepared to wait for him to heal. Injured, he is unable to work, and in his world that makes him more than useless to everyone around him—it makes him a burden.'

'How so?'

'I haven't got to the bottom of his particular circumstances yet as I have only met him once and he wasn't in the mood for talking, but already I know he will be a tough nut to crack. He is only ten, or thereabouts, in body at least. However, his miserable experiences of life have meant an old and wary head now rests on

those young shoulders. I do know his parents are *gone*.'
She mouthed that last word in case Izzy overheard. 'Although I have no clue whether that came by way of bereavement or abandonment. After that, from what I can gather, he has been passed from pillar to post for the last couple of years. After his grandmother died, he was taken in briefly by an aunt, and then most recently by an uncle. In return for that imposition, he had to pay for his board by working in a timber yard by day, loading their carts, and in a tavern by night, hauling barrels.'

'He worked two jobs?' That did not bear thinking about. 'The poor boy.'

'And all those hours for a paltry four and a half shillings a week. Thanks to that greedy uncle who believed it was his due, Jim never saw a farthing of those wages.' Suppressed rage at that hardened her blue eyes to ice crystals. 'But such unjust atrocities are par for the course among those considered too poor and too young to warrant a voice. Jim was unceremoniously cast out of the man's house and deposited with the church within a day of his accident. They gave him sanctuary for a night but were eager to wash their hands of him too so took him immediately to the Cleveland Street workhouse. As he was in no fit state to be any use there and they were already stuffed to the rafters with, as they put it, "infirm paupers who are no good to anyone", after a month they contacted Dr Cribbs and have made it plain they do not want the child back unless he is fixed enough that he can take care of himself.'

Proof if proof were needed that there was always somebody worse off than you, which was a sobering thought after Jasper had pickled himself in spirits last night because he had felt sorry for himself. 'Can the good doctor fix him?'

She huffed out a frustrated breath. 'Maybe...up to a point. The quack who set the bones misaligned the shin bone in his right leg and it will need to be rebroken and reset if he is to have any chance of walking without crutches again, and such an extreme and unpleasant intervention has its own risks and complications.' Unwittingly, she rubbed her own leg, myriad complex emotions skittering across her features before she ruthlessly banished them all with a smile which did not quite touch her eyes. A window into the ordeal of her own recovery. 'Nobody can guarantee its success and the poor boy will have to endure months more suffering on top of what he already has in the last few weeks. It is for the best, of course, to allow Dr Cribbs to try, but the decision has to be Jim's. My current job is to convince him of the need before the bone sets fast.'

'If there is some hope, why does he resist?' Jasper couldn't understand it. 'I mean, look at how the doctor helped you.' Was it still wrong for him to reference her injury despite her openness about it? 'If I interpreted Freddie's frequent appraisals correctly while you were convalescing, there was some doubt in the beginning as to whether you would be able to walk again and now there is no doubt that you can.' Even the pronounced limp did not seem to pain her once her muscles had warmed up. Freddie had done her a disservice in intimating otherwise. His letters had stated Hattie was still as fragile as glass, when the woman beside him was anything but. 'No wonder Dr Cribbs holds you up as a role model for others. You are almost as good as new.' Why the blazes had he felt compelled to add the almost?

If his slightly tactless final comment offended her, she hid it well to ponder her patient. 'But I had the boisterous encouragement and love of a family behind me, along with wealth and privilege. I was never alone like little Jim is. Neither have I been let down or abandoned by everyone I know. I have no idea how it feels to have all hope dashed at every turn, or any concept of how hard his life has been. Right now, he is wallowing at the very bottom of the pit of despair and sees no reason to claw himself out. He has given up on the world and that breaks my heart. Any invasive treatment now might be catastrophic if he doesn't have the will to get better.'

She rapped on the ceiling of the carriage at the corner of Long Acre to make the driver pull over. 'But enough about that.' She offered him an apologetic smile. 'As much as I have already flown in the face of propriety, I fear I shall set the tongues wagging if I allow you to accompany me all the way to the infirmary.'

'Of course.' Jasper tried not to allow his disappointment to show. 'Thank you for visiting. It was very thoughtful of you. And thank you again for last night.'

She waved that away as she bent to stroke Izzy's hair. 'It was lovely to meet you, Izzy.'

'Will you visit me and my papa again, Hattie?'

Jasper wanted to ask much the same but didn't, because such an improper request would be unfair to Hattie who was too good-natured and kind to refuse. Instead, he smiled and came to her rescue, not wanting her to feel beholden to him either. 'I am sure we shall all collide again some time soon.'

'Good day, Izzy.' Hattie touched the tip of her little nose, then did the same to her doll. 'Good day to you too, Mabel.' She straightened and those lovely, empathic eyes locked with his. 'Take care, Jasper.' Then without looking back, she exited the carriage and hurried across the road and, much too soon, disappeared from his view.

'Are you taken for this dance, Lady Anne?' The third besotted gentleman in a row edged towards Hattie's sister as the pair of them perused the refreshment table. Lord Pickering was a handsome devil and knew it. He was also one of the gentlemen her twin had had her eye on. 'For if you are not...'

'She's not,' said Hattie before a beholden Annie felt obliged to turn him down for her sister's sake as she already had with two others. Just because Hattie couldn't dance didn't mean she expected her sister to sit with her in the wallflower chairs as she had loyally declared she would for the first half an hour to 'soak in the atmosphere'.

Then, no doubt, it would be Kitty's turn to pretend her feet were aching, or some other far-fetched nonsense, to justify her shift as nursemaid. Followed, in whatever order her interfering brother had prearranged behind her back, by him and Dorothea. And all because she had begged him to stop cajoling reluctant friends and acquaintances her way and declared Lady Bulphan's ball would be her last foray out this Season if he did.

'My sister would be delighted to dance this dance with you. In fact...' she offered her glaring twin a sickly smile which told her in no uncertain terms that Hattie wasn't the least bit fooled by the family's flimsy charade '...if you are quick, I also happen to know that she has kept the first waltz free, too, as well as all six dances in between.' She announced this at a louder volume on purpose to attract the attention of all the other eligible young men milling about, and like obedient hunting hounds summoned by a bugle, they instantly turned to stare, intrigued. Then, one by one, all clamoured around Annie to claim one of the free dances.

While her sister was surrounded, Hattie poured herself some punch and dissolved into the crowd, taking a convoluted route to the wallflower chairs in case her suffocating brother noticed she was all alone. She nodded to the four other wallflowers in greeting but chose a seat at the back, in the middle of a row because she could use a strategic pillar as camouflage and settled in for the duration.

As she drained the last drops of her punch, another glass appeared over her shoulder. 'Thought I might find you here.'

'Jasper!' She almost dropped the empty cup in shock and attempted to cover the ferocious blush creeping up her neck with mortified irritation. 'I thought I had made it plain that I didn't need saving!'

'Yes, I heard you say that, and before you launch into another diatribe about loathing pity and people feeling beholden, I shall save you the effort.' He had circumvented the back of the chairs and was now shuffling along the front of them balancing another cup of punch on a plate piled high with food from the buffet. 'For neither indebtedness, pity nor guilt have brought me here.' He dropped into the chair beside her, stretched out his long legs beneath the seat in front and crossed them at the ankles. Only then did he remove the cup from the plate and offer the selection to her.

'I wasn't sure what you liked, and as I like it all, I loaded two of everything for us to share but confess I polished off all the little fried cheese things in transit because they were just too moreish.' When she only blinked at him in answer he grinned and balanced the plate on his lap to select something else for himself.

'If you are not here out of a misplaced sense of guilt, then why are you?'

'Two reasons.' Something dainty and wrapped in pastry disappeared into his mouth and the wretch made her wait while he chewed it. 'Firstly, I came to deliver something.' He patted his coat and retrieved a folded square of paper from a hidden pocket inside, waving it at her. 'I promised Izzy solemnly that I would give you this.

'And secondly...' He sighed as his eyes dipped, awkward again and a bit lost. 'Because it turns out that four-year-olds are fast asleep by seven, and as I am avoiding my club for obvious reasons, I am left alone to stew in my own juices and, after the notorious brandy incident, I have come to the conclusion that that isn't wise.' He popped a bacon-wrapped date into his mouth and glanced around him.

'I've never sat in the wallflower chairs before. All the exiled gentlemen hover around the edges and try to disappear into the woodwork, but these chairs rather make a statement, don't they?'

He glanced around him with disdain at their confined space in the furthest corner of the ballroom, and at the overly cheerful few young ladies peppered throughout the seats. They were huddling in groups of two or three so that they could pretend to be engrossed in a riveting conversation, having a high old time, rather than gazing wistfully at their peers dancing. 'I now feel dreadful for every single bottom sat on one and ashamed that I've never taken the time to know any of them.'

Why would he? He was handsome, rich and undisputedly still quite a catch despite his scandalous reputation.

'The young lady in the unfortunate thick spectacles is Miss Winston, the scholarly daughter of an admiral who is so intelligent she scares every gentleman without trying.' Hattie whispered this in his ear while trying not to inhale the seductive woody scent of his cologne. 'Seated beside her is Lady Octavia Trenton.' It felt unkind to mention poor Octavia's protruding teeth or her unremarkable other features. 'This is her fourth Season, so by society's terms, she's already consigned to the dusty shelf of eternal spinsterhood.

'Over there—' she subtly gestured to the three bored ladies tapping their hands and feet to the music '—are the two Misses Bristow, sisters who are well connected but sadly have no dowries or attractive enough *qualities* for such a situation to be ignored. And next to them is the painfully shy and terminally poor Lady Susannah Hargreaves. She is also perennially on a diet, which doesn't seem to work, so stares as wistfully at the refreshments as she does the dance floor. We are all on nodding and smiling at one another terms, seeing as we are all in the same club—and by club I mean the 1813 Wallflowers' Club—which, unlike your den of iniquity, is not an institution anyone would voluntarily want to become a member of.'

Hattie tried to make light of it but could see by his furrowed brow he sympathised with all of the members.

'Lady Bulphan might as well have hung a banner above these chairs announcing this as the place for every lady who is either too old, too plain, too impoverished, too skinny, too plump or—' he nudged her playfully with his elbow '—too wonky to warrant a dance partner.' Then he smiled. It wasn't a polite smile, or an apologetic one. Or a grin, or a fake smile or a flirty one either, for that matter, as she had seen all of those on his expression over the years and none had ever had the effect of this one. It was instead half-heartfelt and half-mischievous, as if they were both firm friends and partners in crime and it warmed her soul.

'Wonky.' She feigned outrage but he refused to bite. 'Is that any way to talk to the daughter of a duke?'

'I am simply being honest. Would you prefer I offered trite, empty and dishonest platitudes instead, Hattie?'

'I can see that you are one of those irritating people who quotes me back at myself.'

'If the shoe fits.' His green eyes were dancing. 'Only you cannot claim to loath other people's well-intentioned pity if you also expect those that respect you to sugar their words. Be wonky and proud. Make no apologies for who you are or what you do. Trust me, that philosophy has served me well for years.'

'Oh, you respect me all of a sudden, do you?' She made a joke of the compliment rather than ask why, folding her arms and tapping one finger on an elbow as if she were waiting for a similar response.

'As a matter of fact I do.' He mirrored her stance by folding his arms too. 'If one ignores your annoying tendency to take offence where none is meant, your stubborn pride and your flagrant flouting of the rules of propriety, you have a number of traits which are admirable.' Remembering the paper protruding from his hand, he thrust it at her, a tad awkward again as if he had admitted more than he was comfortable with. 'But I didn't come here to shower you in flattery, I came here to deliver this.'

Hattie opened the folded square and stared at the childish picture Isabel had drawn for her in chalk. Three exceptionally wonky figures stood in a line holding hands. As the shorter one in the middle appeared to have a doll attached to her chest, she assumed that was Izzy. The tall figure with black sticks for arms, a lop-sided crimson grin and a misshapen top hat had to be Jasper. Which meant the other, with its one big blue eye and one small beneath scruffy swirls of yellow hair had to be her.

'Apparently it is us. Izzy was insistent you have it to remember her by.' He rolled his eyes. A flippant gesture which did nothing to hide the pride in them at his daughter's artistic prowess. 'She's talked about you constantly since she met you, which is no mean feat as she's naturally shy. But clearly you have a knack with children.'

'Tell her I shall treasure it.'

'I promised her that I would also invite you to tea at our house next week. Just the three of us and another huge cake, even though I know that such an invitation is grossly improper, and your previous visit was a one-off borne out of your concern for me, so please take it with a pinch of salt. But that tiny minx has always had me wrapped around her little finger, and I know she will spot the lie if I politely decline on your behalf without doing expressly as she has asked first.'

Of course she should politely decline.

Of course she should!

Escorting him home while he had been drunk had been foolhardy, the second visit had been utter madness but necessary for her peace of mind. A third was openly courting scandal and social suicide no matter how tempted she was to say yes.

'Tell Izzy I would be delighted to accept.' Not at all what she had planned to say, but she was powerless to stop her wayward jaw again. 'I should also like to take you shopping at your earliest convenience so that I can help you with that dreaded list.'

It was his turn to blink at her in surprise, so her possessed mouth ploughed on, while her usually sensible head was already plotting when and how she could manage the promised trip. 'I am expected back at the infirmary on Monday afternoon at three, but my family are so used to my comings and goings there that they will not question me adding a couple more hours to the visit. What about noon? If you have your carriage wait for me on Long Acre, we can sneak to Cheapside as no good member of the *ton* would be seen dead shopping there among the rabble. You can purchase all the regular items and I can deal with all the *unmentionables*.'

'Is that wise?'

'What happened to making no apologies for what I do?'

He went to speak then narrowed his eyes. 'I can see that you are one of those irritating people who quotes me back at myself too.'

As she laughed, a shadow covered Izzy's picture on her lap. It was the slightly paunchy, exceedingly supercilious shadow of Lord Boredom who had crept up with such stealth she hadn't seen him coming. He moistened his lips, a bit like a toad, while he rocked on his heels, openly staring down her cleavage as he did so. 'Did you receive my bouquet this morning, Lady Harriet?'

'She received at least fifteen—which was yours, Cyril?' She was certain Jasper had failed to notice their interloper until she did, but he managed to muster the perfect set down as a response before a startled Hattie had even thought of one. 'Don't tell me...' He clicked his fingers as if this were suddenly a game. 'You sent that enormous, ostentatious bunch of scarlet roses, you old dog.' Jasper winked as Lord Boreham stiffened. 'Or were yours the exotic hothouse lilies which must have cost an arm and a leg?' If Hattie had a knack with children, then he had a knack of insulting someone in such a charming way that they couldn't dare be offended.

'I always suspected still waters ran deep. Right from our Oxford days I knew you were a dark horse where the ladies were concerned. I confess, I never expected we would be rivals for the same one though, Cyril.'

'Well, I...' The other man puffed out his chest like a peacock for a moment then frowned because his 'rival' was now feeding Hattie a titbit from his plate in a manner which suggested the pair of them were long past the polite, tentative stage of courtship and well into the over-familiar. 'I must say, Beaufort, I am surprised to see you here.' Lord Boredom stuck out his flat, non-existent chin. 'This sort of *entertainment* isn't usually to your particular tastes.'

His insulting insinuation was clear, but it was water off a duck's back to Jasper. 'We all have to grow up and settle down some time, Cyril.' He stood and hauled Hattie up with him by the hand. 'Now, if you will excuse us, I promised to show Lady Harriet the terrace.'

Chapter Nine

Jasper stared out of his carriage window, his palm tapping his knee as he scanned the street for Hattie.

For some inexplicable reason, Jasper was nervous. Which was a ludicrous state of affairs when he was a man of the world, when this was just a shopping trip, albeit a clandestine and wholly inappropriate one, and when Hattie was merely a friend. Or at least he assumed that was what she was now that they had reconnected after a couple of years of absence and had talked too much about too many intensely personal things in the last few days to be considered acquaintances. That she was also the off-limits baby sister of one of his oldest friends to boot, doomed their relationship to be platonic for ever if it lasted.

Which it likely wouldn't once the press learned about his plans for Izzy, put two and two together and made one hundred and five and he became the sort of social pariah whom mothers not only warned their daughters about as he was now, but the sort who also ceased being invited anywhere. At least for however many months or years it took the *ton* to forgive him for his latest scandal when he had already been the cause of so many.

Yet oddly nervous he was and not at all by the potential ramifications of both of them being discovered, but more because he had never gone shopping with a lady before. Obviously he had accompanied his mother to the market in Battlesbridge as a child but those trips were quite different. They had certainly felt quite different, although why a visit to the shops with Hattie suddenly felt intimate was beyond him. Except it did. And something about it made him as awkward as a green youth flirting with his first girl.

He sensed her before he saw her, and something peculiar happened in his chest. The relief tinged with a lightness and sense of anticipation that was baffling when they were only shopping for practical things for Izzy.

She beamed as he flung open the door. 'Sorry I'm a bit late.' He grabbed her hand and hauled her in, then tried to fathom why the flesh on his palms still tingled as he pulled closed the door and snapped the curtains shut. 'I forgot that my mother had arranged for the modiste to come to the house this morning, so had to suffer being pinned into several new gowns to ensure the perfect fit.' She sighed as she settled herself on the seat opposite him, looking as pretty as a picture in a bold turquoise muslin with matching ribbons on her straw bonnet which brought out the blue in her eyes. 'Although why it was all so imperative this morning when the Season has barely started, and we girls already have our wardrobes stuffed with new gowns is a mystery to me. But you know my mother.'

'I do and I adore her.'

'Doesn't everyone?' As the carriage lurched forward, it made one fat golden curl poking out of her hat bounce against her cheek and Jasper had to resist the urge to reach out and touch it—which was worrying. 'But talking of measurements, do you have Izzy's?'

'About thirty different measurements to be exact.' Before he had left Lady Bulphan's, Hattie had given him strict instructions to have Mrs Mimms measure her thoroughly, so he produced the piece of paper and held it up for her to read. 'Because my detail-obsessed housekeeper decided to measure everything from the length of Izzy's arms to the circumference of her head.'

She shot him one of her exasperated looks as she snatched the list out of his fingers. 'I knew Mrs Mimms would do a more thorough job than you were capable of.' She folded it back up and tucked it into her reticule, then snapped her fingers. 'And the other list? The terrifying one which had you reaching for the brandy?'

'Ha. Very funny.' But he produced that one too and waited while she scanned it. As she reached the end she pulled a face.

'I fear this all might take more than one trip, Jasper.' Which was surprisingly, and more worryingly, all right with him. 'Let's focus on the main priorities today. The absolute essentials.'

'Which are?' Because he was damned if he knew.

'Well for a start, some suitable furniture for her bedchamber and her nursery.'

'A nursery? I have to furnish two rooms?'

Her exasperation seemed genuine this time. 'Of course you do! One room to sleep in and another to play and do her lessons in.' She gestured to the comfortable luxury of his carriage. 'It is not as if you haven't got empty rooms aplenty and can't afford it.'

'It has nothing to do with the money and everything

to do with the shock of needing a nursery.' Just the word nursery shifted his world further sideways. Changed his fancy house on Russell Square for ever from a busy bachelor's sanctuary to a family home. Except his family, like his entire life he supposed, was destined to be unconventional. To cover how much that paradigm shift affected him he shrugged. 'I did warn you I was clueless about this whole parenting business.'

She smiled at that to let him off, perhaps because he hadn't hidden how his new responsibilities overwhelmed him so. 'I am not much better. The only experience of children that I have is the month of working with sick and damaged ones at the infirmary, but between us I am sure we will work it all out.' The 'we' warmed his soul. 'From my covert enquiries, it would seem that there is a cabinet maker on Old Jewry which specialises in children's furniture. We can start there.'

'We?' Good grief he loved the 'we'. 'Is it sensible for us to go to the same shop together?'

'As it's off the beaten track, I doubt it will be a problem. Besides, I fear you are so clueless, Izzy will end up with a crib and high chair if I leave it to you.'

Gladstone's smelled of sawdust and beeswax. Jasper introduced himself properly, which made perfect sense when anything they ordered would be going to his house on Russell Square, but he blinked in panic as he turned to introduce her to the white-haired cabinet maker the shop was named after. They hadn't thought to rehearse any appropriate excuse for her presence in the carriage. They had been too busy chatting about everything and nothing.

'And I am Lady Harriet… Beaufort.' She suppressed

her own wince which came from using his surname, only partly because she too had panicked at being caught on the hop. The other part was because it sounded presumptuous, coming out so smoothly and with such determination it might appear to Jasper that she had been practising using his name. Which of course she hadn't—at least not consciously—although now that she had used it, she couldn't help thinking how well it fitted. 'His cousin.' She pasted a smile on her face as the man bowed politely, oblivious of the amused face her companion pulled behind his back.

'Yes—my dear spinster *cousin* Hattie volunteered to help me while my *wife* is incapacitated.' He shot her the most sinful and naughty look. 'With nothing better to do with her time than watch the marching of it, she jumped at the opportunity.' He offered the cabinet maker his most serious but pitying man-to-man expression. 'She doesn't get out much.' The wretch was enjoying himself far too much.

'Oh, dear,' said Mr Gladstone, 'Your wife has nothing serious, I hope?'

That question puzzled Jasper who paused for a moment too long, allowing Hattie to get some revenge. 'To be frank, Mr Gladstone, the poor woman is at her wits' end and has taken to her bed—yet again—as it is not easy being married to my annoying cousin.'

'Ah…' Now the poor cabinet maker had no clue how to respond but he recovered quickly. 'How may I help you today?'

'We need some furniture.' Jasper was stating the obvious when this was the fellow's stock-in-trade.

'Quite a bit and in a hurry, Mr Gladstone. Suitable for a child soon to be five.' Who was supposed to be protected from the world for the next few months, so she thought on her feet to keep this secret. 'Our cousin, who lives in the country, has fallen on hard times and cannot afford to redecorate her nursery and what she has is rapidly becoming too small.'

'Yes.' Mr Gladstone nodded. 'Children grow.'

'They do indeed, sir.' Hattie smiled sweetly. 'Exponentially.'

An hour later they hurried out of the shop laughing, after having purchased enough small and pretty furniture to see Izzy right for several years. Jasper hadn't baulked at the price of any of it. If anything, he had added to the cost by requesting special finishes and expensive lilac upholstery because purple was apparently his daughter's favourite colour.

Their convoluted backstory to explain the sale had become more complicated as the minutes ticked by, especially after Mr Gladstone had only been too willing to deliver everything to wherever in the countryside their unfortunate *cousin* happened to live. By the end, the pair of them had been tripping over themselves conjuring plausible excuses but had left him believing that Jasper wanted to deliver it all himself as a surprise for the imaginary woman's birthday in a few weeks.

That went no way to explaining why Jasper had also insisted that the finished articles be delivered to his house in dribs and drabs as soon as they were ready, but once the cabinet maker had totted up the eye-watering bill and heard the purchaser assure him that he would have a man sent over with all the funds on the morrow, he ceased caring.

'I think you just made his year.' His arm felt solid

beneath Hattie's, the temptation to explore the muscles beneath his sleeves almost too much to bear. 'The man couldn't believe his luck to get such a large commission.'

'I am just glad that we were able to do such a good thing for dear Cousin Celia today.' He smiled as he searched the narrow street for any sign of his carriage, then paused to cross the road when he saw it poking out of another street several yards further along. 'The poor thing has suffered enough. Almost as much as my poor, addled wife.'

'We bored spinsters have little else to do than spread idle gossip and I thought some of Mr Gladstone's remedies would do your unfortunate spouse some good.' Gracious, it felt lovely talking nonsense and spending time with such a charming man. Yet another daft thing to ponder where he was concerned, and one which she would no doubt ponder to death in her quiet moments because she had taken to doing that a great deal in the last few days.

Worryingly, and undeniably futilely, the majority of those musings had more to do with him as a man rather than him as a friend in need. A much too attractive and compelling man than a true altruistic good Samaritan here to help should be contemplating. 'And perhaps he is right about the sea air.' She slanted him a glance which felt uncharacteristically coquettish. 'You should take her to Brighton for a week or two as a treat for putting up with you.'

He chuckled. 'I should—*oh, hell*!' Before Hattie could whip her head around to see what had caused his eyes to widen, she found herself being pulled into an alleyway and hurried along it. 'It's the Duchess of Warminster and her pious daughter Felicity!' He hissed this as he hauled her into a doorway because they had hit a dead end. 'What the blazes are they doing in Cheapside?'

Hattie couldn't think of a reason, and not because she thought the Duchess wouldn't usually be caught dead in an area filled with 'the trade', which was little better than 'the great unwashed' in her mind. But because the doorway was small, and with Hattie's back to the wood, his big body had to press against hers to effectively hide himself.

'Are they still there?' Her voice came out in a high-pitched panicked shriek, caused not by the impending prospect of potential ruination, but because one of Jasper's arms was still wrapped around her waist and her bosoms were flattened against his broad chest and getting all manner of inappropriate ideas.

He leaned back slightly to check, giving her bosoms some respite while his hand still played havoc with her senses because it continued to rest on the curve of her hip, then slammed back against them again with his finger to his lips nodding. 'They are literally at the other end of this alleyway. Felicity is frantically rummaging in her reticule. As if she has lost something.'

'Then let us pray she hasn't lost it down here.' Her voice came out croaky this time because her throat had dried, her breathing suddenly too erratic to get enough in her lungs, again caused by her close proximity to him.

Gracious he smelled divine up close.

He had always smelled lovely. The sort of lovely that had a lady's nostrils twitching as he breezed past, but the way that familiar masculine cologne reacted with his skin was a seductive thing of beauty.

She hadn't realised quite how tall he was until now either, because her eyes were level with his lips, giving hers wayward ideas. She blamed her bosoms for that. Who knew that bosoms alone could tempt a lady to sin?

He leant back again, but only his head moved away this time, and Hattie had no idea how she felt about that. The sensible, respectable part couldn't wait for this necessary inappropriateness to end so that her nerve endings could return to normal. The wanton part which he had just awakened wanted to learn so much more.

'The Duchess appears to be telling her off.' His warm breath caressed her cheek, sending a sensitised trail of goose pimples to erupt from the nape of her neck to the base of her spine. 'Felicity has stopped hunting in her reticule. She's wearing an expression of defeat and her mother is wagging her finger.'

Who knew a man's neck could be so attractive and alluring? Alluring enough that she wanted to loop her arms around it. With his head tilted back, she could make out every single follicle of dark stubble growing on his chin and throat, making her fingers itch to trace his face to learn how it made his golden skin feel different from hers. So close she could see the tiny pulse beating rapidly beneath his jaw. She sympathised as Hattie's heart was also beating nineteen to the dozen but for quite different reasons to his, she suspected. Hammering so hard behind her scandalously wanton bosoms it would take a miracle for it not to be knocking against his ribs.

'They're going.' He turned to beam at her triumphantly and she lost herself in his eyes. She watched his smile slip a split second before he realised where his hand was, causing him to instantly snatch it away and put a few polite inches of distance between them. Instead of the relief she had been hoping for, her body immediately mourned the loss.

Jasper turned again so that his eyes remained rooted on the street and at least she was glad of that, because she could already feel the heat of a ferocious blush oozing up her cheeks and branding her a shameless hussy.

'They're gone!' He blurted this out like a hallelujah and practically jumped away. 'That was close.'

Hattie nodded, mortified at the strength of her own fledgling desire, but not trusting herself to speak again in case she gave herself away. By his uncharacteristic stiff yet jerky posture, Jasper clearly wanted to just get away. Fast. 'Why don't I go and fetch the carriage in case they are still lurking close by and I'll signal you from the window if the coast is clear as I dare say the last thing either of us want is to be caught in a compromising position.' She nodded again, trying not to feel disappointed that all her inappropriate, carnal feelings were obviously one-sided. 'It's probably long past time I delivered you to the infirmary anyway.'

And with that, he marched off to get that job done with all haste, his dark brows more furrowed than she had ever seen them.

Chapter Ten

Despite a late and fitful night, Jasper had awoken with the lark. There had been no point attempting to go back to sleep because his mind was whirring every which way, so he decided to bury himself in work until breakfast. There was still close to a month's worth of Reprobates' accounts to go over alongside a mountain of correspondence. Except that hadn't worked to quieten his thoughts either and after an hour of being unable to focus for longer than a few minutes at a time, he had given up to stare out of his study window instead.

His emotions were all over the place. Obvious sadness at Cora's passing and the guilt of missing her funeral, on top of the huge swathe of guilt he already carried as far as she was concerned, mingled with the onerous task of settling her affairs.

Cora had left everything to her daughter. The cottage he had bought them, all her belongings, some treasured family pieces passed from Cora's father and a great many stocks and shares, which he now knew she had spent some of her generous allowance on and which, all credit to her, made Izzy not wealthy in her own right by any stretch of the imagination, but comfortable. Financial independence had meant a lot to Cora in a way that he had never had to comprehend despite his own family's struggles with money. Hardly a surprise when this was a man's world and a woman, and most especially one from Cora's world, was always at the mercy of her masters. As disposable to their betters as that little boy in the infirmary that Hattie had told him about. As the new custodian of all those things, he had to make some careful decisions. He owed it to both Cora and Izzy to do that well.

Then there was Izzy to contend with, which was a whole other hornet's nest of confusion, marred by uncertainty, and an overwhelming fear of inadequacy as far as parenting was concerned. He had been flung in at the deep end, was genuinely doing his best to work it all out and each day revealed fresh challenges he had little clue how to navigate.

She was grieving too and understandably, so much more than he because she really did not understand the concept or the finality of death at all. By day he could minimise her anxieties by keeping her entertained. By night, awful terrors woke her and a week on, it bothered him that they seemed to be getting worse, not better. He had lost count of the many different ways that he had tried to explain that Cora was gone for good in the wee hours when she cried for her mother. It was becoming one of the main things occupying his mind.

That and his guilt and his inadequacies and his impending scandal.

Although the bulk of his pontificating this morning had again been about Hattie. And she was a whole other maelstrom of intense and colliding emotions, most of which he didn't understand. All he did know, or at least thought he did, was that there was a definite connection between them. She seemed to sense exactly what he was thinking and vice versa. They were undoubtedly cut from the same cloth. He was comfortable with her. Able to always be himself when he usually masked his true character, even with his closest friends. However, while Hattie was undisputedly now his friend there were other things floating beneath the surface which he was struggling to ignore. Feelings he wasn't sure were either appropriate or welcome in a friendship.

Attraction was the main concern. Jasper recognised all the symptoms, so was in no doubt that she called to him as a man as well as a friend. The need to see her. The need to look at her. The powerful effects of her smile or her touch or her lush body pressed against his. That impromptu near-embrace in the doorway while they had hidden from the Duchess of Warminster had been pure, unmitigated torture. It had instantly sent him mad with inappropriate lust which had kept rearing its ugly head ever since, leaving him with an overwhelming awareness of his own heartbeat, flesh and nerve endings whenever she was near. There was also a great deal of nervous anticipation before they collided when he knew they would. Like now, where he couldn't sit still because she was due here within the hour for Izzy's tea party.

Or so he hoped even though he had tried to talk her out of it again last night at the Renshaws' annual tuneless and supposedly exclusive *musicale* for the great and the good.

If, indeed, seventy people all gathered around a harpist and a talentless quartet could be construed as an exclusive entertainment. It had been intimate though. The airless room so hot and crammed you had no choice other than to rub shoulders with the great and the good because there wasn't the space to do otherwise. Hattie's summation and a fitting one.

And that was another worrying symptom.

Hanging on her every word. As if actively attending something he wouldn't normally be caught dead at just to spend some time with her wasn't evidence enough. And as if he wasn't burdened by guilt enough that he needed to add an untimely and grossly inappropriate attraction to his best friend's sister to his list of sins. A charitable, good-hearted and respectable young woman who had been nothing but kind to him in his hour of need. Who clearly had more of a soft spot for Izzy than she had for him. A woman whose beguiling eyes and pert figure he had no right enjoying quite as much as he did.

Clearly he was an awful person.

The worst.

Jasper sighed as he gave in to the urge to check the mantel clock for the umpteenth time and almost groaned aloud to see that the minute hand had moved barely an eighth of an inch since the last time he had checked.

In the absence of anything better to do, he decided to knock his head against his desk in the hope that might stop his thoughts spinning, only to jump out of his skin when Mrs Mimms strode in. 'You have a caller.'

'Hattie?' Just to compound his current misery, his foolish heart soared then plummeted as she shook her head.

'Her brother. Told me to be sure to tell you that if you can gallivant at both the Bulphans' and the Renshaws', then you could damned well see him.' She pursed her lips as her eyebrows raised. 'I get the distinct impression he's got a bee in his bonnet.'

It didn't take a genius to work out that bee likely had something to do with his sister. Hattie had intimated her brother hadn't been happy that she had escorted Jasper's brandy-soaked carcase home last week, and his friend had certainly shot him a few daggers last night as he had watched them sat together and laughing at the musical performance. 'Where's Izzy?' It was probably safest to deal with one sting at a time.

'Helping Cook make biscuits for your tea party with Lady Harriet later. I shall keep her in the kitchen till he leaves.'

'You didn't mention the tea party to Freddie, did you?' Because then there would be pistols at dawn for sure.

'I am not an idiot. Although my silence might be moot if she turns up while her brother is still here.' Mrs Mimms pulled a face as her gaze slid to the clock. 'To be on the safe side, I shan't offer him any refreshments whatsoever to speed his exit. In the meantime, I shall send him in and pray for you.'

'It is so nice having someone so staunchly on your side.'

She rolled her eyes at his sarcasm as she bustled out and less than a minute later Freddie Fitzroy strode in with a wagging finger. 'What the blazes do you think you are doing, Jasper Beaufort?'

'And a cheery good morning to you, my friend.'

'Don't give me all that friends rot.' Freddie stopped short of Jasper's desk and planted his feet. 'A decent friend doesn't try to seduce a man's sister behind his back!'

'Actually...' Jasper would suffer the admonishment because his wayward thoughts might well deserve it even if he was not guilty of the charge, but he wouldn't condone blatant hypocrisy. 'Seeing as you went and married George Claremont's sister after both wooing her and then running away with her to Gretna Green behind his back, apparently they do.'

By the way Freddie's eyes began to bulge, that probably wasn't the most sensible way to start this conversation but it was too late to claw it back now, so Jasper dipped his gaze contritely. 'But your point is well made, and a friend should never do such a thing to his best friend's sister—which is why I haven't.' And nor would he. Not only would it be unfair to Hattie and ruin their blossoming friendship, which he valued above all else, with his shocking reputation and the impending scandal about to make it ten times worse, any sort of attempted seduction would also likely send her limping for the hills.

More was the pity.

'Then what the blazes is going on between you?' Freddie began to pace. 'All cosied up at Lady Bulphan's ball, whispering and giggling together. I was prepared to let that slide as a one-off—' his friend paused only long enough to jab his index finger Jasper's way '—then last night happened and you turned up to a *musicale* out of the blue and dominated her time all over again.' Another pause. Another violent point. '*A musicale!* You! Who has never attended one of those awful things in your entire life!' Off he went again, wearing a groove in the Persian.

'Tongues are wagging, Jasper! Insinuations are being made!' When he paused this time, Freddie's clenched fists went to his hips. 'Speculations are being printed in the newspapers! Linking my baby sister and you! With Cora Marlow barely gone a week!' His anger turned swiftly to sympathy as Freddie clearly realised his outburst had touched a nerve. 'My sincerest condolences on that score, my friend, I know she meant—'

Jasper shook his head, not ready to talk about Cora, even to one of his closest friends. He had never discussed the full extent of his relationship with her with anyone—it was, to quote Hattie, nobody's business. 'Thank you.'

Freddie nodded, swallowing his frustration even though this time he had a good reason to expect answers. The anger still shimmered off him in waves. 'As her brother, I demand to know exactly what the blazes are you up to with Hattie?'

'I am not up to anything with Hattie.' It was an unconvincing denial and his friend deserved better, so Jasper huffed to stare at him levelly. 'Nothing beyond rescuing her as she rescued me.'

'Rescuing her?' Freddie threw his hands in the air in exasperation. 'Oh, please! Do I look like I was born yesterday? Who does Hattie need rescuing from apart from an opportunistic chancer like you?' Out came the disapproving finger again, wagging for all it was worth. 'You are taking advantage of a fragile young woman who is in a delicate state! Who lacks confidence and self-worth. You are preying on the vulnerable! Ruining any chance she might have of securing a decent husband who will look after her...'

Jasper surged to his feet, more offended for her than

guilty at his inappropriate attachment to her. 'Oh, for pity's sake! Listen to yourself! Delicate. Fragile. Vulnerable!' He resisted the urge to shake his friend by the shoulders. 'Do you even know Hattie at all, Freddie? Delicate and vulnerable are not adjectives which describe your sister who has more confidence and self-worth than anyone I know. She is determined and tenacious, strong and stubborn and she deserves better from her brother than having him press-gang and cajole eligible gentlemen her way with glasses of sherry at balls on sufferance in the vain hope one might take enough pity on her to marry her!'

Angry himself now, because he suddenly completely understood her frustrations, Jasper began to pace. 'She loathes other people's pity, you idiot, and certainly doesn't deserve it.' He wagged his own finger. 'And shame on you for thinking that she does!'

Freddie's eyes narrowed. 'You like her, you scoundrel!'

'Of course I like her! What's not to like? She is clever and witty, kind and generous, and the most genuine and compassionate soul I have ever met.'

Instead of agreeing, Freddie hit the roof. 'Oh, my God! It's worse than I thought! You not only like her—you're besotted by her!' The accusing finger did not wag this time, just pointed unwavering. 'Stay away from my sister!'

'Freddie, you've got the entirely wrong end of the stick.' Jasper spread his hands placatingly even though inside he was panicking. How to make her overprotective brother understand what was really going on without betraying Hattie's trust and being prevented from seeing her?

When he had to see her.

'Hattie and I are friends.' And that friendship already meant the world. 'After she saved me from making a fool of myself at the Queen's ball when I wasn't in my right mind after I heard about Cora...' He could admit that truth aloud at least. 'Making the Season more bearable for her seemed the least I could do in return. She loathes being viewed as an object of pity, Freddie. Hates all the awkwardness of those conversation partners you foist upon her—but also wants to avoid all the fortune hunters and social climbers who gather in the wings like vultures. Godawful men like Cyril Bloody Boreham and their drooping bouquets and unwelcome advances, who fancy themselves as a son-in-law to a duke and see her as fair game now that she limps.

'If I am guilty of anything, it is of running interference for her sake while distracting myself by feeling useful rather than hopeless.' At least that was the truth too, not that he was ready to admit that it was fatherhood he was hopeless at.

Freddie absorbed this, and to his credit, allowed his own guilt regarding his treatment of Hattie to show. 'I suppose I have been running interference too. Trying to help in my own overbearing and ham-fisted way.' He sighed and finally sat down.

'Help her to what? Find her feet? Find herself? I can assure you she requires no assistance with either. Or are you genuinely trying to help her find a husband because you believe she needs a man to look after her?' Jasper sat too, keen to build a bridge when he sympathised. 'Because if you are, and that is the underlying motive for sending every unmarried and blatantly uninterested fellow you know her way, then it begs the question have you actually asked her if she wants one just yet? Or are you assuming, like Lord Boredom but with less selfish motives, that an uninterested man's ring on her finger is the best achievement in life that she can dare hope for after the accident?'

His friend raked a hand through his hair. 'When you say it like that I feel dreadful.'

'The road to hell is paved with good intentions.'

A throwaway comment which also gave Freddie pause for thought. 'Indeed it is, which is why I am going to have to put my foot down about you dominating Hattie's time in public.' Not at all the measured consequence Jasper had envisaged. 'People are already talking and with your shocking reputation your good intentions, no matter how apparently noble, could destroy hers. Scandals are always worse for the woman. *Always.*'

'Are you still saying I cannot speak to her?' Alarm tinged with hurt bubbled again. 'Even though my intentions and my behaviour have been nothing but honourable?' Which was true. His behaviour, if one ignored the brandy incident, had been that of a gentleman and he really wanted all of his intentions to be honourable.

'Not alone. On that I must insist.' Freddie stood and set his jaw. 'I have never pried into your personal affairs, nor ever sought to judge you for some of your choices as heaven only knows I've not been a saint myself, but I cannot allow certain aspects of your *unconventional* lifestyle and dubious past choices to bring her flawless reputation into disrepute.' He was alluding to Cora. They both knew it although Freddie, like everyone, did not know the half of that shocking story.

'You can converse to your heart's content at any soirée in a crowd where it is acceptable and anywhere else where she is properly chaperoned by a family member. Anything else is not. And I would like your word as my friend and a gentleman that you'll adhere to those parameters.' He stuck out his hand to shake on the bargain. 'Do the decent thing for Hattie's sake. She does not deserve to be sullied by your reputation.'

Jasper had no clue how to respond to that so simply stared, his mind reeling and his heart sore as he reluctantly shook his hand while Freddie smiled the smile of a man who had just offloaded a great weight from his shoulders. 'I am glad we got that all sorted.'

Chapter Eleven

'The most important things are always the hardest to talk about, Jim, especially if you are scared, but things are always easier when you do.'

The boy lay staring out of the infirmary window, speaking when spoken to, but answering mostly in non-committal grunts. He refused to talk about his past or his future, his hopes or his fears. Three visits in and he still wasn't inclined to trust her no matter what she said or did, and Hattie couldn't blame him. The poor thing had had such a hard life and in his mind, even that was over. She had been to that dark place and wouldn't wish it on a soul, let alone a child.

'You do know that you do not have to stay in bed, don't you?'

'There ain't much point in getting out of it, now, is there?'

'Apart from lying down all day and staring at the ceiling being as dull as dishwater. You must be very bored, Jim.' She left her chair to walk to the window, using opening it as an excuse to talk to his face rather than the back of his head. She sniffed the warm breeze and sighed, smiling. 'It is such a lovely spring day… I could take you out in it if you want.'

'No thanks.' He lifted his eyes long enough for her to witness the belligerence in them. 'I can't walk, remember?' That was said as if she were a blithering idiot, in the sort of tone that had it come from one of her siblings she would have bitten back. As almost every response she had received in the hour she had been there had been delivered in much the same hostile way, her patience was wearing thin. So she swallowed the pithy retort on the tip of her tongue, that he likely would be able to walk if he stopped being such a stubborn fool and allowed Dr Cribbs to help him. Losing her temper with Jim wouldn't convince him and would only alienate him further.

'We could use the wheeled…'

'I'm not going in that stupid chair!' He spat that, his freckled face contorted with sheer venom. 'Not that you could push it anyway, you ugly, lame cow!'

Hattie counted to ten and forced another smile as she perched beside him on the mattress, determined not to allow him to force her away no matter how hard he tried. 'I could get one of the porters to push it and we could go feed the ducks. I saw some the other day not too far from here on the way to a friend's, in a lovely little park just off Beaverbrook Square. There are ducklings too and it's a quaint, secluded spot where nobody would bother us. I find a change of scenery always improves the mood.'

'I said no!'

'Maybe tomorrow then?' She hadn't planned on coming to the infirmary again so soon but as she had nothing else on except her mother's knitting circle and she was proving to be the world's worst knitter, she might as well. It wasn't as if she was ever likely to produce a wearable sock. 'If you can be dressed and ready by eleven then…' Out of nowhere, two furious hands lunged with such force that Hattie was thrust from the mattress before she could brace herself, landing hard on her bottom on the floor. The jarring caused pain to shoot up her damaged leg, acute enough to wind her.

'I said no, cow! Didn't you hear me, or are you stupid as well as lame?' His hands curled into fists on the blankets. 'You ugly, limping, worthless, do-gooding hag!'

She tried to get up, using the mattress for support and he smacked his fist on her hand, leaving her beached like a whale and feeling so helpless again something snapped inside. She hated being a victim. Loathed feeling powerless with every fibre of her being.

'I might be lame but at least I am not a miserable, pathetic coward! I am not stupid either, because I had the good sense to accept the doctor's help and I did that because I knew I was worth more than wasting my life in a bed. You make me sick lying there so bloody minded and angry at the world! As if you are the only person who has ever suffered bad luck!'

Hattie used her good leg to shuffle her bottom around so she could use the windowsill as support, then summoned every ounce of strength to drag herself upright. It wasn't pretty but she managed it, and by the time she was standing, she was so furious she couldn't calm down even if she'd wanted to.

'So your bones got broken? Boo-hoo, poor you, so did mine—then the subsequent infection nearly killed me!' Tit for tat probably wasn't the best way to deal with him, but she was past caring. 'But do I go around talking to people like dirt or thumping them? Of course I don't because I am not a martyr who feels hard done by but does nothing to help himself!' Her own fists were clenched now. So tight she could feel her nails digging into her palm. The distant voice of reason cautioned her to count to ten again, but she was so furious she ignored it.

'I am not sure how to break this to you, Jim, but bad things happen all the time to the rest of the inhabitants of this planet too. Tragic things. Unfair and unjust things. Deaths, poverty, hunger, accidents, abandonments, illnesses and injuries! But thankfully, for every snivelling, gutless coward like you who fills every waking moment with self-pity and takes it out on people who do not deserve it, the rest work tirelessly to find a small triumph in that adversity. They rise above it, make the best of it, adapt, work, help others and fight! And thank goodness, as I shudder to think what this earth would be like if it was filled with bitter and twisted surrendering imbeciles like you!'

She wanted to shake him. Punch a wall. Kick something. Hard. But as kicking something would end up with her on her bottom again she settled for a scathing look of absolute disgust. 'Shame on you, you horrid, spiteful and *lame* little boy!'

Hattie didn't wait for a response and dragged her dratted right leg kicking and screaming out of the room, clomped down the stairs and shoved her arms into the sleeves of her pelisse. Then, angrier than she had been since her own accident had crushed all her dreams, she slammed the front door of the infirmary closed behind her.

She ranted to herself all the way to Long Acre and

as she skirted the shabby streets which bordered Seven
Dials, and was still fuming by the time she hit Great
Russell Street where she realised that she was less than
five minutes from Jasper's house. As neither he nor Izzy
deserved to entertain such a grumpy guest, and because
she was likely a good hour earlier than they expected,
she took herself to the small green in the centre of the
square and sat on a bench to calm down. She might have
managed it too until she spied her brother's phaeton
leaving the vicinity of the house she was about to visit.

In case he saw her, Hattie darted behind a bush as
more anger bloomed afresh when she recalled his lecture at this morning's breakfast table and put two and
two together. If Freddie had done what she thought he
had done, then she was going to break his interfering
nose for a second time!

'What did my insufferable big brother want?' Hattie
hadn't bothered shrugging out of her coat before she
marched into Jasper's study. Behind her Mrs Mimms
gave him a wary look as she quietly closed the door and
left them to it. 'And don't you dare try to tell me the
wretch wasn't just here because I saw him!'

'And a cheery good morning to you, my friend.' He
should be tickled to have an excuse to use the exact
same greeting to two separate angry Fitzroy siblings
in the space of half an hour, because such coincidences
usually raised a smile, but he was still in the midst of the
doldrums caused by the eldest who had only just left.
Or at least it seemed as if he had, but with all the fog
in his brain and his current tendency to stare blankly
at nothing for hours at a time, he could be mistaken. To
confirm it, Jasper turned to the clock where the min-

ute hand had only moved on five minutes from when he had last checked it at noon as Freddie left. 'You are early. I thought we said one?'

'We did but...' She let out a frustrated growl as she tossed her gloves on to his desk. 'It has been one of those mornings, and my idiot brother is, frankly, the last straw.' In another quirky, ironic coincidence, her pretty straw bonnet also hit his blotter with a thud. 'I am not angry at you.'

'I am relieved to hear it as I have already been shouted at by a Fitzroy this morning and it wasn't pleasant.'

'Let me guess!' Angry fingers made short work of the buttons of her pelisse. 'You sitting beside me *again* at the Renshaws' following our cosy tête-à-tête at Lady Bulphan's has caused idle tongues to wag, and he doesn't want to see my flawless reputation tarnished by my ill-considered association with a notorious scoundrel with more notches on his bedpost than I have had hot dinners.' She wagged her finger frowning, mimicking Freddie to perfection in both manner, tone and expression.

'While society accepts and understands that the male of the species are at the mercy of their urges, Harriet, it holds its females to a different standard and no decent gentleman will marry a girl who appears to have such loose morals and flouts the rules of propriety so openly as to entertain an infamous and unrepentant rake.' She rolled her lovely eyes heavenwards as she tossed the garment aside and slumped in the wingback opposite.

'Words to that effect.' Good grief it was good to see her, and perhaps, because this seemed doomed to be the last time he ever had her alone, Jasper drank in the sight. 'A tad politer, with no reference to notches and infamy, but perhaps delivered with more malice.'

'But the gist is you are to stay away from his sister.'

Jasper's smile was stretched. 'I believe he managed that line almost verbatim.'

'I hope you told him to go to hell in a handcart verbatim too, as that is precisely what I did when he dared to lecture me this morning! It is beyond me why he feels he has to behave like my father when I have a perfectly good father already. One who treats me like an adult, allows me to make my own choices and who doesn't fuss and carry on like Freddie does.'

She snatched up the paperweight near her elbow and passed the glass ball from hand to hand agitated, at home here already and completely comfortable in his company after such a short but enlightening reacquaintance.

That that had happened so fast was staggering really. Finding an unlikely friendship after almost a decade of knowing one another was one of fate's strange and delightful twists. Which made him all the sadder that the friendship had to end in its current form.

'What infuriates me is that my suddenly holier-than-thou, straw-for-brains brother seems to have forgotten what a shocking scandal he was before he settled down with Dorothea. Either that, or he remembers every moment of his debauchery with the opposite sex with absolute clarity and therefore believes every other man will behave in the same manner to any woman in possession of a pulse.'

'To be fair to Freddie, I am as much, if not more, of a shocking scandal than he was.' And any day now was likely to become more of one because he couldn't hide Izzy for ever, and for her sake he didn't want to. Being hidden away and always having to apologise for who you were was not the life his little girl deserved, and he owed it to Cora to ensure she grew up proud and confident. Acknowledged by someone and openly protected. Which meant that Hattie's brother might have a valid point.

When the news broke—and realistically that was a matter of when not if when the capital had prying eyes everywhere—that Cora's child also bore his surname and lived under his roof, all the worst speculation from the past would be dredged up and embellished as it was shouted from the rooftops. Such infamy might not harm his business—because conversely his wealthy patrons seemed to want him to be every inch the libertine he was painted—but it would harm his social standing. At least in the short term. He'd become a complete social pariah again as far as the *ton* was concerned.

The kind-hearted and noble Hattie did not deserve to be dragged down with him and, as much as it pained him to have to bow down to Freddie's logic, as Jasper knew first-hand, scandals were always worse for a woman, even if none of it was her fault.

While people had patted him on the back during his much gossiped about time with Cora, they crossed the road to avoid her. The gossip about her had been vile and cruel, and he shuddered to think how bad it would have got if they had also learned about Izzy. Which was one of the main reasons Cora had had to leave. 'My reputation is also far worse.'

'Oh, I know that.' Hattie waved that glaring truth away as of no consequence. 'But to be fair to you, it was hardly your fault that you were disinherited and had to open a gentlemen's club to make ends meet.' That she knew that wasn't a surprise when it had been common knowledge for years. 'And maybe you did run a bit fast and loose when you were younger, but—' she gestured to the space around them '—you've become a successful businessman, have made a good home and are determined to raise your child in it when most of the gentlemen of the *ton* tend to brush their indiscretions under the carpet. From where I am sitting you seem to have grown up in the last few years, and done so with admirable decency.'

'Time marches on.'

'It does indeed and with age comes wisdom and all. And while we are about it, why don't we add all the rest of the wise old sayings which are supposed to make us feel better but never do.' She scoffed at them all, her temper calming. That was obvious by the way she gently put the paperweight back in its proper place rather than slamming it down with the same force as she had picked it up.

Part of him wanted to believe his mere presence helped soothe her as hers did him. The other part— the more reasoned and measured part—understood he wasn't being fair in that wish. Just because she had been there in his hour of need did not give him the right to dominate her hours.

She exhaled as she shook her head, exasperation leaking from every pore. 'I am certainly very different from who I was then too—except in my brother's eyes. To him, I am worse than the child I was. To him, I have regressed and changed into the human incarnation of little Izzy's porcelain doll. So fragile, pathetic with my dratted limp, and so suggestible and ignorant of the harsh realities of life that I must be cosseted at every juncture. It is as if he doesn't know me at all.'

'I think I said as much verbatim to him.'

'Thank you.' Her smile warmed his soul and destroyed it at the same time. 'But I doubt he listened. He is too wedded to his outrage. Determined to see seduction at every turn. As if you would seduce me now!' She scoffed at that, her eyes dipping as she shook her head. 'Me, of all people! How stupid is he to consider such nonsense?'

Jasper couldn't decide if she discounted any chance of that because of his reputation, his new circumstances, her lack of attraction to him or her own self-consciousness about her 'dratted' leg.

'So what else did the cretin say when he read you the Riot Act?'

'That I am not to consort with you alone in public ever again.'

She was silent for a moment then her temper surged afresh. 'How dare he! How *dare* he! I am a grown woman, nearing the age of majority, and whomever I choose to *consort* with is no business of his!'

Jasper reached across the table to cover her hand with his, needing to touch her even though he had no right. As always, the innocent contact still reminded him that he was a man. 'We have become fast friends you and I, yes?' She stared at their hands for a moment before nodding. 'Then as your friend, one who cares deeply about your welfare, I have to concede your brother is right. You are a born rescuer to your core, and I adore that about you, but my life is complicated. My reputation has always been precarious to say the least. With Cora gone it has become more so.

'When the world discovers Isabel, which they will, not everyone will be as forgiving as you have been about her existence, and you will be judged by association. Your faultless morals will be brought into question and mud sticks.'

'I do not care about that.'

'Of course you don't, because you are a hopeless rescuer. But I do.' He laced his fingers through hers. 'So I shan't be importuning you again in public. I will not add fuel to a fire that could burn you to cinders but only scorch me. You have already been through enough pain, Hattie, and I will not be the cause of more.'

She digested this and went to argue, but thankfully, an excited Izzy burst through the door just then.

Chapter Twelve

A subdued Freddie guarded Hattie himself at the Countess of Nantwich's ball that night, and that had been a painful experience because she was nowhere near ready to forgive him for ruining her friendship with Jasper, and her outrage did not make for good conversation. She also spent the entire evening watching the door in the hope Jasper had had a change of heart and might walk through it. He didn't, of course, exactly as he had promised, so she had worried about him incessantly as a result.

Tomorrow he travelled alone to Cookham to close up Cora's house and collect her effects, and while he had been all matter of fact and stoic about it as he had told her his intentions in the one quiet interlude that they had had without Izzy, she could tell he was dreading it.

Of course he was. She couldn't imagine how hard it would be to face all that alone, when he had once loved her deeply and they would always share a child.

The thought had so consumed her that she had awoken this morning and decided she would defy both his wishes and Freddie's by seeing him alone once more whether he wanted her to or not. To that end she got the carriage to drop her off at the infirmary early and smuggled herself through the servants' entrance at the back of his house at the unfashionable hour of nine.

Mrs Mimms was surprised to see her but could not hide her relief either, and showed Hattie to his study without announcing her first. His door was open, which meant she saw him sat at his desk lost in thought as he stared out of the window, looking every inch a man with the weight of the world on his back. He snapped around as he heard their approach and the dark shadows etched under his narrowed green eyes were all the confirmation Hattie needed to know she had done the right thing.

'Spare me your silly lecture on propriety, for I am not leaving no matter what you have to say on the matter, and if you try to remove me by force, you should know that I have a legendary right hook as my brother's misshapen nose will testify.' She rested her fists on her hips rather than shake them at him. 'Friends do not desert one another in their hour of need, Jasper Beaufort, and that is that. Friends are there beside you no matter what. *No. Matter. What.*' In case he did try to manhandle her out, she sat in the wingback and stared him down.

'And that door swings both ways. I am the only shoulder you can lean on at the moment because I am the only person outside of this house who knows about Izzy. And without you, I had to suffer a half an hour with Lord Boredom last night, which is how I know to my cost that his foul habit of spraying spit whenever he talks is worse than ever. It was so bad I had to bathe after midnight because I didn't want to sleep with his abundant secretions on my skin!'

After an eternity he gave up glaring and sighed, smiling. 'It is good to see you.'

'And that is my cue to go fetch some tea.' Mrs Mimms backed out of the door, closing it as she went.

'How are things with you today?'

'Me—as well as can be expected after a late night at my club followed by around two hours of sleep. Izzy— not so well.' He leant back in the chair like a man at his wits' end. 'She is sleeping now, utterly exhausted, bless her, after another night filled with bad dreams. She doesn't understand that her mother has gone. Doesn't understand the concept of heaven even slightly. Thinks that a person can return from it, as if Cora has gone on a jaunt somewhere rather than to meet her maker. I just don't know what to do to help her to understand.'

'I suppose it must be confusing for a four-year-old.' Hattie knew that Jasper had been told that a neighbour had taken Izzy in when her mother's fever had worsened while another had tended to Cora who had died that same night. Those two kind women had been trying to protect her from the ordeal. 'I presume she did not attend the funeral.' In the normal course of things, children, especially younger children, were spared the ordeal of the graveside. It was customary still for some to even exclude the womenfolk from funerals, but she couldn't imagine being denied the right to say goodbye as Izzy had. No wonder the child was confused. 'To her one minute her mama was there and the next she was gone.'

When he nodded, something struck her. 'The purpose of a funeral is to say a final goodbye. Izzy hasn't had that so perhaps you should give her the opportunity and take her with you tomorrow.'

'You think I should take her with me to visit the graveside?' His handsome face contorted with distaste. 'How do I explain a grave when she has been told repeatedly that her mother went to heaven?' He pointed to the sky.

'You are right.' Hattie wished she knew the answer. 'Perhaps there is some other way she can say goodbye. A gentler way which would help her understand—but what could I possibly know?' She had no right to lecture him. No relevant experience from which to offer him sound advice. 'I haven't known her since birth, and I am not a parent.'

He exhaled slowly, his eyes searching Hattie's as if weighing her up, the indecision in them still there when he scrunched them closed. 'Can I entrust you with a secret that you can never tell another living soul *ever*— no matter what?'

'Of course you can.'

'Do you swear it?' His eyes opened and locked with hers so intently it made her uneasy because the message in them was clear. Whatever he was about to confess was momentous.

'On my life, Jasper.' Because the moment seemed to need it, she reached across the blotter to grip both his hands. 'You can trust me with anything.'

His fingers curled tight around hers as he whispered, 'I am not a parent either. Izzy isn't mine.'

Whatever her whirring mind had thought he might say, that certainly wasn't it. *'What?'* she stuttered, flabbergasted. 'But she is the image of you.'

He tugged one hand away to reach into a desk drawer, then placed a small oval enamel on the desk between them. 'She is the image of Cora.'

Hattie blinked at the tiny portrait. At the intense hazel gaze and dark curls. The contours of the face. The angle of the nose. The colouring. It was like looking at Isabel as an adult. 'But I do not understand. Cora was your mistress. Everyone knows that.'

'Everyone thinks *that*...but she and I never...' He raked a hand through his own dark hair as if searching for a polite way to explain and when he failed, shrugged. 'We were never lovers.'

Uncle Jasper! A slip she had put down to the peculiarities of their situation, all linked to his daughter's illegitimacy. Yet now, the odd expression Jasper got whenever the little girl remembered to call him 'Papa' had to be re-evaluated.

'But...you loved her. You told me so at the Queen's ball.'

'Of course I loved her. She was my friend. My oldest friend.' His smile was wistful. 'We grew up together. Cora's father was the stable master at the Battlesbridge estate, so we knew each other practically from birth. As things were always fraught between me and my objectional sire, I tried to spend as little time as possible in the house when he was in it. I used to escape to the stables when I was home, bothering her father who always had more time for me than my own. As the years went on, Mr Marlow struggled to cope with the workload.' That memory furrowed his brow.

'He had bad rheumatism, not that my father would have had any sympathy because he couldn't afford to pension anyone off, so Cora and I worked together to hide his condition. Knowing her father would be dismissed and replaced if my tight-fisted sire got wind of his increasing infirmity, by the time I was seventeen Cora and I did more and more of his job, but…'

Jasper blew out a breath. 'I was young and selfish. I grabbed the chance to go to Oxford with both hands to get away from Battlesbridge and am ashamed to say that once I got there, I enjoyed having too much of a high old time that I neglected to check on them quite as often as I should have. Cora and I exchanged letters in the first few months—her more than me because her father was ailing and she was worried sick—and then they suddenly stopped.

'To my shame, I was relieved. Not hearing of their difficulties made it easier to put their precarious situation out of my mind, and because I have always had such a fractious relationship with my father, I avoided going home.'

He settled back into the chair, his expression enough to tell her being so open about his past did not come easy, so Hattie avoided asking any of the questions which popped into her head in case they caused him to clam up.

'By then, I was also coming to realise that the Battlesbridge finances were not as healthy as my father wanted the world to believe. I had creditors knocking at my door asking why they hadn't been paid for the books or the lodgings that I needed to study. When my reminders to my father were ignored, I started to find creative ways to pay them myself. That summer after months of uncharacteristic silence on her part and thoughtless abandonment on mine, when I finally returned home, I discovered Mr Marlow's secret had found its way to my father's ears and he had been dismissed and the pair of them evicted.'

Hattie could see his deep guilt at that atrocity but bit her tongue to tell Jasper it hadn't been his fault because she could sense there was more stored up inside that he needed to share. A boil needed to be lanced fully to heal. 'Then what happened?'

'I fell out further with my father, tried to find them—searched all summer long—but they had disappeared without a trace. By autumn, I had to give up because around the same time my maternal grandfather passed away. He left me some money, and because I had also used the summer to uncover the full extent of the dire Battlesbridge finances, I decided to help. As we seemed to need money fast, the quickest route to getting it appeared to be via reckless games of chance.'

'You gambled it?'

He scoffed at that, baffled that she would even think it. 'I am not daft, Hattie. Even at nineteen I knew that the only real winners in such uncertain pursuits were the house, so I quit Oxford as my second year was due to start and I spent my entire inheritance on purchasing the building on King Street and then robbed Peter to pay Paul to turn it into The Reprobates'.'

'And lived a high old time while you were doing it.' Hattie remembered those years well as Jasper had been a regular fixture at their house in Mayfair whenever Freddie and George Claremont were home, where she blushed and stuttered around him awkwardly. 'As I recall, you were always in gossip columns with your hedonistic carousing in some of the most dubious places in the city, and apparently broke hearts here, there and everywhere.'

He didn't deny it but had the good grace to appear chagrined. 'It was good for business, for who would visit a club designed for sinners if it was run by a saint? I was still learning the ropes, so I made a point of visiting every hell from Teddington to Tilbury to discover what worked and what didn't.'

'Oh, it was all research, was it?'

'Not all.' He offered her a sheepish shrug. 'I never claimed I was a saint, Hattie. But with hindsight I can see that all that *carousing* was also a small and pathetic rebellion against my awful father, which seemed irrationally fitting at the time. He had always disapproved of me so much without me trying, in my immature head I decided I would dedicate myself to truly earning his censure seeing as he had reacted to my forays into business by publicly cutting me off. Not that he had the funds to support me by then, but appearances are everything and I was a disgrace.'

He huffed, clearly irritated by the difficult relationship he had with the man. 'It is not a period I am particularly proud of, but in a strange sort of way I never would have found Cora again without it, so I cannot regret it.' He opened his mouth as if he was about to continue and then thought better of it. After a pregnant pause he shrugged. 'But thankfully I found her and you know the rest.'

Hattie folded her arms and glared. 'I assume from that patronising comment, you consider the rest of that story too shocking for my tender ears?'

'It is not a pleasant tale.'

'But it is significant, Jasper. Significant enough that you have given Izzy your name and are prepared to cause a huge scandal and take the secret of her paternity to the grave.'

He glanced away to stare out of the window and she

groaned. 'If you think a woman like me, one who has been to hell and back, and who now spends her days trying to help children who have suffered at the hands of the very dregs of society will shatter like glass at an unpleasant tale, then you are no better than Freddie and do not know me at all.' When he still refused to look her way, she kicked him lightly under the table. 'Oh, for pity's sake just spit it out, Jasper; I know you want to. I shan't stop nagging or leave until you do.'

His eyes turned to hers slowly, thoroughly, a begrudging half-smile on his face. 'One night I went to a notorious gaming hell...' She rewarded him with the ghost of a smile of triumph in return, as if she never doubted he would see sense and come around to her way of thinking, and he rolled his eyes.

'It was in the thick of the docks, well away from the glare of the authorities. As low a place as you could possibly imagine. The definition of a den of iniquity. I had never ventured somewhere quite so base before and cannot deny some of the wretchedness and depravity on display shocked me despite already being three sheets to the wind. I went to the bar to find the fourth sheet and one of the, for want of a better word, *ladies* of the house sidled up behind to whisper in my ear and offer herself as a distraction for the night. As I am sure you have already guessed, that lady was Cora.'

'Oh, Jasper.' She reached for his hand again and squeezed. 'You must have felt awful.'

He winced at the memory. 'To be honest, I cannot decide which of us was more horrified. She tried to run away while I hit the roof, and because she feared her employer, she eventually grabbed me and dragged me to a filthy back room as if I were a client, where we sat for hours and I learned every bit of the awful truth of our years of separation. From the hand-to-mouth subsistence life she and her father endured immediately after their eviction, to the rapid decline in his health where she first had to sell herself to pay for his medicine, to his death, to how she had ended up as little better than an indentured whore in that hell.'

'You rescued her.'

He nodded. 'I had to. I owed her. I had let her down grievously. If I hadn't abandoned her to go to Oxford or had answered her letters, none of what happened to her might have happened. She became the hostess of my club and lived with me in the cramped little apartment above it—quite platonically.' Hattie had no idea quite why he felt compelled to clarify that but was oddly relieved that he had.

'Soon after, she realised she was with child. Before you ask, she had no clue who Izzy's father was and wasn't inclined to ponder it as it had happened at that dreadful hell in the docks. Because all the gossip about the pair of us did wonders for the business and because my patrons adored her, we concealed Izzy's existence for her first few months and carried on as if we were a couple.

'But as Izzy grew, as children are so prone to—' he smiled at that '—and she started crawling, that arrangement became impractical. It wasn't fair to keep her hidden indoors and neither of us wanted her to grow up tainted by our scandal, which I know is ironic given where we currently find ourselves. As soon as I had profit enough to be able to afford a cottage somewhere where nobody knew about her past, I bought one. Cora was happy, my business was booming and Isabel blossomed.'

His eyes locked with hers, myriad complex emotions swirling in the emerald irises. 'Life was good. Or at least for a while it was. Until now.' His gaze dipped, lost in sorrow again for a moment. 'But I made a solemn promise to Cora just after Izzy was born that I would raise her if anything happened, and there is no better way of honouring that promise after the way I had let her down than claiming her daughter as mine.'

His eyes lifted to hers once more, cautious, as if she would judge him unfavourably for sacrificing himself for an old friend and her daughter. 'And now you genuinely do know the rest. That is why I want to do right by Izzy despite being totally clueless and ill equipped as to how to do it.'

He fell silent as Mrs Mimms came in with the tea, snatching his hand away too late for her not to raise an intrigued eyebrow, and then sat awkwardly after she left as he awaited Hattie's verdict. Yet even with that extended pause it took Hattie an age to formulate all her racing thoughts into words. She wanted to tell him that she was proud of him and that he might well have a few notches on his bedpost, but he had gone up several more in her estimation.

Instead, she reached for his hand again, smiling as she embraced the warm feelings this complicated, sensitive, likeable man gave her. 'Nobody is perfect, Jasper. All we can ever do is our best and sometimes even that falls woefully short. Yesterday, I am ashamed to admit that because I allowed him to get to me, I lost my temper with a confused and abandoned ten-year-old boy who called me an ugly, lame, old hag before pushing me over.'

'Jim?'

She nodded.

'I wouldn't feel guilty about losing your temper as it sounds to me as if he had it coming.'

'Maybe...' She shrugged this time. 'But perhaps, now that my temper has cooled, with the benefit of hindsight I can see that my outburst could just as easily do some good for our relationship as it does bad. Only time will tell. But what I already know is that when I see him today, I will not make that mistake again because out of every misstep or failure we learn, and we come back stronger and better equipped.' Her thumb caressed his palm of its own accord and she decided not to stop, using the flimsy excuse of him needing the contact to justify the intimacy when she needed it just as much.

'I know you carry an enormous amount of guilt over Cora—much of it unnecessary in my view—but you are not ready to accept that yet. What your father did to her all those years ago would likely still have happened even if you had been there. Because you can only hide such things for so long and you would not have been listened to by your father then either. So you can punish yourself for what happened to her afterwards, blame yourself for not being there all you want, but it does not change the two fundamentals which no amount of self-flagellation can deny.'

'There are two?' He wasn't convinced but was humouring her.

'First and foremost, you have more than made up for it afterwards and secondly, Cora must have had faith in you because she entrusted her daughter to you, secure in the knowledge that you would do the job right. You are as much, if not more, of a rescuer than I am, Jasper, because you care too much. That is why I couldn't be more certain that you will excel as Izzy's papa. You built a business from the ground up and rapidly made a fortune to save her mother, so I can only imagine what mountains you will climb for her daughter. But even you can only ever climb each mountain one step at a time.'

He squeezed her hand, obviously touched. 'At least one of us has faith in me.'

Faith suggested some room for doubt, whereas Hattie was certain he wouldn't fail. He was as stubborn as she was and twice as resourceful. 'Seeing as you are as hopeless a rescuer as I am, and seeing as we are both tenacious and relentless in that endeavour, why don't we take on this first mountain together and between us, work out how to help Izzy say goodbye to her mother?'

Chapter Thirteen

Jasper couldn't imagine the web of lies Hattie had spun her family to be stood here with him at the very edge of dusk in Richmond Park, but after the ordeal closing up Cora's house alone yesterday, he was glad she was. He also had no idea where she had got the delicate Chinese lantern from, but it certainly held Izzy transfixed as the three of them stared up at the emerging stars from their blanket.

'Isn't heaven beautiful?' For the last half an hour Hattie had conjured a world beyond theirs which Izzy seemed to understand. A world where every single star in the sky was a soul living in a faraway paradise.

'Which one is Mama?'

Hattie bent her head level to the little girl's and narrowed her eyes, squinting at them all as if considering. 'It's hard to tell right now but we will know soon enough. Have you got the gifts?'

Izzy nodded, her gaze never leaving the sky as she rummaged in her coat pocket for the pretty silk handkerchief which had once belonged to Cora. A tiny square infused with love because Hattie had solemnly made her kiss it and hug it before it was tied around a small, folded picture which the child had drawn this afternoon expressly for her mother.

'Then let us attach it to the lantern.' She sat back on her hands to allow him and Izzy to tie the precious but light cargo to the lantern. 'Now I think we are ready to send it to your mama.'

'Do you think she will like my picture?'

Jasper hugged his new daughter. 'She will love it and treasure it until you and she can be together again.' Just as he would this precious gift.

'And I will definitely be going to heaven too?'

'Definitely, Izzy. So will I, and one day the three of us will be together again having tea parties in the clouds.' He hoped that was true too. Hattie's version of heaven was one he wanted to exist.

Izzy gently held the lantern out to him to light, but then pulled it back to scan the sky with the uncertainty of an anxious four-year-old. 'How can I be sure she will get it?'

'The lantern will know the way, won't it, Jasper?' Hattie seemed to know exactly the right answer to every question.

'It will.' For some reason he was finding this informal, unorthodox ceremony more moving than any funeral. Maybe because there was no expectation that he mask his emotions, as here, cloaked in darkness, he knew Hattie would not judge him for them. 'And don't forget your mama is watching, so she'll be looking out for it too.' His voice caught and she stroked his back and took control for him.

Hattie smoothed her hand over Izzy's hair. 'Are you ready to say farewell?'

'Why farewell and not goodbye, Hattie?'

Where such a question would have flummoxed Jasper, Hattie answered the child without a moment's hesitation. 'Because farewell is a temporary state of affairs, and not for ever, whereas goodbye is final and you will never see that person again. Now hold that lantern tight and do not let go until I tell you.' That reassuring hand smoothed his back again.

With tears in his eyes, Jasper struck a match and lit the lantern, and they all held their breath while it glowed and filled with heat.

'It is time,' whispered Hattie and Izzy let go, and the lantern floated gently upwards. 'Farewell, Cora.'

'Farewell, Cora.' Jasper's tears fell and he let them as he grabbed Izzy's hand.

'Farewell, Mama, I shall see you soon.'

'She will be waiting.' Hattie reached for his hand as the three of them watched the light soar ever higher. 'But in the meantime, she will be always watching you from afar, so whenever you miss her, all you have to do is look up at the stars and you can be sure she is smiling back.'

For several minutes, the lantern rose and bounced on the cool evening breeze, the flame within getting dimmer and dimmer as the candle burned down, until it flickered and died.

'Has Mama got my gift now?'

'Yes, she has, poppet.'

He cuddled Izzy close while still holding Hattie's hand, his heart filled with sorrow but oddly bursting with love and so much gratitude for the extraordinary woman sat beside him it humbled him. All this had been her idea and it was as perfect a send-off as it was poignant.

Then, the oddest thing happened as they watched the night sky in companiable silence together. A shooting star danced across the heavens in an arc, so fast if they had blinked they would have missed it. Yet none of them did.

As Izzy oohed and ah-ed with wonder and Hattie proclaimed it was Cora waving thank you from afar, Jasper sighed with relief. Oddly secure in the knowledge that whatever strange but scientifically explainable phenomenon of the cosmos had just occurred, it had also somehow possessed the mystical power to take some of the guilt he had carried for so long with it. And while doing that, and quite unexpectedly, it had miraculously also managed to wipe some of his cluttered slate of guilt clean.

Chapter Fourteen

'If you think I am going to leave you alone in the dark, you can think again, madam.' Jasper did not care if this was the mews behind her house or that she was quite capable of looking after herself or that the Avondale carriage might return with her family at any moment. It would be a cold day in hell before he abandoned her to this back alley at night. 'I am still seeing you to your garden and I will not be swayed from that. As you so forcefully pointed out two days ago, friends are there beside you no matter what.' The stubborn minx couldn't argue with her own logic. 'I would take you all the way to the back door if I wasn't scared Freddie might shoot me.'

He also couldn't deny that he was in no hurry to be rid of her either. There had been something wonderful about riding in a nondescript hackney through the quiet back streets from Russell Square to Mayfair. Talking about nothing in particular and everything in general. Unchaperoned. Unjudged. Unwatched. Unburdened.

All most likely unwise in its impropriety but he hadn't cared about that when he had insisted, nor did he care about it now. After the day he had had—the week, the month—being with Hattie right now was a balm to his battered soul. It also, bizarrely, felt like a new beginning although he had no clue of what beyond the next chapter of his life.

'But what if somebody sees you?' For a woman who claimed to care little for propriety, when it came to the crunch, the cracks in that bravado began to show.

For all her assertions to the contrary, she cared about her reputation because she understood that the loss of it would likely have catastrophic consequences for her future. Scandals were always worse for the woman as he and Cora had learned first-hand. The press had been relentless uncovering her past and smearing it over the gossip columns, until the whole *ton* had finally known how she had earned her living in the docks. Nobody cared to consider the motives for that act of desperation. Those truths about the cruel ways of their world were not something the aristocracy wished to learn. Not when it was always easier to look down their noses and cast judgement rather than develop a social conscience.

Jasper cared deeply about Hattie's reputation too and wouldn't intentionally harm it for any reason. Yet a selfish part of him was still wounded by her concerns of total ruination by association because clearly he wasn't the sort of man she wanted to be trapped with. Which hurt a great deal when he was coming to think that Hattie was exactly the sort of woman he wouldn't mind spending eternity with.

Where the blazes had that thought come from?

His heart raced while his mind quickly rationalised what had made him think such an outrageous thing, and then slowed when he could justify it all with the handy excuse of tonight. He hadn't known how to help Izzy but Hattie had been his rock and he had clung to her, and so, by default, it stood to reason he was feeling particularly close to her right now. It had nothing to do with her arm feeling so wonderful in his that he never wanted her to let go. Or his ongoing and inappropriate attraction, which he was determined to conquer for her sake, although he felt that keenly tonight thanks to the intimacy of their current situation and the odd lift in his mood after the peculiar behaviour of the heavens earlier.

'They won't see me, Miss Nervous, because it is pitch black out here with plenty of shadows to hide in if need to do so arises, so you shall be spared the awful chore of being compromised and forced into marrying me.' *And why the blazes had he said that?* And why had the comment sounded so petulant, all of a sudden, when he was in no position to be thinking of her in that way anyway?

Because his emotions were all over the place, obviously!

Hopefully?

Jasper was a wreck.

An exhausted, raw and vulnerable shell of his usual self. Who bizarrely felt lighter and more himself in this precise moment than he had since he had first discovered Cora had died. A ridiculous emotional contradiction which made absolutely no sense if he analysed it in any detail.

Therefore, he decided he wouldn't. He wouldn't judge himself so harshly, would instead ignore it all just for tonight and not overthink his feelings for Hattie at this precise moment as they were likely as transient and unreliable as his oddly buoyant mood was. All part and parcel of this unusual and exhausting day.

They circumnavigated a jagged pothole as they neared her back gate and her hand tightened around his elbow while their bodies brushed from shoulder to hip. To his shame, Jasper couldn't pretend he didn't enjoy that too despite his best efforts to ignore it. The unusual circumstances and friendship aside, there was nothing platonic about the way his nerve endings reacted nor the manner in which his eyes kept wandering her way and feasted when she wasn't looking. If he wasn't a walking scandal about to happen, if he had reconnected with her over a month ago when everything hadn't gone to hell, Jasper was in no doubt he would have pursued the overwhelming attraction irrespective of her brother's warnings.

He would have had to.

Because everything about Hattie drew him like a magnet, from her kind heart and clever brain to her pert bosom and delicious peach of a bottom. Enough, perhaps, that, if his circumstances had been different, he would have been tempted to seriously consider courting her in the official sense. Surrender his heart and plight his troth.

That had never happened to him before.

He had never met a woman who made him contemplate that sort of a future. One filled with familiarity and family, of companionable days and sultry nights.

Sultry nights!

So much for easing up on himself when such incendiary and inexcusable thoughts most definitely needed reining in when he had her so inappropriately to himself in such an opportunity-rich setting!

It wasn't sensible to contemplate sultry nights in this deserted alleyway in his addled state, not even hypothetically, when she was too near, he didn't want to leave her and his body was already responding.

'I never asked—what do your family think you are doing tonight?' A change of subject might get his mind back on the noble path and away from its out of control and ungentlemanly whirring. 'When I could have sworn tonight was the night for Lord and Lady Brampton's annual ball.' A ball which was one of the cornerstones of the Season and which nobody who was anybody ever missed.

She instantly cringed. 'Half an hour before they left, I told them I was in so much agony I couldn't possibly go as I could barely stand.' Between their side-by-side bodies he felt her hand pat her own thigh. 'And because they all walk on eggshells wherever my dratted leg is concerned, nobody questioned the outrageous lie. I went to bed and pretended to be asleep, and as soon as they were gone, I crept out the back and hailed a hackney.'

She hung her head as if she had committed high treason. 'I am appalled at myself for manipulating their concern for me to suit my own ends. I even avoided Jim and the infirmary today so that I could attend my mother's latest dreadful Keep a Ragamuffin Warm in Winter knitting party where I sowed some subtle seeds to her and my sister-in-law Dorothea that my injury was bothering me. I didn't want my meddling brother accusing me of making it up to avoid another awkward stint on the wallflower chairs or being cornered by Lord Boredom wishing I was somewhere else.'

Even the dark could not hide the bleakness in her eyes before she waved that away, and he felt guilty for abandoning her when she hadn't abandoned him, irrespective of whether or not that was the best thing to do to protect her from the *ton*'s censure. 'But at least I am now four dreary society functions and almost two weeks of hell down and only have another six months of purgatory to go.'

'I wish I could save you from them.' Not because he owed her at least that, because that was a given, but because he understood tonight was their last hurrah. Neither of them had referenced it but they both knew all her clandestine, charitable visits to his house and shopping trips could not continue and he had been rightly banned by Freddie from dominating her time and risking her reputation in public.

He was doing the right thing by putting her needs above his own, but Lord, he was going to miss her.

'I do not need saving but...' Then she grinned, a naughty, sinful, alluring grin which re-awoke his overwrought and suggestible frayed nerves—or more specifically one particular nerve ending—with a bang. 'Should you happen to accidently on purpose burn the Duchess of Laindon's Grosvenor Square town house to the ground tomorrow at around eight, it would be much appreciated. Especially as I've used the excuse of my dratted leg up now thanks to you.'

'Consider it done.' They stopped at the Avondale back gate, both smiling at the joke but neither really meaning it. 'What's a bit of arson between friends?' Jasper sighed and allowed his true emotions to show. 'Thank you for today and for everything, Hattie. Your timely and unswerving friendship has meant the world to me.'

She turned away from him to open the gate. 'Don't you dare say goodbye to me, Jasper Beaufort. Don't you dare.' When the lock wouldn't budge she bashed it in frustration. 'This is a farewell and nothing more.' She growled at the stuck gate and spun around to lean against it. 'In fact, I plan to convince Jim to come feed the ducks with me at that little park I discovered off Beaverbrook Square the day after tomorrow. We shall be there around noon if you and Izzy happen to stumble across us.'

She had done enough.

Been kind enough.

Rescued him enough.

Risked enough.

'I am starting to think you are a bad influence, Hattie Fitzroy, with all your outrageous lies and machinations.' He had to be noble. Be unselfish and do the right thing, not least because he had promised her brother and a promise was sacrosanct.

He had to save her from her own rash but admirable tendency to rescue above all else, and most importantly, he had to be the bigger person and stop allowing her to rescue him. As much as it saddened him to do it, it was time to say goodbye—for her sake.

Jasper nudged her out of the way, going to war with himself as he attempted to open the blasted gate. 'But if I am going to be led astray, I might as well do it in style and bring a picnic.' Clearly, she was scrambling his wits, or he was the most selfish man who ever walked the earth—or both. Annoyed at himself and yet incapable of retracting his outrageous acceptance of her invitation he huffed in double defeat. 'But in the meantime, this gate is locked from the inside.'

'I didn't realise they locked it while the family are out, else I'd have brought a key!' Panic skittered across her lovely moonlit features now. 'What am I going to do, Jasper? How am I going to explain being out when I claimed I couldn't walk!'

He scanned the size of the wall, which wasn't much taller than him. 'Can you climb?'

'I used to be able to but thanks to my dratted leg I have no idea and...' As she was flapping he placed a finger over her lips, regretting it instantly because he was desperate to kiss them.

'If I heave you upwards and you sit on the top, then I can climb over and help you down.'

She blew out a breath as she nodded. 'That might work.'

Jasper crouched and cupped his hands, and after several misstarts while she tested which limb would work best, she plumped for leaning heavily on his shoulder to stand on her bad leg, so that she could use the good one to launch herself upwards. Except while she threw both arms over the top of the wall, she lost momentum and simply dangled, her delectable bottom level with his face.

There was no gentlemanly way of manoeuvring her, so with an apology and a wince which was more for himself than for her, he filled his hands with her distracting backside and pushed. Thankfully, that did the trick and with some effort she managed to straddle the wall, but not before her womanly body gave his wayward one even more ideas it had no right having. Such carnal and erotic ideas her brother had every right to want to shoot him for.

As Hattie watched, Jasper hauled himself up to sit beside her then almost groaned aloud at the sight before him because the Avondale garden was sunk lower than the alleyway. Which meant the six-foot wall they had climbed had a drop of at least eight on the other side, so getting her down wasn't going to be either pretty or proper, and would involve a great deal more manhandling, which he wasn't entirely certain he could cope with.

But it couldn't be helped. He had to step up in her hour of need, just as she had so many times already in his, and if that played havoc with his urges, then he would just have to manage.

Thanks to his long legs and upper body strength, Jasper managed to lower himself down far enough to be able to jump the short distance to the lawn below. He took a deep breath to steel himself for the inevitable torture to come, then held out his arms. 'I think the best thing for you to do is to swing your legs over backwards while using your arms to hold the top of the wall.'

Hattie did not look convinced. 'I am going to die, or worse, I shall break the other leg.'

'You shan't do either as I will catch you. The alternative is you stay up there until one of the servants spots you and raises the alarm because they think the house is being burgled or your family return—either way the jig will be up and Freddie will kill us both. Come on…' He stretched up his arms. 'I have got you.'

Reluctantly she twisted and began to do as he said, dangling first one shapely leg then the other over the edge as she clung to the brickwork for dear life. To assist, he tried to take her weight by reaching for her waist but ended up having to grapple with her bottom again. For the sake of his own sanity, he grabbed her silk-clad right ankle to position it in a foothold, only to have her snatch it away and flail in panic.

'I didn't mean to hurt you!' Now he felt dreadful,

remembering too late that it was her right leg which had been damaged. 'I'll be more gentle!' Yet despite that reassurance, she still did everything in her power to stop him from catching it and his tenuous grip of her began to fail. 'For the love of God, Hattie! Let me help, woman!'

He lunged and caught her calf again in the nick of time, and she froze but finally allowed him to guide it to a protruding brick to steady herself while using himself from head to waist wedged against her as a support. A position which was such pure, unmitigated torture he decided the most prudent course of action was to speed up the proceedings rather than slow them down. In desperation, he wrapped his arms around her waist and suffered the feel of his cheek buried in her bottom for only as long as it took for him to pull her free. He staggered backwards and almost fell, but she had the great good sense to twist at the last moment enough to brace her arms on his shoulders before she slithered all the way down his body until her feet found the floor.

'That was close.' Off balance, she giggled, her palms splayed against his chest to steady herself, her warm breath caressing his face, those equally distracting pert bosoms now flattened against his ribs while his hands learned the exact shape of the curve of her hips. Information they did not need so hot on the heels of enjoying her bottom. 'For a moment there, I thought we were done for!' Then she smiled up at him and managed to completely bewitch him in the process. 'Thanks for catching me and getting me home. At least now I won't have to convince my idiot brother *not* to meet you on the duelling field.'

Jasper should have chuckled back. Offered an ac-

ceptable flippant comment along the lines of 'happy
to be of service' or 'all's well that ends well'. Put some
polite distance between them. Bid her goodnight. Behave like the good friend she deserved. The *platonic*
and steadfast good friend she deserved.

But he didn't.

Instead, he stared deep into her eyes. Allowed one
finger to twirl in a stray curl which bounced against
her cheek and heard himself say, 'Frankly, Hattie, some
things are worth duelling for.'

And then, because he meant that with every fibre of
his being, he closed the distance between his mouth and
hers and nearly—*very* nearly—kissed her lips.

Chapter Fifteen

Hattie had no clue what a peck on the nose meant beyond a disappointingly chaste gesture which still left her feeling flat the following evening. Especially as, for a split second, she had been convinced Jasper had intended a more romantic sort of kiss which she would have welcomed had his lips not suddenly changed direction at the last moment.

Fortunately—or unfortunately because she was still in two minds about it—she had mustered the strength from somewhere to stop herself from dragging him back and kissing him properly herself. Aside from being presumptuous and unladylike, although neither of those things had particularly bothered her in the moment, it was her inexperience and lack of confidence in her body which had prevented her from finishing what she had been convinced he had intended to start.

But had he really, or was she merely hoping he had so much she'd imagined it?

And therein lay the crux of the matter.

Somewhere in their short reacquaintance, he had gone from being a person she was worried about to someone she cared about. That she could be herself with Jasper was the icing on the cake. Around him, she never felt like an ugly, lame, old hag—to paraphrase Jim— and that was because Jasper never ever treated her as if she was broken. While she did not agree with all of young Jim's angry summary of her body—because she wasn't ugly, at least not above the waist at any rate, and at twenty she was a long way off old—she was lame and she was no longer perfect and just because Jasper enjoyed her as a friend did not mean that he found her attractive in other ways.

She might be inexperienced in romantic relations, but even she knew there was an ocean of difference between liking a member of the opposite sex and *liking* them. The latter, from what she could make out, involved heated looks and lingering glances. Lust and longing, and while she was now categorically experiencing both for Jasper, she could secretly swoon for him as much as she wanted but it was no guarantee he would swoon back.

Besides, he was, without a doubt, a man of the world. One who likely did have more notches on his bedpost than she had had hot dinners, exactly as Freddie had cautioned. He was also a handsome and charming devil who could still have his pick of women. He might well currently be the scandalous owner of a notorious gentlemen's club and about to be a worse scandal once the news of Izzy leaked out, but he was also a wealthy peer and the heir to a dukedom and such things tended to overrule society's most fervent objections given time. Hattie sincerely doubted there was a debutante this Season who would rebuff his advances if he made any, and she remembered with the utmost clarity how successful a flirt he could be as she had witnessed it plenty of times in the past while never ever being on the receiving end of it.

Even recently, at the two social functions he had assisted her at, while he had flirted shamelessly with Annie, Kitty, Dorothea, Hattie's mother and half of all the other ladies he had briefly collided with, it had never once occurred to him to flirt with her. That not insignificant detail spoke volumes so, with that in mind, she probably had misread the apparent signals last night. For surely a man on the cusp of romantically kissing a woman would have no issue flirting with her first?

And then, of course, he had just done the unthinkable and felt her dratted leg as he had helped her off the wall, so knew the limp was the tip of the iceberg. As he had manoeuvred her calf and her ankle to safety, he had to have felt the misshapen bone, the wasted muscle and the scars. Even two thick layers of woollen stockings could not hide those and Hattie had foolishly worn silk in deference to the warmth of May, and silk was too thin to hide anything. Therefore, she was not surprised he might have been repulsed by it—because she certainly was—and even if he had been on the cusp of kissing her, she understood why he might have rapidly come to his senses. Which altogether made it unsurprising that he had pecked her nose and then hightailed it back over the wall as if the snarling hounds of hell were after him.

One thing was for certain—if he never mentioned the awkward incident again, neither would she. Least said, soonest mended, and she would rather have him as a platonic friend in her life than not in her life at all...

'Are you aware that you are muttering and pulling

faces?' Opposite her in the carriage, Annie was staring at her as if she had gone mad. 'For if you are not you might want to talk to Dr Cribbs as you are clearly losing your marbles.'

'She has been very distracted all day.' Kitty wiggled her brows. 'I caught her sighing and staring out of the drawing room windows after breakfast.'

'If I didn't know better, I would say she was in love,' added her mother with a wink at the rest of them, oblivious that her innocent teasing had actually struck a nerve. 'She has that air about her, don't you think? But alas, it cannot possibly be that as she refuses to meet anyone no matter how many eligible gentlemen her brother throws her way.' It was meant as a flippant chastisement because her mother despaired of her lack of interest in the press-ganged bachelors on offer and she wanted her happily married, but the comment still made Hattie's cheeks heat. Because she never missed an opportunity to torment her, Annie, of course, noticed this straight away.

'Oh, my goodness, she's blushing!' Her twin reached over to prod her cheek, so Hattie swatted the accusing finger away. 'Perhaps there *is* a man she has her beady eyes on after all.'

'If there was, I would need opera glasses to see him from the wallflower chairs.' Hattie schooled her features into her most peeved mask. 'The only one who pursues me with any fervour is Lord Boredom, and frankly I wouldn't have him if we were the last two people left on earth. But if you must know and you are genuinely interested in the reasons for my current distracted mood, the cause *is* a vexing male.'

'I knew it!' shouted Kitty and Annie in unison.

'Vexing does sound promising.' This time her mother winked at her father in her trademark mischievous manner. 'I have always found you extremely vexatious, dear.'

'As have I you.' Her father smiled back at his wife soppily.

Annie pulled a disgusted face at both their parents before prodding her again. 'What is his name then? Which one of Freddie's acquaintances has caught your much too picky eye?'

'His name is Jim.' Hattie rolled her eyes to give gravitas to that lie. 'And before you all start bouncing around and shaking the carriage in your excitement, he is a ten-year-old patient at the infirmary and not a suitor. One who has suffered a similar injury to mine but who has endured far more in other ways.'

As that truth felt much more solid, she continued, glad that her quick thinking had calmed her teasing family completely. 'I am trying and failing to convince him he needs his leg broken again so that it can be reset and he can walk. But nothing I have said and done so far has worked. That is also why I am at the infirmary so much at the moment.' Thank goodness they were in a carriage and not a church as Hattie deserved smiting for all her copious recent falsehoods. 'But I am determined to wear his stubbornness down if it is the last thing I do.'

'Oh, the poor thing.' Her mother patted her knee, all thought of a mystery suitor banished now. 'But well done you for persevering. If anyone can convince him, it will be you, Hattie. Nothing defeats you when you set your mind to it.'

'Thank you, Mama…' Clearly she was the world's worst daughter, but when opportunity knocked, you had to let it in. 'To that end, I have decided to redouble my efforts. The more hours I put in at his bedside, the more chances I have at success.' That was almost the truth because she had decided that was the best course of action to win over Jim. Just in case the Almighty also realised half of those extra hours would likely be spent with Jasper and Izzy, she quickly checked outside the carriage window for a thunderbolt from the heavens. 'It is for his own good.'

'It is, dearest, and I am sure he will thank you for your tenacity one day soon.' Then her mother cupped her cheek, tears in her eyes. 'We are all so proud of you, Hattie. So many people would have given up after all you went through, but not my daughter. She not only fought tooth and nail for her own recovery but now she fights for others too. You are a credit to this family, darling.'

The overwhelming guilt made her toes curl, but she managed a smile, and thanked her lucky stars that the carriage finally lurched to a stop outside the Duchess of Laindon's town house.

Inside, Hattie made short work of removing her cape and losing her family, and instead made her way to the empty wallflower chairs well before the dancing started. At least that way, she hoped she was making her own statement, that was here by choice rather than drifting here despondent and ignored when every other debutante was claimed by a partner. She was about to lower her bottom on to one, when a sound came from behind.

'*Psst!*' She turned towards it and then gaped at the unexpected sight of Jasper partially hidden behind a potted palm in the alcove.

'What are you doing here?'

With his finger to his lips, he glanced around him like a spy then ushered her over. As soon as she was within arm's length he tugged her behind the palm too and grinned. 'Rather than burn this house to the ground as you requested, I've had the most brilliant idea.' His green eyes were dancing in a much too disarming fashion, reminding her of all the things she found attractive about him and sending her silly pulse racing. 'Because good friends are there beside you no matter what, I've finally worked out a way to save you from both Lord Boredom and the crushing boredom of the wallflower chairs without breaking any of Freddie's rules.'

'If it involves us hiding behind this plant pot all night, I can tell you right now that will not work. Freddie watches me like a hawk and has taken to following me around at these affairs like a bad smell unless I am sat with another wallflower pretending to have a good time.'

'That is the beauty of my brilliant idea.' His smile was doing outrageous things to her insides. 'As it involves sitting with the other wallflowers!' He threw up his hands with a flourish as if he expected applause. '*All* of the other wallflowers!'

She threw up her own palms in confusion. 'I really do not follow.' As she dropped them, he caught them both in his and instantly sent her pulse spiralling into chaos.

'The 1813 Wallflowers' Club!' When she still blinked back bewildered, he laughed. 'Your own idea, Hattie Fitzroy! But you were quite wrong about nobody wanting to become a member! Nobody wanted to join The Reprobates' until I made it appealing and then everyone wanted to join, which is exactly why I refuse to let just anyone join the Wallflowers' Club. Its very exclusivity is what will make it so attractive.'

As the unholy trinity of his presence, his smile and his touch was scrambling her wits, she tugged her hands away and folded her arms before she glared down her nose at him. 'Stop speaking in riddles, Jasper.'

His smug smile suited him too much. 'Freddie has stipulated that I cannot consort with you alone in public, has he not? So let's *never* be alone in public. Let us use his rules and bend them to suit us!' His excitement was evident and the chandeliers picked out the most distracting amber flecks in his eyes. 'And in the process, we two hopeless born rescuers can rescue every other wallflower, both male and female, while we are about it!'

He caught her hands again, which while the contact was supremely distracting, at least prevented hers from smoothing his lapels as they wanted to. 'We form our own exclusive little club in the wallflower chairs made up of all the people society deems not quite good enough or too scandalous to dally with at these affairs, and we show our enjoyment by having a raucous, high old time rather than apologising by trying to blend in. We host our own entertainment within an entertainment and to hell with the rest of them!'

'That is…um…' How exactly was she supposed to construct a sentence when his thumbs were tracing lazy circles on her fevered skin? When his laughing eyes and conspiratorial whispers were seducing every fibre of her being?

'It is genius is what it is, Hattie Fitzroy, utter genius! If I make a point of dancing the odd dance with an outrageous flirt at each entertainment, and flirting with a few others under Freddie's nose, he'll also realise I have no inappropriate designs on you!' She smiled because he was smiling, even though that last comment wounded and the thought of him dancing with shameless flirts while he flirted with them churned the jealous acid in her gut. 'So go round up the other wallflowers that you know and I shall meet you back at our chairs in fifteen minutes with their male counterparts.'

It actually took him closer to twenty minutes to return herding a handful of similarly ignored gentlemen like sheep. Together with her usual companions in the forgotten chairs, they made an eclectic if motley bunch. Jasper facilitated the introductions between the ladies and the gentlemen—the two poor but plain Misses Bristow, the plump and shy Lady Susannah Hargreaves, the bespeckled bluestocking Miss Winston and the toothy Lady Octavia were now joined by their male equivalents. Lord Marbury had a charming manner but barely stood five feet. Another fellow had an unfortunate stutter. Two weren't blessed in the looks department at all and the last was so scandalously bankrupt and in debt that everyone knew it. Or as Jasper had whispered to her alone while sending hot shivers down her spine in the process, the *ton* knew the gent didn't have a pot to piss in.

Jasper then procured a footman who promptly delivered them all alcoholic beverages, and with a few choice and entertaining stories from their new, self-proclaimed but deprecating host who claimed he was just too scandalous for anyone discerning to want to associate with, the newly formed 1813 Wallflowers' Club were soon all laughing together. The bond of being excluded from the rest of the festivities and the relief at finally having others to talk to who were in the same boat united them quicker than weeks of acquaintance would normally.

As a consequence, the hours flew by and miraculously, Hattie had a wonderful time despite her brother's constant staring—or outright glaring.

It took Freddie two hours to venture over, and like an admiral inspecting the fleet, he rocked on his heels beside Jasper and asked, 'What is going on here then?' To which a straight-faced Jasper replied with something deadly dull about Miss Winston's fascinating recent study of the unique flora and fauna of Hyde Park—a topic which she had never once commented upon but nodded sagely alongside her new hero as if she had.

'Join us, Freddie!' He had then invited her brother to sit on a chair among them. 'You might learn something, for I never knew there were so many different species of snail living in London.'

'I only wish I could.' Her brother's eyes had then darted hither and thither searching for an escape. 'But I fear I am being a bad husband by neglecting Dorothea for so long.' And with that, he had scurried away but continued to watch the proceedings sporadically from across the ballroom with an expression of bewilderment, clearly in two minds as to whether he had had a lucky escape or had been thoroughly hoodwinked.

Then, their exclusive new club had laughed conspiratorially, and shared stories about the worst aspects of being a wallflower, prompting Hattie to confide in them about Lord Boredom. Which meant when he approached and tried to pick her off for a conversation while Jasper danced with a very pretty young widow, her new friends ran such swift but subtle interference, the unwelcome interloper was squeezed out of their closed ranks until he gave up trying and sloped off with his tail between his pompous legs.

When her father waved and signalled that the family were about to leave, Jasper moved closer to her chair, obviously pleased with himself. 'I think that went well. Enough that it kept you from hiding out the night in the retiring room or getting sprayed with unwelcome spit.' When she rolled her eyes at that he nudged her playfully, unaware that the brief contact caused a ripple of goose pimples to bloom on the back of her neck. 'Admit it, I came up with the perfect solution to your predicament.'

'It wasn't the worst way to spend an evening.' If she ignored how much his one dance with that flirty widow had bothered her.

'Is that your way of saying, *Thank you, Jasper for being my gallant knight in shining armour*?'

'A true knight doesn't require affirmation of his shining status by reminding the damsel in distress of his efforts on her behalf, and then shamelessly courting compliments.' She quirked one brow, trying to appear peeved and failing miserably. 'That is very ungallant of you.'

'Then I shall make amends by being ungallant all over again at the Earl of Burstead's ball on Saturday. Shall I meet you in the wallflowers' chairs around nine for the next club meeting?'

'Nine suits.'

'Marvellous...' Jasper stared at his shoes and kicked an imaginary speck of dust, awkward all of a sudden which was most unlike him. 'Marvellous...and...um...

while we are discussing our calendars…will Izzy and I still see you tomorrow at the duck pond?' A question which shouldn't have sent her heart soaring but did.

Neither had mentioned her reckless, improper offer all night, and after he had found a noble way to continue their friendship in public, she hadn't wanted to bring it up in case it made her appear keen to be more than his friend. 'I wouldn't importune you further under all normal circumstances, Hattie, you understand but…' His smile was a little shy. Boyish. Utterly charming. 'But Izzy caught wind of it and wants to bring a picnic for us as well as the ducklings…and I confess I am intrigued to meet your tiny tormentor, Jim.'

Her words tripped over themselves in their hurry to get out. 'We shall be there.' Or at least Hattie would. Wild horses wouldn't keep her away now no matter how improper it was. Convincing Jim, however, was a whole different matter. And if by some miracle she did manage to get him to the park, given his explosive temper and tendency to fling about cruel insults willy-nilly, she should probably prewarn Jasper of his character. 'But I shall apologise in advance if Jim doesn't behave with the expected courtesies. He is…'

'Lost and floundering and in dire need of rescuing too.' He idly rubbed the back of her hand and sent a bolt of longing ricocheting through her system before he noticed what he was doing and snatched it away. 'If only we knew two hopeless rescuers who could work together to save him from himself? Maybe a double-pronged attack is what is needed to crack your tough nut?'

'Maybe it w—'

'Hurry along, Hattie, the carriage is outside.' Freddie's command as he marched towards the wallflower chairs brooked no argument. Because the interfering idiot couldn't help himself, her brother glared at his friend for good measure. 'Good to see you, Jasper. Why don't we catch up over billiards soon? At your scandalous club perhaps, seeing as you while away most of every night there?' The clipped invitation was loaded with unsubtle meaning, and by Jasper's amused expression he understood that 'billiards' was a flimsy code for another lecture. 'Or at White's tomorrow afternoon?'

'Tomorrow is already filled to the gills with ghastly chores, old boy.' Jasper's eyes flicked briefly to hers, amusement making those distracting amber flecks dance just for her seeing as she was the 'ghastly chore' in question. 'So is all of next week. Some of us have to work for a living.'

'Yet you still found the hours to be here.' Freddie was like a dog with a bone.

'All work and no play makes Jasper a dull boy. Besides…' he offered her brother a nonchalant shrug '…the club only ever gets busy after these affairs wind down so I am not really needed there, and being seen in public like this is good for business. And you did say that I could converse with Hattie in public, didn't you? As long as we were in a crowd.' If he noticed her sentry's narrowed eyes, he hid it well and slapped him on the back, laughing as if he was purposely teasing his old friend to get a rise out of him. 'But it *has* been ages since we last caught up so I'll find an evening next week and you, me and George can make a night of it. Relive our wild youth and lament the fact we had to grow up.'

'Splendid.' Freddie grabbed Hattie's arm and wound it through his as if he owned her. 'Goodnight, Jasper.'

'Goodnight, Freddie.' Jasper smiled at his friend and then his eyes locked with hers again briefly, an intense glance she felt everywhere, before he bowed politely with mischief in his striking emerald eyes again. 'Fare thee well, my Lady Harriet.' A courtly goodbye as if he truly was one of the knights of old, and one, to Hattie's inexperienced ear, which sounded a great deal like flirting. 'I would kiss your hand in a friendly, platonic manner as is deemed entirely proper by the rest of society at these sorts of occasions, but fear dear, untrusting Freddie here might misread it and have a fit if I do.' Then he winked at her, purely to vex Freddie of course, but like a dolt, Hattie almost sighed aloud at that small crumb.

Chapter Sixteen

'Whether he likes it or not, Jim needs some fresh air.' Hattie had commandeered a nurse to assist her in getting him dressed now that Dr Cribbs had agreed a change of scenery might do his most cantankerous patient some good.

Obviously, she had been sketchy on the details, allowing Dr Cribbs to think she was taking Jim on a short wheel to the bakery around the corner rather than the park, and that she would be properly chaperoned as he had queried without specifically mentioning by whom. Being rushed off his feet, the good doctor accepted this before he was distracted by more work, leaving Hattie free to basically do as she pleased. While all the lies she was telling to people who did not deserve it bothered her, the need to see Jasper overruled her niggling conscience.

Besides, now that they would always be in the midst of the Wallflowers' Club in public, if she did not see him today, then who knew when she would next have an excuse to see Izzy and him alone?

At least that was how she was justifying this im-

proper trip to herself, despite not believing that justi-
fication at all.

'Do whatever it takes to get him ready for an outing
but don't tell him that I am here.' Her best chance of getting Jim to comply was to have him sat in the wheeled
chair before she made her entrance. 'I am not his favourite person at the moment. The last time I saw him,
neither of us behaved particularly well.'

'I figured as much as he sulked for hours after you
left.' The kindly older nursemaid smiled in sympathy,
recognising Hattie's guilt before she discounted it. 'Although I suspect it might have hit home as he's asked
about you a few times since, in his own charming way,
enquiring as to your prolonged absence while pretending to be relieved by it. But it doesn't fool me. He might
outwardly pretend to hate you but he's simply making
you earn your stripes.'

'Let's hope so.'

Hattie visited with some of the other patients while
the nurse did her bidding, trying to focus on them rather
than Jasper with little success. At least her preoccupa-
tion with him prevented her from overthinking how to
behave with Jim or formulating a plan of attack when
her gut told her to take her lead from the boy and work
on that.

Jim, who undoubtedly *was* floundering and lost and
in dire need of rescuing exactly as Jasper had said,
blinked in shock as she strode through the door as if
he had not expected to ever see her again but quickly
covered that with a scowl.

'Well look what the cat dragged in.' He was sat in the
wheeled chair and dressed in a set of clean but scruffy

clothes, either charitable hand-me-downs or the clothes he had arrived in.

'Did you honestly think I was so lily-livered I would allow one tantrum from a frightened little boy to dissuade me from coming?' She sauntered towards the bed defiantly. 'I am made of sterner stuff than that, Jim.'

'Only because you want me to do as you say. To roll over and do what you want.'

'I just want you to get better.'

'I won't get better!' The venom with which he spat the words was echoed by the utter despondency in his eyes. 'Stop lying and pretending that I will!'

'I am not lying.'

'Adults always lie.' He turned his head away. 'So go away, you stubborn old hag, before I push you over again.'

'Do you honestly think another tantrum might work on this stubborn old hag when the last one failed?' To prove she wasn't the least bit afraid of him and his temper or wounded by his insults, she sat on the exact same spot of the mattress he had pushed her off only a short time ago and offered him a wry smile. 'But seeing as we are on the topic of your tantrum, I should like to apologise for mine.' As she had intended, that threw him, and his jaw dropped.

'I am sorry for losing my temper with you the other day, Jim. I would have come to apologise to you sooner, only I had to support a good friend who has lost someone close. But I am here now, later than planned but determined to make amends.' Hattie suppressed the urge to reach out and touch him because Jim was a long way off ready for that yet. Instead, she shrugged and smiled. 'Just because you were cruel to me, doesn't give me the right to raise my voice or to resort to insults in retaliation. I am usually a better person than that and I am sorry.'

By the confusion behind his freckles, he hadn't expected an apology, nor knew how to react to one. 'I shouldn't have called you a coward either, Jim, that was uncalled for, and I retract those awful words as I suspect you have had to be braver in your ten short years than a person like me, with my spoiled upbringing, could possibly imagine in a lifetime.'

'You've got that right at least.' A begrudging admission which could not disguise how shocked he was at her words. If she were a betting sort, Hattie was prepared to wager hers had been the only apology he had ever received in his life. 'You wouldn't last five minutes in my world.'

'I wouldn't.' She sat back and looked him dead in the eyes. 'But then I sincerely doubt you would last five minutes in mine either. It's not easy being the daughter of a duke.'

'Oh, boo-hoo, poor you.' Sarcasm dripped from every syllable, but she was impressed he could quote her quite so aptly and with such cutting precision. 'How you must have suffered in your father's fancy mansion, sipping tea with your little finger in the air and embroidering your pointless days away.'

She shrugged, unoffended, as he made a valid point. 'I've always been useless at embroidery. I can't paint, or draw, or sing, or play an instrument either, so I am probably the least accomplished duke's daughter that ever lived. Which rather exacerbates my current problem, as the sole purpose of an aristocratic young lady like me is apparently to be so perfect and accomplished that

I can catch the discerning eye of an aristocratic man, marry him and make more aristocratic babies. Now that I am, as you so rightly pointed out, an ugly, lame, old hag, nobody discerning wants to marry me, so I have no purpose any more. I have outlived my usefulness. I am only twenty, yet as far as my shallow world is concerned, my life is over.'

'You're not...*that* ugly.' By the way his features scrunched, even that much of a begrudging apology hurt him. 'Someone will likely still want to marry you.'

'Oh, there's someone, all right.' She shuddered for effect. 'Lord Boreham has tossed his hat into the empty ring, but he is pompous and dull, spits when he talks and only wants me so he can benefit from my father's connections. And there is the not insignificant detail that he also makes my flesh crawl.'

She folded her arms and stuck out her chin. 'I am certain I deserve better than that! And, after giving the matter a great deal of thought, I have decided I deserve better than being an aristocrat's wife too. Just because that is what is expected doesn't mean that I can't do something else, does it? There's a whole wide world out there and not just the one I was born into, so why should I allow other people's stupid opinions and prejudices to dictate what I do next? And so what if I have one leg shorter than the other? How dare they condemn me to the ash heap on the back of it. I am going to prove every single last one of those naysayers wrong by gripping my life by the lapels and living it to the full just to spite them!'

'How much shorter is it?'

She stretched out both legs and hitched her skirts up enough so Jim could see her boots. 'Two inches, or thereabouts.' Sensing they were turning a corner, she decided to continue being honest with him. 'When I first broke my leg, I also punctured a lung, so as saving my life was the physician's main priority, fixing my leg was an afterthought. By the time my chest had healed, the bone in my shin had set badly and our family physician believed there was nothing else that could be done. I could barely use it, it was so misshapen and weak. Fortunately, that is when Dr Cribbs came along and reset it, and now I can use it again, so what is two inches in the grand scheme of things?'

'Did it hurt?'

Adults always lie.

'Yes. A great deal. Enough that I regretted my decision for months afterwards.' Was this the right way to get him to agree to the same? Hattie had no idea, but she was determined to be the one adult he could rely on. The one who always told the truth, no matter how difficult it might be for him to hear. 'Doctor Cribbs had to break the bone in two places to straighten my leg again. I had to wear tight splints for three months afterwards with no guarantees that his intervention would work. Then it took a lot of hard work and exercise and many more months to get to where I am now. Having the bone re-broken wasn't an easy option but as you can see…' she stood and did a little lopsided jig which shocked him almost as much as her apology had '… I don't need either crutches or wheels to get around nowadays.'

He was silent for several seconds, staring out of the window with the look of a boy with a thousand questions and the most pressing was whether or not he could trust her. She left him to ponder it, understanding that if she pushed too far too soon, he would only lash out in fear and close her down. Eventually, he turned to her, his expression still suspicious.

'Who died?' The change of subject was abrupt, but that he was curious about her enough to want to test her excuse was a breakthrough.

'Her name was Cora Marlow. She was a little girl called Izzy's mother. Izzy is only four, so she is still very confused and frightened by it all. So frightened she's been having nightmares.' Even the cynical Jim could not hide the flash of sympathy—or perhaps empathy—which played across his features. 'I was going to take you to meet her and her...father—' the truth of Jasper's paternity wasn't hers to tell '—to see if the pair of us could take her mind off her fears for a little while we feed the ducks.'

Hattie was already sitting on a bench near the pond when he and Izzy arrived at noon. Beside her was a boy with a mop of sandy hair sat in a wheeled chair who glared at him warily as Jasper waved a cheery hello. Only his companion waved back, and the sight of Hattie smiling instantly buoyed his mood but did nothing to alleviate the strange butterflies which had inhabited his stomach since last night.

He wanted to blame those on the continued impropriety and risk associated with yet another clandestine meeting with his friend's baby sister, and while that indeed played on his mind and niggled his conscience, he had a sneaking suspicion that there was more to his nerves than that.

Hattie was getting under his skin.

Or to be more specific, she had already got under it

and despite knowing that another meeting, and one in the great outdoors no less, was playing with fire here he still was. Prepared to get burned.

Thank goodness she had been right about this little park in an unfinished corner of Bloomsbury being secluded. There wasn't another soul in it and, if he forgot how selfish he was being in meeting her and tried to be a bit noble, he genuinely did not want Hattie to get burned too. It probably spoke volumes that he himself thought this was worth the risk. A tiny part of him, a part Jasper was thoroughly ashamed of, thought being caught in a compromising situation with her might not be a bad thing. At least if they were caught and propriety dictated he had to do the decent thing, he could stop pretending he wasn't interested in her in a way he had absolutely no right to be.

'Hattie!' Izzy rushed towards her and was enveloped in a hug. 'We brought cake for us and bread for the ducks.' She slanted a glance at the boy who was pretending not to notice the affection. 'Is this Jim?'

'It is Jim.' Hattie wrapped her arm around his shoulder and Jasper watched the boy instinctively stiffen. 'Jim Bradley, this is Isabel…' She realised her mistake and shot Jasper a panicked look.

'Isabel Marlow-Beaufort.' To cover the awkward moment and show the boy some respect, Jasper stuck out his hand. 'And I am Jasper Beaufort.' If Jim struggled to trust, tossing around airs and graces wouldn't help him. 'I am very pleased to meet you, Jim. Hattie has told me all about you.'

The boy took his proffered hand and shook it but said nothing, all the while sizing him up as if the cut of his coat alone was the only measure of the man who wore it.

While Jasper knew how to bide his time, Izzy didn't and stared at the wheeled chair with interest. 'Do you have to sit in that because you cannot walk?' She looked to Hattie for reassurance. 'Because Hattie said that you can't.'

'I can walk.' The boy set his stubborn jaw. 'If I wanted to. But I don't.'

Well, that set the tone nicely, or so Jim no doubt hoped, but Jasper hadn't built a business based on hospitality without learning how to charm the most difficult to please.

'If you tell me that you managed to push that chair and this strapping young man in it all the way from Covent Garden, Hattie, I shall be impressed.' Deflection was the answer here, Jasper would wager—deflection, humour and a large dollop of selective deafness. 'How is it possible that a wonky wallflower can haul a heavy load almost a mile and yet cannot dance a step?' He shot her a saucy look daring her to react in kind and she didn't disappoint.

'I can dance. If I wanted to. But I don't. At least with *you* at any rate.' She folded her arms. A motion which did wonders for her bosom, which in turn played havoc with his good intentions. 'A wonky wallflower I may be, but I still have standards.' She nudged Jim as an aside and whispered at volume out of the side of her mouth, 'Don't you dare mention that I got a porter from the infirmary to push you or that I bribed him to leave us here and not come to collect us for an hour.'

'An hour!' Jasper dropped the wicker basket he had brought with him and sat beside it on the grass as an excuse to stop contemplating her bosom. 'Then we had best get cracking if we are going to eat all this food and feed the hundredweight of bread Izzy insisted on bringing to the ducks.' As he unpacked things, he purposely thrust the muslin-wrapped fruitcake at Hattie and the plates at Jim, so the boy had to be convivial and hand them around. 'Now, who wants some lemonade?'

Chapter Seventeen

'Thank you…for this.' Hattie idly watched Izzy and Jim as he taught her how to scatter a handful of bread-crumbs to the enormous gaggle of assorted waterfowl which had gathered around them. Jasper had pushed the boy's chair to the pond's edge once their confection-ary repast was done and then had tactfully withdrawn to allow the children to be children. For all his pride and stand-offish belligerence towards the two adults, young Jim seemed to have the patience of a saint where Isabel was concerned. 'I don't think he has been out-side in weeks.'

He turned to smile at her and was grateful she con-tinued to watch the water because his breath caught in his throat. With the May sunshine picking out the stray strands of gold in her hair and the gentle heat warming the apples of her cheeks, she looked gorgeous. Having discarded her thin pelisse as well as her bonnet, the light fabric of her summer gown hugged her curves like a second skin. The square neck revealed a mini-mum amount of cleavage but enough for him to enjoy the gentle rise and fall of her chest as she relaxed back on her hands. 'The fresh air will do him good. It will do us all good.'

Jasper's mood was already lighter. 'It's therapeutic, isn't it?'

She nodded then closed her eyes and tilted her face to bask in the sun, unwittingly showing him such a perfect profile his finger longed to trace it. She had the most kissable lips he had ever seen. Pink and plump and begging to be plundered. 'I had forgotten quite how much myself. I used to always be outside and yet nowadays I seem to always be inside.'

'Says the woman who claims to walk at least a mile a day.' He wrenched his eyes away from her mouth long enough to check on Izzy before his lack of willpower dragged them back.

'I do—because I have to. But that is essential exercise not fun like riding or revelling in the glorious sunshine as I am now.' Still with her eyes closed she inhaled deeply then sighed the air out, the motion so sensual, her features suffused with such pleasure, his body and imagination reacted simultaneously.

Once the image of a similarly relaxed and sated Hattie lying on his pillow, her wheaten curls fanned out in a haphazard halo around her head, her delightful breasts rising and falling beneath the gauzy cover of his sheets lodged itself in his mind, there was no evicting it. He knew already that image would haunt his nights for weeks to come, stored in his memory alongside the image of her most intimate smile and the sultry feel of her body plastered against his as he had helped her down from the wall.

In another life, the one before Izzy, he wouldn't have resisted the temptation to make that fantasy a reality.

But now, he had to do the decent thing and settle for the daydream. Wonder what it would be like to taste her lips, peel her clothes off layer by layer and explore her lush body slowly with his hands rather than succumb to the overwhelming urge to do so.

'I will endeavour to spend more time enjoying the outside from this day forward exactly as I used to. I shall sit for at least half an hour here and gather my thoughts in the sunshine out of sight of the rest of society. That shall be my next milestone.' She sat up straight and smiled at him as she tapped her forehead. 'I always need one to aim towards.'

'Milestones?'

'One of Dr Cribbs's wise philosophies, which I now follow to the letter—like walking that daily mile—as he has never steered me wrong.' She plucked a daisy from the grass and twirled it in her fingers. 'When the journey ahead seems vast and daunting, it is always easier to break it into smaller achievable chunks. Much like stopping at different inns along the Great North Road on your way to Scotland. We planned my recovery together in much the same way, never mentioning the final destination which seemed so unachievable in the distance and instead focusing on the next achievable milestone in getting Hattie back.'

She held up the daisy. 'The first was to get through the procedure.' She picked another daisy. 'The second was to allow the bones to heal again.' As she explained, she chained the two tiny flowers together then sourced a third. 'The next was to be able to stand on my leg, then strengthen the muscles, then to learn to walk with crutches.' With each mentioned milestone she picked another flower and began attaching it to the previous stem. 'And here we are.'

'I suspect you have omitted several important milestones in that summary.'

She shrugged but didn't elaborate. 'It's been a long journey. Two years' worth. Not helped by my own impatience and tendency to try to jump ahead several milestones when I know that never works, and then disappointing myself because I failed to get there as fast as I wanted.'

'But you found Hattie at the end of it.'

'Most of her.' She sighed as she threaded some more daisies together. 'What is left of her, and by that I mean the old her. The new Hattie is still a work in progress. The same in many ways but necessarily different.' Unconsciously she rubbed her leg, her expression more wistful than sad. 'As one door closes, we must force open another and grab what is behind it by the lapels. Find new paths and new milestones to make up for those we can never return to.'

'Like dancing?'

'Dancing, running, climbing. Galloping across the fields with the wind in my hair.' Only the last was said with regret, and as if she had revealed too much she focussed on the delicate chain she was making. Behaviour that was telling yet Jasper understood he needed to tread carefully while he challenged it.

Rather than search her face for the truth, he snapped his own daisy from the lawn and ensured his response was casual. 'If you can sit on a chair, you can sit on a horse, Hattie.'

'I know... I could ride if I wanted to...' She dropped the daisy chain in her lap and stared towards the pond.

'But I don't.' Her smile was wistful. 'After the trauma of the accident, despite my annoying tendency to look too far ahead, that is one of the few milestones I am not ready to contemplate yet. I shall never say never as I am too stubborn for that but...' her eyes slanted to his, as honest and open and vulnerable as he had ever seen them '...for now, I console myself that I will get back in the saddle again the moment I need to. The new Hattie isn't as devil-may-care as the old one. She is not as brave.'

'For the record, having had the pleasure of meeting both, I much prefer the new Hattie to the old.' Without thinking, he cupped her cheek before he fastened his little, floppy daisy behind her ear. 'She is resilient and resourceful, compassionate, kind and funny, so clever she is wise beyond her years and is, without a doubt, the best, bravest person I have ever met.'

'Are you and Hattie going to get married, Papa?' Neither of them had noticed Izzy approach, and they both jumped apart in surprise at her voice so close.

Poor Hattie blushed wide-eyed at the question, clearly horrified by it, but being four, Isabel failed to notice. 'Only my mama promised that one day I would have a proper family to live with and brothers and sisters too. And Mrs Mimms thinks Hattie would make me a good new mother and is convinced the pair of you like one another because she said to Cook that you always look at Hattie as if you want to eat her for breakfast.'

He considered countering with a denial but was too mortified that he had been so transparent, and was so unnerved by that, to trust it wouldn't come out sounding false and thereby confirm he was guilty as charged.

So, instead, he settled for ruffling Izzy's curls, laughing for all he was worth while willing himself not to blush like a virgin. 'Clearly I need to have a few stern words with Mrs Mimms and Cook for wasting time on silly gossip. You have all clearly gone daft in the head if you think I would ever marry Hattie!' He jumped up and avoided running for the camouflage of the trees in order to die quietly by doing his best impression of a criminal not caught red-handed.

With his hands on his hips, he bent towards the young blabbermouth. 'Why have you abandoned poor Jim?' Deflection was his last hope of not spontaneously combusting with embarrassment.

'We ran out of bread for the ducks.'

'Then let them eat cake!' Like a drowning man grabbing ineffectually at some random passing driftwood in the hope that it could save him, he snatched up the remains of the fruitcake and marched it down to the water's edge as if his life depended upon it.

'That was a nice outing yesterday, wasn't it?' Hattie smiled at Jim as she settled him by the window despite feeling anything but happy a full day on. 'That hour of sun has brought the colour back to your cheeks.'

'It was all right, I suppose.' From him, this was tantamount to gushing praise.

'Thank you for taking such good care of Izzy.' When the adults had been out of earshot, he had chatted to the little girl non-stop and made her laugh. Such consideration hinted that a kind heart beat beneath Jim's hard exterior. An undeniably badly bruised and battered one, but one which still cared. 'It was so nice to see a smile on her face.'

'Izzy's all right.' He stared out of the window. 'That

toff you brought was all right too, despite the plum lodged in his mouth.'

'Jasper cannot help the world he was born into any more than you or I can.'

He scoffed at that. 'It must be so hard to be born rich.'

'Do not allow that aristocratic accent to fool you. Jasper is a working man, just like you. In fact, he owns that club over the road.' She pointed to The Reprobates', which was already a hive of activity in preparation for the night. He would be there soon—or was already there now because he usually stopped by in the afternoons to check on things—and she had no idea how to feel about that. Having Jasper within spitting distance after his insulting reaction yesterday was not something she was comfortable with.

Not yet at any rate.

Maybe in a day or two, once she had come to terms with his abrupt disgust, she would be more inclined to forgive him. Right now, she was angry and wounded at his lack of thought for her feelings. While she might be reconciled to his lack of romantic attraction to her—for she understood that she was hardly the catch of the day any longer thanks to her dratted leg—they were friends and he could have handled Izzy's innocent question better than he had. Let them both down gentler.

His stomping to the pond furious that such a preposterous, unpalatable idea had been proposed in the first place had also stomped all over her brittle self-esteem. It had also rather negated his pretty compliments from only seconds before they were interrupted. Compliments which had meant the world until he ruined them all by being so offended.

Jim rolled his eyes. 'As if he needs to work! The cost of his fancy boots alone is more than most honest folk earn in a year.'

'Have you ever heard the phrase about not judging a book by its cover Jim?' A phrase which Jasper could do with heeding himself! 'Because those fancy boots and everything else he owns were all bought and paid for on the back of Lord Beaufort's hard graft. He set up that club when his family ran out of money. Built it from the ground up. He earns every single penny he spends.' Even while disappointed at the wretch, she clearly still felt the compunction to defend him. What a hopeless case she was. A total doormat. Grateful for his crumbs despite knowing inside she deserved the whole loaf.

Why, oh, why did she not have the wherewithal to have set little Izzy straight herself by stating that she wouldn't marry the thoughtless devil if he was the last man on the planet!

That question had plagued her all night as she had tossed and turned and flagellated herself for her own stupidity. But no! Her usual proud bravado had deserted her. Instead, she had remained mute, gaping like an idiot while blushing like a beetroot, hoping he would drop the tiniest hint that she was growing on him in some small way which transcended the platonic.

Afterwards, pride alone forced her to pretend nothing untoward had happened whatsoever when they bade each other their overpolite goodbyes. Even though she was dying on the inside and left so self-conscious about her ugly limp and scars that she still wanted to cry or rage at the heavens for cursing her so.

What a pathetic fool she was!

Jim was silent for a moment while he watched the

comings and goings at the front door of The Reprobates', then he turned to her with the first smile he had
ever offered her. 'You fancy him, don't you?'

'I...er... I m-most certainly do not!' A fresh blush
crept up her neck and burned her cheeks as she stuttered
that unconvincing response and Jim grinned.

'Liar. You've taken a fancy to Lord Toff and it's
as plain as those red blotches all over your face.' He
touched one and made a sizzling noise before collaps-
ing in a fit of the giggles.

Rather than deny it further and risk turning purple in
the process, Hattie decided to brazen it out. 'Go ahead,
have fun at my expense. What would a ten-year-old
know about such things anyway? You barely know me
so have no clue what goes on inside my head. Or are
you a mind reader now, Jim?'

'It don't take a psychic or a genius to work out what's
obvious. Any more than it takes one to notice that the
pair of you are dancing around it and both pretending
you don't fancy one another.'

'Oh, for goodness sake,' Hattie huffed, exasperated
as she stood and made a great show of neatening the
corners of his already tidy bed. Trying not to be buoyed
up that the child in the chair behind her thought there
was hope after Jasper had practically shouted that he
thought everyone had gone daft in the head to think he
would ever marry her. Now she really was grabbing at
straws if she was pinning fresh hope on the observa-
tions of a surly ten-year-old!

'I think I should ask Dr Cribbs to check your head
when he checks on your leg today as that clearly got
knocked when the cart ran you over. Jasper and I are
friends. Nothing more. In fact...' The phrase 'the lady

doth protest too much' sprang to mind and reminded her to shut her mouth before she hanged herself.

But she had already leaked too much for the canny Jim. 'Just friends, are you? The sort of friends who have to bribe porters so they can sneak off to see each other in private. The sort who stare at each other longingly and weave daisies into one another's hair.' His finger slowly pointed to her ear and remembering the silly flower, Hattie blushed scarlet.

That was yet another thing she wished she had dealt with differently yesterday. Especially as she had forgotten it was there and gone home with it still tucked behind her ear, and then had to lie to her mother about how it came to be there. Worse, Hattie was still furious at herself that she had kept the thing. That she had been compelled to press that insignificant, wilted weed between the pages of the book on her nightstand and then continually reach for it all night and pathetically ponder if it might have meant something after all.

'You are reading too much into nothing.' Exactly as she was with that stupid daisy and Jasper's compliments, or his readiness to continue finding ways to meet her. Or his disappointing nose kiss. How daft was she to fall for a man who was never going to return the sentiment?

'Of course I am.' His smug grin called her a liar too until it melted into something which looked a great deal like sympathy. 'Although I understand why the pair of you have to pretend, as I don't suppose it's the done thing to be getting all lovey-dovey when his wife has only just died.'

'She wasn't his wife. She wasn't even his—' She clamped her jaws shut. 'It is complicated.'

'Clearly.' He shook his head, smiling, and then it split into a grin as he leaned towards the window. 'Talk of the devil... Seems like your fancy man has just arrived at work.'

'He isn't my fancy man.' But she couldn't stop herself from taking a peek at Jasper alighting from his curricle through the window and then dashing up the steps into his club. 'And that is the end of this ridiculous conversation!'

And a rather decisive end to the last remnants of her futile hope, as Jasper knew she was in here. Even if he had failed to spot the Avondale carriage passing him on the road on its way home, she had told him she would be here today specifically at this time a good half an hour before he had weaved that daisy into her hair, yet he strode into his club without as much as a backwards glance at the infirmary. Which all suggested she was an out of sight, out of mind sort of friend, instead of one in the front and centre as he was for her.

'Even though you fancy him and he fancies you?'

'Why on earth would a man like him fancy a woman like me when he could have anyone?'

'I notice you didn't deny your feelings for the toff.' Jim folded his arms, amused, looking older than his years. 'It's funny to hear someone who is so adamant that a little limp isn't going to stop her fall at the first hurdle and hide behind it when a man is involved. Who's the coward now, Hattie? What happened to grabbing life by the lapels?'

The wretch had her there and he knew it. 'I am not discussing your silly flight of fancy any longer.'

He smiled at her, his expression teasing as he aptly aimed another one of her pearls of wisdom right back at her like an arrow. 'The most important things are always the hardest to talk about, Hattie. Especially if you are scared.'

Unwittingly, he had given her the perfect opportunity to not only change the depressing and humiliating subject, but to bring up what she had come here specifically to talk about. Because heaven only knew it was time to stop torturing herself with unrealistic nonsense and to refocus all her attentions on doing something with a proper purpose.

'Is that why you refuse to talk about Dr Cribbs fixing your leg, Jim?'

Silence all of a sudden as the shutters came down with a bang.

'I know you are scared, Jim, but with every passing day, as your bone sets harder, the less chance you have of him doing the best job possible. Look at me...' Calm reason and honesty were going to be her new mantras with him now that she knew him better. 'For me, the months of delay meant that some of the damage was irreversible. You are lucky that yours is still—'

'I'm not lucky!' The flash of anger told her she had pushed too far again. Either that or she needed to push harder. 'This isn't lucky!' He pointed to his splinted legs. 'This has ruined everything!'

'Only temporarily. Once you are healed...'

Tears filled his eyes before he could cover them with a snarl. 'Once I'm healed I get to limp back to the Cleveland Street workhouse! The place useless people from my world get sent to when nobody else wants them!'

'That will only be temporary too.'

'They said that to my gran, and she never came out!' His eyes were wide with panic now. 'Nobody ever comes out of that prison alive, and nobody lasts in there that long!'

'That is why you don't want to be fixed, isn't it?' Understanding suddenly dawned as bright as the sun. 'Because they will only have you back if you are.'

'I'd rather take my chances on the streets begging for coins with the rest of the cripples than ever set foot in that stinking hellhole again!'

'Then surely that's all the more reason to get fixed?' Hattie nearly jumped out of her skin at the sound of Jasper's voice behind them. As her head whipped around, she saw he was leaning on the door frame. Goodness knew how long he had been there or, heaven help her, how much of their conversation he had overheard.

Chapter Eighteen

Jasper pushed himself away from the frame and sauntered in, his eyes briefly flicking to hers in discomfort
before they locked with Jim's. 'You have more chance
of finding gainful employment with a reasonably able
body than you do without.'

'Shows what you know, *Your Lordship*!' Ashamed
and afraid, Jim lashed out. 'I'm no use to anyone lame!
You need a strong pair of legs to lift and carry! Not that
a spoiled toff like you would understand.'

'I understand that there are better jobs than hauling
barrels, young man.' Jasper's tone was more of repri-
mand than pity as he stood tall and proud in front of
the window, commanding the boy to look up at him
rather than away. 'Do you know your letters and your
numbers?'

'What do you think, idiot!' This was spat with such
venom even Hattie, who had been at the receiving end
of Jim's sharp tongue many times, was taken aback.

But Jasper wasn't the least bit cowed by the tone or
the insult. Outwardly, he found them amusing and simply raised his brows as if he wasn't fooled by the bra-

vado for a minute. 'Then it occurs to me that a sensible chap would use his long convalescence to learn and better himself. Plan for a proper future rather than wallow in impotent self-pity while he waits for others to decide what is to become of him. There are plenty of good jobs for the literate which pay better too, and none require a strong pair of legs, merely legs that work.'

In one fluid movement and without pausing, he sat on the mattress and rested his elbows on his knees, relaxed. 'I have such a vacancy myself for an apprentice jack of all trades and seeing as we are currently neighbours—' he gestured out of the window towards his club '—and I am in the process of hiring a governess to begin Izzy's education anyway, I would be happy for you to attend those lessons on the understanding that if you apply yourself diligently and always try your hardest, that apprenticeship will be yours.'

That knocked the wind out of Jim's sails. To be frank, it had also knocked it out of Hattie's. As they both blinked at him, stunned, Jasper stared at Jim levelly.

'The wages are ten shillings a week to begin with, plus board and lodging of course.' A king's ransom for a child like Jim who had barely scraped a third of that with two jobs. To Hattie, it was obvious Jasper was making this all up on the hoof to help Jim out while saving the boy's pride, but Jim didn't know that.

'It goes without saying that if you prove yourself to be a lazy and rude ne'er-do-well, or a dishonest and untrustworthy scoundrel, I shall toss you out on your ear. I will not accept thieving, malingering or surliness in any way, shape or form. I would also expect you to continue with your lessons after your recovery as I need an educated apprentice, one who can learn every aspect of my business, and will adjust your hours accordingly to fit those in. You'll get every Sunday and Christmas Day off. From both work and your lessons.'

A slack-jawed Jim couldn't believe his luck and was already so thoroughly seduced he just kept staring at Hattie, bewildered as if he was hallucinating.

'It also means having your leg fixed by Dr Cribbs is non-negotiable, young man. And your employment and your wages start the day you have that procedure.' Then, as his green eyes stared unrelenting, daring Jim to be stupid enough to turn him down, Jasper stuck out his hand for the boy to shake. 'Do we have an accord, Mr Bradley?'

Overwhelmed and entirely lost for words, Jim nodded and produced his own hand.

'Splendid.' Jasper pumped it vigorously, then stood, slapping the boy on the back as if they were now the best of friends. 'Once the procedure has been done, I shall arrange the first times and dates of your lessons through Hattie. Now if you will excuse me, Jim…' Those unrelenting, unreadable green eyes locked with hers. 'I need to borrow her for a minute.'

She followed him outside into the hallway with the fakest smile he had ever seen pasted on her face. But as her blue eyes were as hard as nails Jasper knew she was angry at him for yesterday, just as he had suspected she had been when she had offered him her clipped goodbye at the park.

He also knew, despite all his mortifying behaviour yesterday, exactly what she was most angry about. He knew because he had replayed the same awful sentence over and over again in his mind ever since he had uttered the damn thing. For how on earth could she be anything other than hideously insulted to be told that everyone had clearly gone daft in the head if they thought he would ever marry her!

At the time, he had intended a very different version of that dreadful sentence, one where their roles were reversed. But at the last moment, he had become flustered and reasoned that saying what he had intended would also be a confirmation that Izzy, Mrs Mimms and his blasted cook had got things right. So the sentence had come out garbled and he had unintentionally hurt the one person he never wanted to hurt. He had seen that in her eyes the moment he had barked it out and still saw it now as she waited primly for him to speak.

'Hattie, I...' Good grief this was awkward. 'I wanted to...' What? Explain? Retract? Confess? 'Yesterday...at the park when Izzy...' Her lovely eyes widened in horror then began to blink rapidly, momentarily putting him off finding the right words to correct his callous mistake. 'I handled things badly and for that I am sorry.'

Her breezy roll of her eyes was as fake as her smile had been. 'Children will be children and it really doesn't matter.' Before he could counter, she briskly filled the silence. 'That was a lovely thing you just did for Jim. Thank you. If I had realised it was his reluctance to return to the poor house which had caused him to refuse treatment, I would have handled things differently from the outset, but Jim is a stubborn boy and a proud one. Yet you managed to give him hope where none existed before, and all by thinking on your feet as I presume you haven't yet hired a governess for Izzy, have you?'

She was trying to let him off lightly by changing the subject, and it would have been so easy to let her.

However, brushing his behaviour aside would not banish her hurt and he knew he wouldn't rest until he had rescued her from that.

Which necessitated a level of honesty he had hoped to avoid for the sake of their friendship. 'In my hamfisted way, I insulted you yesterday. It wasn't intentional and it certainly wasn't meant how it sounded.'

'Please, Jasper…' There was an air of panic about her expression. 'Let us not discuss it. I can assure you that there really is no need. Izzy asked a ridiculous question which neither of us were expecting, so you answered in a manner which I took no offence at. It is just as well that you did, because I was so shocked by the question I couldn't think of a single response and…' She was babbling again, a clear sign that she was nervous, and he sympathised entirely because so was he. 'If you hadn't nipped it in the bud, she would have only asked worse. So…'

He caught her hand and gently traced her fingers, staring at them rather than her initial response to his confession in case she was thoroughly appalled by what he was compelled to say. 'The truth is…' This was probably a mistake. A huge, ill-considered mistake which could kill their friendship stone dead—and maybe that was for the best in the grand scheme of things. For her at least.

'If my life wasn't as complicated as it currently is and wasn't about to implode in a scandal, you are exactly the sort of woman that I would want by my side. You mean the world to me, Harriet Fitzroy.' The sheer truth of that absolute fact made him dizzy. 'And I meant every single word I said to you yesterday, right up to the moment I put my big, fat, clumsy foot in it because Izzy had hit a raw nerve. If I could...*if only* I could... I would send you a hundred robust crimson tulips every single day.'

With one eye scrunched closed he risked looking at her with the other to gauge her reaction and she simply stared at him in wordless shock. Or perhaps horror. Which was likely his cue to leave, seeing as he had no right to question which it was.

'Anyway...' How to kill a perfectly good friendship in a single moment, or two if he counted his insult yesterday. 'I just wanted to explain my reaction.'

As all she seemed capable of doing was opening and closing her eyelids, he shrugged apologetically, then to spare them both more awkwardness, strode towards the door.

'Jasper—'

He slowed but did not turn around.

'How much of my conversation with Jim did you just hear?'

Not at all one of the many sentences he had foolishly hoped she would say after he had just bared his heart. 'Enough to know that Jim's grandmother died in the same poor house he will return to if nothing else turns up.' As the silence stretched, he could feel her eyes on his back, hear the cogs of her mind turning. The intense weight of the significance of the moment. When he could bear it no longer, he twisted to find her watching him, not so much warily as in question. 'Why?'

'No reason.' She shrugged and worried her bottom lip as if she were in two minds about saying something.

About doing something.

Until her expression shifted again to one which he could not decipher. One which could have been either fear or anticipation. It was most disconcerting.

'There must have been some reason, or you wouldn't have asked.' Whatever it was, good or bad, he needed to know. Needed either the kindling to feed the glimmer of hope inside which stalwartly refused to die or to snuff it out completely.

'It is just that Jim said something quite profound before that...' As her uneven, wary footsteps brought her slowly closer, the air in the narrow, empty, clinical hallway seemed to shift and change. 'He called me out on something...and he was right to.' She stopped a foot away from him, allowing Jasper to see every bit of indecision and uncertainty in her lovely eyes before she smiled shyly. 'I can hardly lecture others about gripping life by the lapels if I am too scared to do it myself, now can I?'

Jasper had no clue what that meant but nodded, a knot in his throat and a bigger one in his gut. 'I suppose so.'

As the world slowed to a standstill and the charged atmosphere crackled around them, he watched her palms reach out to smooth his lapels. Her touch so gentle he barely felt it, yet bizarrely also felt it everywhere. He held his breath as she finally gripped the fabric in her fingers, his heart racing because whatever was going on felt so profound. Almost as if this was one of those defining moments where the path of his life was about to drastically alter.

For the longest time, she stared resolutely at his chest. After an eternity, her eyes finally lifted, and she tugged his face towards hers slow enough for him to consider all of the reasons why he should put a noble stop to this and discount every single one. And because while his spirit was willing to be the knight in shining armour she deserved, his flesh and his heart were too weak to do what was right by her, he sighed against her mouth in surrender as she tentatively pressed her mouth to his.

Her lips were soft but deadly, overwhelming him from the outset and firing his blood. In one last futile attempt to be a gentleman and a friend, Jasper fisted his hands at his sides and tried to restrict himself to merely tasting her rather than devouring her. That deprivation lasted seconds before he lost himself completely in a kiss so tender and honest, the emotion floored him. Because Hattie felt like home—or at least the part of his which he hadn't realised was missing until this moment.

Still not daring to touch her he deepened the kiss, and it changed instantly into something else. A desire he could not control or wanted to. When her arms looped around his neck, his snaked around her waist, pulling her closer until her heart beat against his. Exactly where he wanted it. Strong and steady and so right his swelled in his chest.

After that, all reason was gone and he was glad to be rid of it, feasting on her mouth as his greedy hands explored the shape of her curves.

Hips, thighs, bottom…

Later, he would have a vague recollection of lifting her while he staggered backwards towards the wall, her hands in his hair, her tongue dancing with his before approaching voices in the distance dragged them both back to reality.

As they jumped apart, and because she looked every inch like a woman thoroughly ravished, he had had the wherewithal to neaten his hair, tuck in his shirt and do up his waistcoat, although he had no memory of how it had become undone. But by the way the skin beneath still thrummed from her touch, he knew her hands had explored his flesh beneath the barrier of his clothes.

'How is our patient today, Lady Harriet?' If Dr Cribbs noticed Hattie's kiss-swollen lips or Jasper's erratic breathing as he came around the corner reading his notes, his expression leaked no clue.

'Thanks to Lord Beaufort's timely interference, Jim has agreed to have the operation.' To Jasper she looked as guilty as sin, as well as like rumpled sin incarnate. All his doing because he had been unable to control himself. If the physician hadn't disturbed them, he shuddered to think what sort of a state she would be in as he had been seconds away from unlacing her gown and pulling the pins from her hair.

'That is splendid news. Well done.' The doctor consulted his notes again and the long list of things he had to do. 'How about I schedule it for tomorrow around ten?' He searched Hattie's guilty face and as if she realised her aroused nipples strained against the soft fabric of her bodice, she folded her arms to cover them, her gaze briefly darting to Jasper's and her cheeks colouring because they both knew she had moaned her pleasure as his thumbs had teased them.

'The sooner the better.'

'I am assuming you will want to be here when it happens?'

All the colour drained from her face as Jasper witnessed the flash of fear in her eyes, which typically she covered before she steeled her shoulders.

'Of course I want to be there. Jim will need someone with him who cares.'

'Ten o'clock sharp then,' said the doctor jotting that

down. 'Shall we explain everything to him together now?' He smiled at Hattie and she nodded again.

'Yes…of course. Let me just show Lord Beaufort out first.'

'Of course.' Doctor Cribbs began walking forward with purpose once more. 'I shall check on some of the others while I wait.'

She watched him leave, her arms still tightly folded, gently worrying her bottom lip as if she could still feel the brand of his on it. When she finally turned back, she was deliciously awkward. 'That was close.'

Undeniably a little too close and guilt swamped him. Another five seconds and she would have been ruined and all the choice in her future taken away. 'I lost my head… I'm sorry.'

She stared at her shuffling feet. 'I think we both did, so please do not apologise. Besides…' her gaze lifted to his, shy but defiant '…I started it.'

'But I allowed it to get out of hand when I should have exercised some restraint.' Good grief he wanted to kiss her again. Haul her into his arms and to hell with the consequences. Unfortunately, as they would both have to live with those consequences, and her worst of all, he had to be sensible. Had to put her needs above his no matter what his selfish soul wanted. 'I am a wing and a prayer from potentially the mother of all scandals, Hattie, the last thing I want to do is embroil you in another alongside it.'

The arms folded again. 'What does that mean?'

'It means that I will not put you in a compromising position.' He would not let her down like that. Wouldn't be able to live with the guilt if he did. He had to take the moral high ground, no matter how much his heart screamed otherwise. 'Therefore, I can only be your friend—for now at least, but—'

'I see.' She bristled, clearly not seeing at all. 'Five minutes ago, you claimed to want to send me a hundred crimson tulips but after one kiss we are back to being just friends again.'

'Only until I have weathered the scandal and...' Jasper raked a frustrated hand through his hair, his sensible head at war with his heart and soul. 'What I mean to say...what I have absolutely no right to ask is...' He tried to stall the selfish question, or at least rephrase it, but he did not possess the willpower to hold it back. 'Would you wait for me, Hattie?'

'Wait?' She was frowning but at least the hurt was gone.

'Only until the dust has settled and you and I can...' He shrugged, blushing himself now too because he had never laid his feelings so bare in front of another living soul, and especially not one who held the power to shatter him with her answer. 'Explore what we just started.'

She furrowed her brows while she digested that, making him sweat on her decision for at least half a minute before she answered.

'Only on one condition.'

'Which is?'

'That I shall concede to being your friend in public, Jasper—for now.' She grabbed his lapels again and rose on tiptoes to place a lingering kiss on his mouth. It was nowhere near as passionate as their last kiss but still heated his blood all over again. 'But never in private.'

Chapter Nineteen

Hattie was a mess in the carriage on the way to the infirmary the next morning. Such a mess she feared she wouldn't be able to hide it from Jim any better than she had been able to hide it from her own family over the breakfast table.

While Kitty and Dorothea had tried to fill the void of silence with idle chatter to take her mind off things, her parents and her two siblings understood why she sat quietly, lost in her own thoughts. They understood because they had been there when she had undergone the exact same procedure that that poor little boy was about to endure, and they knew what a horrific and painful ordeal it had been.

Her mother, who had been the only one in the actual room as Hattie's leg had been rebroken, was as white as a sheet as she sipped her tea yet had still repeatedly offered to swap places with her today to spare her the trauma. Spare her the pain of dredging up her own awful experience and reliving it second by second as Jim suffered the same fate.

As tempting as it was to accept, Hattie had refused

on two counts. Firstly, because Jim had never met her mother and it had been Hattie who had been the one to convince him that this was for the best. And secondly, because she did not need to be stood in the operating theatre later to relive her past, she had spent all night doing so.

Not even the fresh memory of her spectacular kiss with Jasper and his awkward but glorious request that she wait for him could block out her fragmented, horrific recollections of her operation of almost eighteen months ago. Fragmented, as at times, when it had all become too much, she had blacked out. Those dreadful gaps in her mind would be filled today, and the nightmare which she had kept locked in a box since the day it had happened, would be free again to haunt her.

Yet it couldn't be helped, and as much as she wanted to curl into a ball and hide until it was all over, she would not let little Jim down in his hour of need. Therefore, she had forced a matter-of-fact serenity over herself at the breakfast table. Adamantly stated she had to do this and that was that, then tried to choke some dry toast down so that she had something to settle her roiling stomach, even though the food had not stayed in her stomach for long. But at least she had been able to hide that aspect of the morning from her family before she had bidden them a good day and reminded them that she wouldn't be home until dinner tonight, or maybe later.

Nobody had argued because they all understood she would not be able to leave until she was certain Jim was going to be all right.

She prayed with all her heart that he would be, though the odds were evens at best. If he survived the shock and escaped infection, there were no guarantees the bone would set properly a second time and there was more than a good chance it would end up in a worse shape. A fact which made her doubt her insistence that he should consent to the operation. It was that doubt which was destroying her now, but she was adamant she could not let it show. For Jim's sake, she had to be the brave one today and the soothing voice of calm, and she would be, just as soon as she managed to stop her own hands from shaking.

The carriage made its final turn into King Street and Hattie sucked in a calming breath. She allowed the carriage to stop and still remained in her seat, needing those extra moments to compose herself before she became the solid rock for a terrified little boy to cling to. Only when her mask was properly fixed in place did she alight, managing to sound in control as she told the driver not to expect a message recalling him until well after eight tonight.

Stalling for time, she stood on the infirmary steps and watched the carriage leave, then sagged in relief at the sight of Jasper revealed on the opposite pavement behind it. He waited for the vehicle to trundle away and checked the coast was clear before he came across the road.

His hand moved to touch her before he stopped himself. 'I've come to take your place. Mrs Mimms is taking care of Izzy for the day, freeing me to be with Jim in your stead. There is no need to put yourself through all that again, and I cannot allow you to do it. Sit with him before and stay with him after, but there really is no need for you to be present while the operation takes place.'

She shook her head. 'There is every need. Aside

from the inescapable fact that we both know that I am incapable of deserting anyone in distress, Jim has put his trust in me and me alone, and I will not be another adult who lets him down.'

'Then let me at least be there with you...' She silenced him with another shake of her head.

'No, Jasper. He barely knows you, and agony is such a personal and private thing he should not have to endure it with a stranger. I have to do this for him, and you know that. If it were Izzy, wild horses wouldn't stop you from being with her because you are who she would want. I have become rather fond of Jim and, although he hides it as if his life depends upon it, I believe he has developed a fondness for me, too. I am the only person who knows what he is about to go through and therefore, I am the only one who can help him through it. I made a promise to a lost and frightened child and, like you, when I make a promise, it is sacrosanct.'

Because she needed the contact more than she cared about propriety, she reached for his hands and squeezed them tight. 'But it means the world that you offered and that you are here, and I shall be all the stronger knowing that you are nearby once this is done.' She wanted to hold him. Wanted him to hold her so that she could absorb his strength but had to settle for laying her palm over his heart. 'Go to work, Jasper. Take your mind off this and when it is done, I shall send word to your club. I am sure Jim will appreciate a visit here later—almost as much as I will.'

Work, she had said, to take his mind off things.

As if that was going to happen! He had stared religiously at the hands of the mantel clock in his office above The Reprobates', both of which now pointed at noon. He knew the operation was to have commenced at ten and he had paced the floor relentlessly in the two hours hence, constantly checking his window to watch the street below or stare at the infirmary. Yet still there was no word from Hattie, which surely could only be a bad sign.

Rather than pace some more, he decided enough was enough, and went to grab the coat he had long discarded in his anguish only to be interrupted by his doorman.

'You've a caller. A lady, apparently.' He raised his brows as they both knew such an occurrence was a rarity indeed at a gentlemen's club. 'Told me to tell you her name is Hattie.'

'She's here!' His coat forgotten, Jasper bounded for the door and took the stairs two at a time in his haste to get to her. He skidded to a stop on the polished marble where she waited in the atrium, except the sight of her did not fill him with joy despite her feeble attempt at a smile.

'It's done.' She looked and sounded exhausted. Her usual English rose complexion was as pale as milk. Her posture slumped. Her hair a dishevelled, ratty mess. Her lovely eyes lost and harrowed, focussed not on him or her surroundings but on something which wasn't present. As if she had just stumbled off a battlefield rather than out of a hospital. 'The laudanum has finally kicked in and he's sleeping now—thank God— so at least he will get a few hours of relief before the next ordeal starts.'

Jasper had a million questions, none of which mattered when it was clearly she who now needed looking after, so he wrapped his arm around her and silently led her up the stairs.

She allowed him to settle her on the enormous chesterfield in his office and sat stranded in her own thoughts while he arranged for some tea to be brought up. Only when his door was firmly closed, and she cradled a steaming cup in her hands, did he sit beside her and cuddle her close.

'Do you want to talk about it?'

'It was every bit as dreadful as I anticipated it would be—and some.' She rested a heavy head on his shoulder. 'That poor boy... Even though I have been through that hell already, if I could have swapped places with him, I would have.'

'Of course you would have.' He kissed the top of her head. 'Because you are a hopeless rescuer to your core.'

'Maybe, but...' She barely shook her head. 'It turns out it is easier to go through it than it is to witness it, powerless to take another's pain away.'

'Oh, Hattie.' He wished he could take her pain away but knew he couldn't. 'You mustn't feel guilty, although I know you do. What has happened today was a necessary evil, done for Jim's benefit. And like you, one day he will thank Dr Cribbs and us for bullying him into it.'

'You are right... I know you are right but...' Emotion choked her voice. 'It brought everything back, Jasper... *everything*. The smells, the awful sounds, the sheer barbarism and excruciating agony of it all. The fear...all so raw and visceral, having to hold him down... I hated that part most of all but knew it was necessary.' Before the cup fell from her shaking fingers, Jasper took it, then hauled her into his lap and held her tight.

'For someone who feels another's pain quite as intensely as your big, kind heart does, Hattie, this was always going to rip you to shreds.'

'I never wanted to have to think about it ever again. Never wanted to remember it all with such clarity or watch another living soul suffer the same, let alone a child.'

Jasper kissed her head again. 'Then you probably should have thought about that before you decided to volunteer at the Ragamuffin Infirmary, or at least done so at a distance by knitting socks rather than getting personally involved.' He smiled as he stroked her hair. 'But you are not made that way.'

'I know... I hate knitting.' She laughed without humour. 'I suppose I have rather brought this on myself. Poor Jim is the one who has suffered the worst today, and yet here I am, feeling sorry for myself. Wallowing in my own pit of self-pity when this isn't about me.'

'A wise friend once told me that sometimes we all need to surrender to the self-indulgent futility and give it an airing because if we don't it festers.'

The half-hearted chuckle was real this time rather than pained. 'I see you are going to be irritating by quoting me back at myself again, Jasper Beaufort.'

'Everyone needs a shoulder to cry on sometimes, Hattie Fitzroy, even someone as brave and indomitable as you. And for the record, I am honoured that you chose mine.' She twisted slightly to smile up at him and he, because he couldn't help himself, kissed her.

'We are each other's knights in shining armour, you and I, and when I promised to rescue you from all the horrors of the Season, I never stipulated it had to happen in a ballroom. My shoulders are yours to cry upon whenever they are needed, whether that be in public or in private, and my services as your knight run the gamut from sitting next to you on the wallflowers' chairs to mopping up your tears. Whatever it is that you need, if it is in my power to do it, your wish is always my command.'

Because he wanted to kiss her again, he tucked an untidy coil of her hair behind her ear. 'You look tired.' An understatement. 'I will lay money that you did not sleep a wink last night.'

She shrugged but didn't deny it. 'I had a lot on my mind.'

'As the worst is over and your patient is sleeping, why don't you grab the chance for a quick nap?'

She instantly bristled, sitting bolt upright on his lap. 'I am not going home!'

'I do not recall suggesting that you should?' It did not take a genius to work out that the only way he would currently get her back to Mayfair was bound, gagged, kicking and screaming, and knowing the tenacious Hattie as well as he did, he did not fancy his chances even then. 'Sleep here.' He patted the sofa. 'Just for an hour to get some colour back into your ghostly complexion.'

She stubbornly discounted that suggestion straight away. 'There is too much going on in my mind, I am too distracted by my past and Jim's future that I know I wouldn't sleep a wink even if I tried.'

'Then why don't I try to distract you from all your futile, racing thoughts in some other way. I could read to you. There's a copy of *The Times* on my desk. I always find their column on stocks and shares more soporific than counting sheep. Or better still, I could grab one of my ledgers and recite all the columns of figures in all their monotonous glory. Or I could have a hot bath drawn for you. Nothing eases tension like a nice bath. Or I could—'

She placed a finger on his lips and seemed to stare into his soul. 'Or you could just carry on holding me and tell me that everything is going to be all right.'

Chapter Twenty

Hattie awoke feeling warm and safe.

It took a few moments to realise that was because she was sprawled atop Jasper, snuggled within the cage of his arms.

Shamelessly sprawled on top of Jasper, because her head rested on his chest, her hand was splayed on his abdomen and her bad leg had hooked itself between his and was held in place by the solid weight of his palm on her thigh. It was a considerably more intimate position than the way she last remembered them. She recalled being swaddled in his lap, her cheek against his neck as he softly whispered reassurances against her hair while his fingers toyed with it. They had been upright then. That they weren't now must have meant that either he had lowered them back once she had dozed off or, by the slow, rhythmic motion of his breathing, he had nodded off too and their bodies had found a comfortable way to sleep entwined.

Whichever it was, it was rather lovely as well as highly improper.

Hattie lifted her head to assess the best route off

the chesterfield without waking Jasper, but as she was wedged against the back and her only option was to roll over him, that was unlikely to happen. Besides, he would only worry if she miraculously managed to sneak out without him noticing and that wouldn't be fair, so instead, she kissed his cheek.

'I should go, Jasper.' Then, for good measure she placed a soft kiss goodbye on his mouth.

His lips responded sleepily, and he sighed his appreciation, the hand on her thigh sliding possessively upwards to her bottom. 'Don't go yet.' His mouth was fully awake when it found hers again. 'Stay for just a little bit more.'

The next kiss was thorough, and she revelled in it irrespective of the impropriety. Then she decided she did not care if it was improper because everything about her relationship with Jasper was technically improper anyway. What difference would a bit more impropriety make? She would be just as ruined if they were innocently found together in the little park with the duck pond as she would be here in his arms.

In fact, she decided, as she gave herself completely to the kiss, there was considerably less chance of that happening here than there. Besides, being ruined by Jasper wouldn't exactly be the end of the world. In many ways, it might well be the start of it, so she kissed him some more.

He rolled to reverse their position and that was when she first became aware of the intriguing changes in his body and the insistent bulge which pressed against her lower abdomen.

Hattie knew what that was. One couldn't spend half one's life in the countryside and not notice how the farm

animals procreated, and she had since filled all the gaps
in her knowledge on the intricacies in human anatomy
by flicking through the many medical books scattered
around the infirmary. She also knew that if that part of
Jasper wasn't at rest like the rest of his big body, then
something rather marvellous was afoot.

He desired her.

Her!

The wonkiest wallflower in the whole of Christen-
dom.

It was heady knowledge to be armed with and instantly gave her wayward body a whole host of seriously
improper ideas. Ideas which were much too tempting
to ignore.

Feeling bold, she deepened the kiss, using her tongue
and teeth to tease his mouth to play along, until he
growled and took control again.

'I've dreamed of this.' His teeth found her ear and
nibbled softly. 'Craved you incessantly for weeks.' His
whisper sent a delicious shiver down her spine. 'Tried
to resist you but I can't.'

How wonderful!

'Then don't.' Intimacy was one of those milestones
she had feared, yet suddenly, with Jasper, that fear felt
redundant. If he wanted her and she wanted him, why
fight it? Especially as this felt so gloriously right. Another moment to grab life by the lapels.

Because he seemed to like what she was doing and
because the bottom of his shirt was untucked, she allowed her fingers to trail up his warm belly, to follow
the crisp arrow of hair which led the way from his navel
to his chest, and then to trace the shape of his nipples.
They puckered instantly and he moaned against her

mouth, the hard, male part of him now pressed against the apex of her thighs and awakening all the feminine nerves which lived there.

'You're killing me.' His kisses were languid and lazy, but intense, as if he were in no hurry to get the job done despite his obvious ardour, so Hattie responded in kind while her palms learned the unique pattern of the bunched muscles in his back. When one of his hands found her breast, she arched against it, murmuring encouragement until he slipped his fingers beneath the fabric of her bodice and freed it. The fresh afternoon breeze blowing through the windows whispered over her skin at the same moment as his fingertips grazed the sensitive tip and she sighed her pleasure, feeling decadent and seductive and ripe for the picking.

Jasper moaned too, whispering her name as his lips trailed along her jaw, then down her neck, and finally encircled her aching nipple. 'You're so lovely, Hattie.' His breath teased that sensitive flesh more and she felt beautiful. Powerful. Overwhelmed.

Wanton.

'So perfect.' The fabric of her skirts caught and ruched as he hoisted them upwards, so she adjusted her body to make that easier. 'How on earth am I supposed to keep resisting you when I want you so much?'

'I want you too, Jasper.' Of its own accord, her body opened for him and then hummed and blossomed as his covered erection pulsed against the most sensitive part of her. Instinct told her to hook her legs around his to bring him closer. 'All of you.' And never a truer word was spoken. There was an ache in her womb which needed to be filled. Parts of her body which screamed to be touched.

'I need all of you too, Hattie. All of you.'

Propriety dictated that she should have been out-raged when he reached between their bodies to caress between her thighs, but by then she was so lost in the sublime sensuality of his touch that she had quite for-gotten the meaning of the word. Instead, she surren-dered to it. Welcomed it.

Within seconds, she became a puddle of fizzing nerve endings and a willing captive to her own plea-sure, needing every stroke on that needy bud more than air. Craving every caress in a way she had never desired anything else ever. Desperate to climb higher and higher and step ever closer to the edge. To fly.

Then all at once—much too soon but far too late—her body pulsed and shattered as she cried out into his mouth, then floated slowly back to earth like an au-tumn leaf caught on the wind. Tumbling and twisting in utter, utter bliss.

When she came to, he was smiling, the tip of his nose nuzzling hers gently, but his eyes smouldered with so much desire it re-awoke her body in an instant. In case he thought this was it, she had to let him know. 'I still want all of you, Jasper. So *very* much…' She did not recognise the sultry timbre of her own voice or her as-sured and bold touch, yet did not hesitate to be the one to reach between them this time and boldly trace the shape of him before she began to unbutton his falls with impatient fingers. 'Every last inch.'

Those unusual green eyes instantly darkened to al-most black before he smothered her mouth with a kiss so carnal it left her both breathless and desperate for him again. 'Then we had best get these clothes off.'

In one fluid motion, his flattened palm smoothed her stocking down her thigh to her calf.

Then he froze.

Jasper stared down at Hattie in a mixture of insatiable need and sheer horror, completely torn in two.

Good grief, what had he done!

The guilt weighed so heavy he could barely breathe. She had come to him overwrought and vulnerable, needing a friend in her greatest hour of need and instead of being her rock as she had always been his, he had seduced her! Put his needs above hers and taken advantage with shameless abandon.

He wasn't entirely sure how things had gone so far or quite which of them had instigated it. One minute he had been sound asleep, dreaming about making love to her and the next she had been in the throes of ecstasy, by which time and undeniably wide awake and out of control, he had needed to witness the unadulterated, erotic beauty of that happening.

Somewhere in between, he had lost the ability to think and now she was sprawled beneath him on the chesterfield in his office. Her hair a tangled mess around her head, her mouth swollen from his ardent kisses, one perfect breast exposed to his hungry gaze alongside the damp, golden curls between her open thighs. The errant, ungentlemanly hand which had brought her to a shuddering, noisy climax still hovering on the stocking he had almost ripped to shreds in his blind, animalistic passion and his painful erection jutting against her fingers through his half-opened falls and positively screaming for release.

He snatched his hand away and fisted it in case it

was tempted to finish what it had started, took a deep breath and slowly rolled his body away, then sat on the edge of the chesterfield with his back to her. His head in his hands and his heart in his mouth.

'Jasper?' Hattie reached out and trailed her hand down his rumpled shirt, stoking his unsatisfied lust further when he was trying to dampen it down. 'What did I do wrong?' The hurt in her voice broke his heart and added to his guilt. 'Has something displeased you?'

'Of course not... You were perfect but...' Her touch was killing him. The urge to haul her into his arms and decisively finish what he had started was making it impossible to think straight, so he leapt up to save them both. 'This isn't right.'

'Why?' Her wounded eyes dropped to where his breeches strained, his manhood throbbing like a traitor beneath her gaze. 'Don't you want me any more?'

He choked out a bitter laugh as he gestured to the undeniable evidence to the contrary. 'What I want and what I deserve right now are two very different things.' Ashamed, he stood and used the back of a chair to hide behind in case his body refused to comply with his head. 'What I deserve is shooting for taking of advantage of you.'

'You really didn't, Jasper.' She pulled her stocking back up before she struggled to sit thanks to her hopelessly twisted skirts, rucked tight and trapped beneath her hips. 'I can assure you that I didn't mind in the slightest.'

He struggled to speak.

Struggled to answer with anything coherent because his head and his body had gone to war. He knew that he couldn't, in all good conscience, take advantage of her further but…she was like a siren tempting him. He had never wanted a woman more than he wanted Hattie in this precise moment. He could still taste her kiss, feel the potency of her desire. Still see the vaguest hint of her swollen sex beneath those inviting wheaten curls as she wrestled with her knotted clothing.

He sincerely doubted he would ever forget the sight or the sounds of her surrendering to her orgasm, or the sublime feel of the silken walls of her body convulsing against his fingers. Because his Hattie had approached her pleasure with the same single-minded enthusiasm as she approached everything—head first and to hell with the consequences.

But he did not have that luxury.

He had to think of the consequences—for her. Because he was wholly in the wrong here and he could not live with himself if he ruined her life, as he had Cora's, by putting his needs first. Especially when, if he gave in to them, all of the dire consequences of it would be hers to bear.

The stigma of complete ruination. The disappointment of her family. Denying her the right and the time to decide if he could be the one once the dust had settled. Trapping her in a marriage which might very well suit him but might not ultimately suit her. Instantly becoming a mother to a child which wasn't hers, and inevitably, if he gave in to the temptation to make her his in every sense of the word, perhaps to even have to deal with the immediate prospect of their own baby in her belly. And all because he couldn't control his desire for her when she had come to him in distress.

'This is too soon, Hattie. Just weeks. It has happened

too fast. We…' he shook his head, needing to own the blame for it all '…*you* are not ready for this.'

'But, Jasper…'

He vehemently shook his head because he could not allow her to make him feel better. He deserved all the guilt he currently felt. Deserved it and needed it to help him do what was right. 'We've only just started to get to know one another and rushing through the different phases of love…' The intensity of his erection made it hard to pace, but he did anyway, hoping against hope that it might make it subside and cease controlling him.

'Well, it's like your milestones, is what it is…those phases cannot be rushed no matter how keen I am to get to the final destination and I certainly shouldn't have taken advantage of you just now when you came to me for comfort.'

His eyes latched on to her breast again so he winced and turned away, gesturing ineffectually with a flapping hand. 'For the love of God, cover yourself, woman, and give me a fighting chance here, when I am trying to be a gentleman.'

'I think that ship has sailed, don't you?' She padded behind him and wrapped her arms around his waist. 'And good riddance to it, so why don't we finish what we just started?'

It would have been so easy to succumb. So easy to swivel in her arms and lose himself and his guilt in her kiss. Carry her back to the sofa and bury his needy body to the hilt inside her and to hell with the consequences, but Jasper couldn't.

Wouldn't.

Not until his scandal had passed and she was truly certain he was worth it. He loved her too much to live with her regret and was saddled with quite enough guilt already of his own.

'You are in no fit state to make such a decision today and if we are to have a future together, and I hope with all my heart that we do, it will not happen because I forced your hand.'

Good grief! He loved her!

Loved her!

Which meant that not only was his head spinning but the floor had just been ripped from beneath his feet.

'But, Jasper...'

He stayed her with a lacklustre shake of the head, the flimsy control over his urges and with it, all his good intentions, too close to shattering at the slightest temptation. 'The most sensible thing to do right now is to try to carry on as if this never happened.' Jasper turned and without looking back, walked on leaden feet to the door because for him, forgetting this before he lapsed into aged senility would take a blasted miracle. 'Repair your clothing and I'll meet you downstairs. I am sure poor Jim is counting the seconds until he sees you again.'

Chapter Twenty-One

'I declare the second meeting of the 1813 Wallflowers' Club open.' Miss Winston made the toast and they all clinked glasses, delighted for once to all be at an evening entertainment during the Season because they had each other.

Every member of their exclusive little club was at the Earl and Countess of Nethermayne's ball except one, and Hattie hadn't a clue if Jasper was coming. They hadn't had time to discuss it yesterday before they returned to the infirmary, and after, because he had been too busy lecturing her on the need to take things slowly before he bade her the most distant and polite farewell of their reacquaintance.

And all because he was convinced that she was the one who needed time to consider all of her options before she gave herself to him, that her current feelings for him might wane as the initial fraught circumstances which had thrust them together calmed and that she may develop second thoughts when his scandal inevitably broke.

She wouldn't, of course, because when something was right it was right, but he had been too busy being noble and feeling guilty for apparently taking advantage and ravishing her to hear reason. That she had heartily encouraged the ravishing was apparently by the by. But as a gentleman as well as her friend, he was dutybound to do what was right by her, even if that meant stepping aside to allow a worthier fellow to steal her away because all he cared about was her happiness. That was all stuff and nonsense.

His raw and misplaced guilt had made him deaf to any of her counterarguments, so she had given up, reasoning that he might be more receptive after he had ceased flagellating himself. Once he realised that her feelings weren't transient, that she had thoroughly enjoyed what they had done and could not wait to do it again, she hoped he would realise that the last thing she needed was for him to be noble about *that* side of their relationship. That while she admired and adored his strong morals and sensible head and always would, she wanted him to thoroughly lose his head and discard those morals whenever they were alone. That she wanted to be wanton around him.

Jasper had awakened a part of her which she had not realised existed and there wasn't a cat in hell's chance of putting it back to sleep now that it was up. In fact, in the two days since he had first touched her, she had had to touch herself in bed at night because her body craved his so. She supposed she should feel guilty or ashamed for that weakness, but couldn't because it had been necessary in order get some respite and some sleep. But never enough because the release was nowhere near as satisfying, no matter how hard she tried to imagine that it had been him who had brought it about.

It hadn't taken long for all his seemingly noble excuses to whittle away her self-esteem though either, and that had kept her awake as well. Meaning that now she harboured enough doubt about his motives for not completing their lovemaking having something to do with her dratted leg.

Thanks to her wantonness, he had seen the damn thing, albeit partially as it was still encased in a stocking, and perhaps the sight of it had dampened his ardour. For there was no doubt that one minute he couldn't get enough of her, and the next he couldn't get away fast enough.

Hattie hated that she thought that. Hated herself that she was so readily prepared to believe that. But there was absolutely no denying that she had offered herself to him on a platter and he had refused when, from her limited experience of the urges of men, such a thing was considered inconceivable. If Freddie's constant warnings were any gauge, some men were supposed to be incapable of controlling their urges, and if the number of alleged notches on Jasper's infamous bedpost was another reliable gauge, it did beg the question why she wasn't now one of them.

He had also avoided her completely today. She had arrived at the infirmary early to sit with Jim and left so late she had barely had time to change to come here, and he hadn't stopped by for a second when he had to have been at his club at some point during that time. The niggling voice of doubt in her head told her that that also spoke volumes.

But then again, would his desire have been quite so evident if he did not want her? Even after they had stopped and he had paced, it had still been there. Bulging in the most intriguing manner against his breeches...

'Good evening, Lady Harriet.'

She squeaked in shock and then blushed like a beet-root. While wool-gathering over the pleasures of the flesh, when everyone else in the Wallflowers' Club had made their way to the chairs, she had remained standing while she pondered Jasper—or more precisely a particular part of Jasper—which meant she had left herself a sitting duck for Lord Boredom to capture.

'Would it be too forward to tell you how lovely you look this evening?' Her only official suitor grabbed her hand and placed a lingering kiss on the back of it which made her toes curl and had her thanking her lucky stars that she was wearing gloves. 'Ravishing in fact.'

Hattie pulled her hand away and forced a polite smile, subtly searching around her for a means of escape. Unfortunately, the rest of the 1813 Wallflowers' Club were already engrossed, laughing at a story, so none noticed her predicament. Neither were Annie nor Kitty anywhere to be seen. Even the overbearing, interfering hawk Freddie had his back to her on the opposite side of the ballroom, so she was well and truly stuck for now.

'Good evening, Lord Boreham.' She bobbed a lack-lustre curtsy, staggered by the irony that not all kisses were equal, and neither were heated looks. When Jasper had gazed at her in desire she melted like a puddle, yet when Dribbling Cyril did it, as he was now, she would prefer to drown herself in a puddle than witness it. 'Thank you for the kind compliment.' The implication of which made her want to gag. In case she did, she glanced around again unsubtly for any potential reason to escape but unfortunately, her indifferent efforts were wasted on him.

'I am pleased to finally catch you on your own, Lady

Harriet, as I have been most desirous of having a proper conversation with you for some weeks now.' In case she was oblivious of his intentions, he leaned closer, dangerously within spitting range. 'But I believe you have already worked that out, haven't you, because of the many bouquets I have diligently sent to your residence.'

'Yes…' Hattie's false smile was slipping. The effort of keeping it nailed in place was making her cheeks hurt. 'I have been meaning to thank you for those, but…' She faltered while she tried to come up with a plausible excuse for ignoring them, only to have him sidle closer and nudge her.

'There is no need to explain your reticence, my dear Lady Harriet, for I know how this game is played. It does not do for a young lady to appear too grateful of a gentleman's attentions in the first instance, even one of my *stature*.' A spray of spittle accompanied the word 'stature', which landed on her cheek. It took every ounce of willpower not to claw the offending blob off with her nails. 'As you understand, we hot-blooded males need the thrill and the challenge of the chase. And be in no doubt, for a comely *prize* such as yourself—' more spittle sprayed on the pronounced elongation of the zed and the self '—I am fully prepared to chase and chase for as long as it takes until *you* have thoroughly caught me.' He licked the superfluous drool from the corners of his mouth as he winked, and Hattie wanted to vomit into her champagne glass.

'I can assure you that I have no desire to be caught, Lord Boreham.' At least not by him. 'While I should have thanked you for your bouquets from the outset, I also should have told you to desist sending them because I am afraid that I am not interested in you in that way at all and never have been.' Because she felt that point needed emphasising, Hattie repeated it. 'You must hunt elsewhere, Lord Boreham. Chase someone else. I am sure there must be plenty of ladies who would appreciate a man of your superior stature—but I can assure you that I am not one of them.'

'Naughty, naughty.' He wagged his pudgy finger in front of her face. 'You are a tease, my lady. But I have caught your hint.' He wiggled his eyebrows as he stared at her bosom. 'You are going to need a few more flowers to warm you up.' He tapped his nose then reached for her hand again to kiss, but as she attempted to wrestle it from his grip, another hand swooped in and claimed it.

'Sorry I am late.' Jasper said this while moving at speed, dragging her with him towards the sanctuary of the wallflower chairs. To ensure Lord Boredom knew that his services were no longer required, he smiled at the odious toad over his shoulder. 'Thank you for keeping her entertained in my absence, Cyril. It is much appreciated.' Then, for her ears alone, he whispered, 'If I were you, I'd burn those gloves now that he has slobbered all over them.'

'Something I had already decided to do at my earliest convenience, I can assure you.' Then because she couldn't help herself, she beamed at him as they shuffled along a row of chairs to get to the others. 'I didn't think I would see you tonight.'

'Sadly, I cannot stay long because I am needed at the club but…well… I wanted to see you…to talk to you first.'

'For another lecture warning me off?' Hattie stripped off one of the soiled gloves and tossed it in disgust on to the chair in front, then pulled at the other.

'No lecture.' Behind the cover of the chairbacks in front, he caught her hand and slowly tugged off the glove, tracing his index finger down the exposed skin as he did so. 'I merely desired the *platonic* public pleasure of your company this evening.' The heat in his stormy green gaze was anything but platonic. 'However, I give you fair warning, should an opportunity present itself and we happen to find ourselves in private for few moments, I plan to use every single second to kiss you until we are both senseless.' And with that he turned to greet the others as if he hadn't just undressed her with his eyes, seduced her with his words and made her hungry body yearn some more on the strength of a single, brief touch.

It was quite some time later that her brother noticed them sat together and stalked towards them.

'Well…isn't this a surprise?' Freddie's disapproval was palpable. 'What on earth has dragged you here when I thought you were swamped with accounts at your club? Or at least that is the excuse you have been using to fob me off all week. In fact, you used it again only this afternoon when you replied to my note.'

Her brother's eyes narrowed as they bored into Jasper's. 'Yet apparently it appears that you can find the time to attend another ball and chat to my sister at length even when you cannot spare one of your oldest and dearest friends half an hour for a quick game of billiards.'

'I could spare you half an hour now, old boy.' Jasper smiled as if butter wouldn't melt in his mouth. 'In fact, I came specifically to lure you into Nethermayne's billiard's room as your sister here will confirm, and was only chatting to Hattie while I waited for you to finish waltzing with your wife.' Freddie's suspicious gaze slid to hers, so she nodded.

'That is the case, Freddie.'

'So shall we?' Jasper was up like a shot, and as if she was now completely forgotten, he slapped her brother on the back as he led him away.

She had watched them leave, then an hour later watched her brother return alone. Half an hour after that, when there was still no sign of Jasper returning and she was sick and tired of pretending she was having a good time, Hattie took herself to the retiring room to lick her wounds in private. She was halfway down the silent corridor when Jasper's smiling face appeared from behind a suit of armour.

'You took your time.' He caught her hand, pulled her through a door then tugged her into his arms as he simultaneously closed it. Total blackness enveloped them. Not a single crease of light leaked from anywhere. 'I was on the cusp of giving up all hope.' His arms snaked around her waist. 'I was going to give it another two, maybe three hours of pining here, and then I was going to go. Four at a push. Five at the most.'

The exaggerated desperation in his tone made her giggle. 'Where are we?' She could not even see the outline of his face.

'In a linen closet.' His lips seemed to have no trouble finding her neck. 'I didn't want us to be disturbed.' They nuzzled the sensitive skin beneath her ear. 'I've been going mad thinking about you.'

'What happened to the man who urged caution?' She arched her neck to give him better access. 'The one who was determined to be noble. The one who wanted to wait until his impending scandal had completely blown over before he explored things between us further?'

His talented mouth fused itself to hers, and took several lazy, languid moments to drive her mad with lust before it answered. 'It turns out there are two Jaspers.'

'Two?'

'Two.' He nibbled her bottom lip twice. 'The sensible, noble and decent one who is determined to do right by you and the incorrigible, selfish and reckless one who wants only to have his wicked way with you. The saint and—' his palms slid up to cup her breasts '—the sinner. They went to war at around eight o'clock this evening, where I am devastated to have to inform you that the forces of evil wrestled the forces of good into complete submission.'

He kissed her deeply again, his palms boldly tracing her bottom. 'As I expect that state of affairs to be far too fleeting—because the new Saint Jasper of Selfless Sacrifice is too strong an adversary not to rise up again ready to do battle for your honour—I thought it most prudent to strike while the iron is hot and give Sinner Jasper a chance to waylay you.'

'I think I like Sinner Jasper.'

'Good—then make the most of him…' His mouth found her other ear and tortured it. 'Because I am only allowing him five minutes of freedom before I force the shameless scoundrel to unhand you.'

'Can't you make it six?'

He managed to shake his head while still kissing her. 'I daren't. In six minutes, he will thoroughly ruin you, whereas in five he will just ruin himself.'

Chapter Twenty-Two

'I swear, this is the final straw!' Freddie paced his study while Jasper scanned the newspaper his friend had just slapped on his desk. 'I've tried to be reasonable. Tried to honour the bargain we *apparently* made for Hattie's sake.' He paused only long enough to glare. 'But now this has gone too far!'

The *Bugle* was a tawdry rag, if not the tawdriest, and famously the most salacious and inaccurate, but even so, Freddie had a point. This was a damning article.

Not for him so much, of course, as he had years of form when it came to being a scandal and they expected nothing less, but society always most harshly judged the woman. In the month since he had first ravished her, after every ball they met at, there had been an increasing amount of speculation regarding the exact nature of his relationship with Lady Harriet Fitzroy.

It had been made worse by the unfortunate and published sighting of them in broad daylight in Covent Garden on the morning of Jim's operation, which meant that Jasper now also had to subject himself to a twice-weekly lecture from her increasingly suspicious brother who refused to believe they were just friends when the press clearly didn't.

Most of the articles were tame innuendo, suggesting but not outright declaring any firm suspicions. Whenever the gossip became too rife, Jasper worked doubly hard to cast the theories into doubt. Usually by openly flirting and then dancing with another woman before he disappeared early to head to his club. But in this one, they had painted Hattie very much the victim, while also turning her into everything she would hate. A pathetic, foolish, fragile creature who was so happy to receive the scraps from any man's table that she was prepared to turn a blind eye to almost anything.

The Hattie of this article was an object of pity, and worse, one who deserved it.

It broke his heart for him to imagine Hattie reading this hurtful rot even if it was all a pack of lies. The headline alone was vicious. Jasper did not have to read far past *The Wandering Eyes beside the Limping Lady* to get the full gist of the story which had sent Freddie into a rage.

According to their 'sources' the *Bugle* had concocted a convoluted scenario in which Jasper was stringing Hattie along as a ruse to get closer to her prettier sister Annie, who was the real object of his affections. While the 'imperfect' and 'universally pitied' sister gazed upon him in 'undisguised love and adoration', he apparently gazed longingly at the dance floor at the other Fitzroy and bided his time. Last night, again according to 'three respected witnesses', the opportune moment had finally presented itself and he was apparently seen 'in a tryst' with the object of his secret affections on Lady Warburton's terrace at precisely five minutes past midnight.

'Has she seen it?'

'Yes.' Freddie dropped heavily into a chair. 'And of course she laughed it away, because that is what she does, but for a moment there was genuine hurt in her eyes.'

Hurt which Jasper knew only too well as in the last month, he had also unintentionally put more of that there than he was comfortable with. Enough that the guilt was eating away at him. He hadn't slept a wink tossing and turning about their argument last night, although technically it wasn't an argument and more cross words.

Only the words had been hers and she had been cross. And undeniably wounded when she had accused him of blowing hot and cold because he was different by day from how he was by night. Then, for the briefest few seconds, her lovely blue eyes had been filled with pain before she had stalked off after leaving him on Lady Warburton's lawn with one final flea in his ear.

A flea he was struggling to dislodge. 'I am starting to think that all your seemingly sensible and selfless justifications about protecting my welfare are more for your benefit, Jasper, than they are mine!' She had said this down her nose with squared, proud shoulders. 'That it is you who is uncertain—or perhaps ashamed—of me!'

That she questioned his certainty was one thing, when he had never been more certain of anything in his life as he was about his feelings for Hattie. But that she thought for one second that he was ashamed of her...

That was not only unpalatable food for thought, it had also been a bitter pill to swallow. Because after a great deal of soul-searching as he had stared listlessly at his bedchamber ceiling until the sun rose, he could see why she might think that. She was wrong of course, because he loved her with all of his heart and wanted her by his side and in his bed more than life itself, but he had never expressly said so.

He had always held back from admitting the truth in case his feelings made her feel beholden towards him and she used them as an excuse to lash herself stoically to his side and to hell with the dire consequences to herself.

If they had a future together—and he was adamant about this—then it would happen because they both wanted it and not because she had been forced, coerced or herded towards it by society's expectations or his selfish needs or his impending scandal.

'Both my mother and my father have also seen it and they are fuming at the allegations.' Freddie tapped the newspaper between them on the desk. 'I hope, for your sake, that there is no truth in this?'

'What do you think?' Frankly, Jasper did not know quite where to start with the inaccuracies that had been printed, but because there was more than a grain of truth to parts of the article, had to choose his words wisely. 'Not only have I never ogled or coveted Annie, we only chatted briefly last night so heaven only knows how they came to this nonsensical diatribe.' The very thought was laughable, so he choked out a chuckle and hoped it sounded convincing.

Although he had danced a waltz with the other Fitzroy sister two nights previously to put the gossips off the scent, stupidly thinking that if he was seen with Annie it gave credence to the argument that his relationship with her twin was because he was a good friend of the family.

'Do I need to remind you that you stood sentry duty opposite me for most of the night as usual, Freddie?

And you and I were playing cards together long after midnight. Where you cheated and rinsed me out of five guineas!' He pushed the newspaper away in dismissal. 'I think I would remember an illicit tryst with Annie on the terrace at the same time.' That at least was all true.

Jasper had, however, and much to his continued shame and chagrin, enjoyed a tryst on Lady Warburton's terrace a little before midnight. Except, as had become the norm in the last four weeks when his need for her overpowered all of his noble intentions, it had been Hattie who had been with him. Hattie whom he had lured on to that terrace with the precise intention of having his wicked way with her.

The constant need to do that was sending him insane.

The thrice-weekly five minutes he allowed his inner sinner loose certainly weren't helping him control his urges where she was concerned. If anything, those heated, fevered clandestine mini-ravishings over Hattie's clothes were exacerbating the problem of his inappropriate, out-of-control, unsated lust for her. That he only dared allow them during the rigid confines of a public entertainment, where her brother watched them like a hawk, also made them dangerous.

The shocking truth about last night which Freddie had every right to want to castrate him for, was that he and Hattie had almost been discovered *in flagrante* on Lady Warburton's terrace. A scandal barely averted thanks to Freddie's beguiling sister's quick thinking and a convenient raised bed filled with roses which she dragged him behind. If it had been down to him, Jasper had been so consumed with her and the ticking clock on his self-imposed time limit that he wouldn't have noticed a military marching band go past unless they stomped their hobnails all over him.

Afterwards, when she had said that she thought it was daft that they kept pretending nothing was going on when everyone suspected it, and he had responded with his usual cautionary reminder that he would not consider openly courting her until the dust of his impending scandal had settled, it had caused a tiff. So Jasper had stayed on and played cards at the ball, rather than head to his club before the ball finished as usual, so that he could pour oil on troubled waters once she had calmed down. Except by the time the game was finished Hattie had gone.

And now this.

It was near impossible to look his friend in the eye and lie again about his relationship with Hattie only hours after filling his hands with her luscious, sensitive breasts, and not feel guilty.

All the lies heaped on lies were getting out of control and the crushing guilt from all quarters was killing him. Guilt for the lies. Guilt for the rot printed in the gossip columns. Guilt for the shocking liberties he kept taking with Hattie's delectable body and the intense guilt for his inability to put what was morally right and fair over what his heart wanted and his body craved.

All things considered, being her friend in public while not quite being her lover in private wasn't working out so well in either theory or in practice. And Hattie's complete ruination, like his other impending scandal, was as good as inevitable now that the *Bugle* knew too much, unless something changed drastically to prevent it.

'I insist you demand a retraction! Hire a lawyer and

sue them for libel because it isn't fair that Hattie's good name gets dragged through the mud with yours day in and day out.' Freddie stood and wagged his finger. 'And I've asked this before and was talked out of it because you seemed to make her happy, but this time I mean it.' He snatched up the paper and waved it like a sword as he stalked to the door. 'From this point forward, stay away from my sister! Both of my sisters!' He pulled it open but could not resist one final barb before he left.

'And if I find out that you have been stringing Hattie along, Jasper, toying with her affections and giving her false hope after everything she has been through, I swear to God I will strangle you with my bare hands, disembowel you and feed your entrails to my dogs!'

The door slammed and Jasper slumped back in his chair as those words hit home. The last thing he would ever do was string along the woman he adored, but he could see how to others it might seem that he was. Worse, he could see that she might think it too. She was certainly becoming more frustrated by his constant demand that they wait.

That he was only doing so for her sake did nothing to wipe the hurt from her expression whenever he kept her at arm's length when they visited the little duck pond she adored so much, or she wheeled Jim into his lessons. Or when she begged him not to stop and he tore his lips away during one of the short trysts he allowed himself thrice weekly to avoid outright ruining her.

Blowing hot and cold exactly as she had said.

What a fool he was! In doing the right thing, it was clear he was making them both miserable. And now he was making her family miserable too.

'Has he gone, Papa?' The question from behind made

him jump. The sight of Izzy's little eye blinking at him warily from a crack in the other door made him uncomfortable. Her next question rubbed more salt into an already gaping wound. 'Can I stop hiding now?'

'Of course, poppet.' That she felt the need to hide at all when he was supposed to be doing right by her too was criminal.

Instead of announcing Izzy as his daughter to the world as he had promised Cora, and waiting for the inevitable dust to settle as he had promised Hattie, or leaving his sister the hell alone as he had promised Freddie, he was instead skulking around waiting for the axe to fall and hoping that it wouldn't.

Because he wanted to have his cake and eat it. Didn't want what they had to come to an end. Because he knew his scandal might tear them apart and he wanted her more than he wanted to do the right things he was supposed to.

He lifted his little girl into his lap and cuddled her close. 'I think it's time we both stopped hiding.' Which was the right thing for everyone—except him. 'I think it's time to grab life by the lapels and give it a good shake.'

Because if you loved someone, you had to let them go, no matter how terrified you were to do it. If they came back, and he prayed to God that Hattie would do just that once the gossipmongers moved on elsewhere— then they were always yours. If they didn't…

Well, Jasper would climb that mountain a step at a time when he came to it. But at least he would climb it secure in the knowledge that he finally was doing the right thing by the three women in his life and his best friend, and could therefore climb the damn mountain without being weighed down by guilt.

Chapter Twenty-Three

'The quote he personally gave the columnist from *The Times* confirms everything we knew and worse.' The Duchess of Warminster was enjoying today's great scandal far more than was dignified, probably because Hattie had been included in it. Not directly in *The Times*, which as the main source was trying to remain above reproach, but in every other gossip column's interpretation of it.

'Lord Beaufort fathered a child with that lightskirt he was sleeping with all those years ago, and now that the hussy is dead, he intends to bring up his daughter here in town.' She lowered her knitting to stare straight at Hattie. '*His daughter.* An unashamed acknowledgement written in black and white for all to read. I cannot imagine what he is thinking to openly flaunt the illegitimate offspring of his harlot to the *ton* quite so brazenly as a fait accompli.'

Hattie knew Jasper would never deny Izzy was his if he was asked outright, because they had discussed it many times. They had discussed it because that was how he had expected the truth to come out, and so had she. That it had apparently not leaked out at all because Jasper had gone to *The Times* of his own free will had completely knocked her for six along with the rest of society. But, or so she had read with a slackened jaw over her coddled eggs at breakfast, maybe he was tired of all the speculation and most especially of all the unfair, unfounded and malicious gossip about the nature of his relationship with Lady Harriet Fitzroy.

He was an old friend of the family, that was all, and to suggest that he had any sort of a relationship with either Fitzroy sister was grossly untrue. To that end, now that he had set the record straight and to spare her and her family from further scurrilous defamation, he was removing himself from society for the rest of the Season to concentrate on his business and his daughter.

Never mind the removal of himself felt like abandonment to her!

If this was another one of his idiotic attempts at being noble and selfless, then it had fallen well shy of the mark. Hattie was furious at the wretch for making such a momentous and transformative decision, not only without telling her, but on the back of their first ever argument!

How dare he fail to include her in the decision!

As if her feelings for the wretch were of no consequence!

'It is as if he expects us to accept his indiscretion without censure and blithely carry on as if nothing has happened, when I know most of the good *ton* would rather cross the road now than acknowledge the acquaintance.' The Duchess of Warminster grimaced as if she found it all beyond distasteful. 'It is a good job he has taken himself out of the rest of the Season as I hear invitations are being rescinded here, there and everywhere. He has burned his bridges with half of Mayfair.'

'And how do you know that already, Your Grace, when you only read it over breakfast with the rest of us and it is not yet noon?' Hattie could not keep silent even though she had been warned in no uncertain terms to do just that by both her shocked parents and her overprotective brother over their own breakfast table.

But how exactly was she supposed to keep her mouth shut and her head down while a complete travesty was occurring to someone she held dear, even if she was rightly fuming at the cretin? It made her blood boil to think of people scurrying outside to gossip about things they had no concept of. Berkeley Square had been filled with busybodies all morning, all shaking their heads with appalled expressions on their faces, as if Jasper had committed a murder.

'Because bad news and scandal travels fast, Lady Harriet.' That, Hattie did not doubt. Already the story had been printed everywhere and exaggerated and embellished so grossly in certain newspapers it bore no resemblance to any truth whatsoever. 'It goes without saying that *we* must all follow suit and give him the cut direct from now on—but you especially would do well to distance yourself from him as soon as possible. Now that he has absolved you from any part in this outrageous scandal, I suggest you do the same with your own public remonstrance and rebuttal, and *The Times* is as good a place as any. The sooner you do that, the less damage all the other nonsense will do to your good reputation.'

The other nonsense was the persistent and much too close for comfort but widely printed new theory that

Jasper had nipped in the bud the rumours about them because he feared she thought of him as more than a friend. And that he, as a future duke, albeit one with an illegitimate daughter in dire need of a mother, did not feel the need to saddle himself with 'the Limping Lady' simply to procure Izzy one. Only the dreadful *Bugle* had used that specific nickname—but even so the implication hurt. Especially as Hattie couldn't entirely discount it herself.

Jasper had certainly not been in any hurry to investigate under her skirts again since she had wantonly showed him everything that lurked beneath them— including her dratted leg. He had blown hot and cold since that afternoon. All over her under the camouflaging cover of darkness and as prim as a priest during daylight hours no matter how alone they were.

And they were regularly alone during the day when not in the public glare. She had moved heaven and earth to ensure it, and he had deftly spurned every single advance she had made. Even when she threw herself at him as she had on the morning of the Warburton Ball when they had been alone in his carriage, the curtains closed, while on another clandestine shopping trip to Cheapside. Yet that night, he had almost got them caught thanks to his rampant desire on the terrace!

'Indeed, Hattie.' Like her sanctimonious mother, Lady Felicity Claremont was acting exceptionally pious this morning. 'You should make it known that you are insulted by any suggestion that you harboured any affection towards Lord Beaufort, or that the scoundrel had earmarked you to be his by-blow's new mother, stating that you find such an inexcusable imposition as ridiculous as you do abhorrent. Make it plain that any interest was entirely one-sided and that you never did anything to court his attention.'

She offered a sickly smile to the rest of the ladies in the room. 'Those of us who know the truth understand that he went out of his way to pursue her in the wallflower chairs, and she was only being polite in indulging his presence because she found it difficult to escape.'

Of course her sanctimonious eyes flicked to Hattie's dratted leg at that, in case she hadn't been reminded enough about its unattractiveness this morning. Then in a condescending aside to her recoiling elder sibling and Hattie's sister-in-law, Dorothea, the little witch Felicity could not resist one final barb thinly disguised as familial concern.

'As I said to Lady Critchley when Mama and I collided with her on our walk over here, the threat to dear Hattie's good reputation aside, just because she is no longer what she once was and lacks the droves of suitors that the rest of us debutantes have queuing, does not mean she would ever stoop that low!'

Before either Hattie's tight-lipped mother or twin sprang forward to scratch the girl's eyes out on her behalf, she decided to put the stuffy Claremonts in their place herself.

'While I hardly think an alliance with a future duke could be construed as "stooping low" by anyone's standards, I personally admire and applaud Lord Beaufort's decision to raise his daughter at home rather than flagrantly ignore her existence as so many of the gentlemen of the *good ton* do.'

As it was too difficult to pretend to knit while seething, she dropped her misshapen disaster of a sock in her lap. 'It is a mystery to me why it is considered more of a crime against decency to love and acknowledge your child, than to abandon them to a life of poverty as that libertine Lord Stevens continues to do with his well-documented *indiscretions*.'

As Hattie had intended, the ensuing silence from that bombshell was deafening, not least because the well-connected future marquess Lord Stevens was currently the mean-spirited Felicity's most ardent suitor. As both Annie and Kitty gaped at her boldness, Felicity's mother looked ready to combust with indignation. Dorothea, for her part, continued to stare at her knitting like a startled deer while Hattie's own mother looked quietly impressed, so Hattie decided she might as well continue.

'His family dismissed the housemaid he had impregnated three Christmases ago, didn't they?' Words no genteel young lady should ever say in public without the whole two-faced fabric of society crumbling under the weight of its own sordid hypocrisy.

'We all bore witness to that commotion, didn't we, as nowhere do curtains twitch with quite as much enthusiasm as they do here in Berkeley Square.' And that had been quite a commotion because the poor unfortunate maid refused to go quietly and had brought the squalling babe to Lord Stevens's front door demanding he provide for it.

'But we are all supposed to turn a blind eye to that because she is a servant and he denies it, and that is the neat and tidy *done* thing to do. Sweep it all under the carpet where it belongs and never mention it again. Never mind that it is morally reprehensible and downright callous! For heaven forbid an aristocrat should admit to a mistake and make amends for it as Jasper has done. Frankly, if I had droves of suitors like you, Felicity, I know which sort I would prefer.'

In case the opinionated chit was unsure of the answer, Hattie glared directly at her. 'I would pick only those with the highest moral standards rather than the purveyors of the most atrocious and despicable double standards.'

After several stuttering misstarts, the Duchess of Warminster finally found her voice. 'You have no right to speak to my daughter like that!' Typically, she looked to Hattie's mother to do the chastising. 'Coarse language like that might be the way all the filthy miscreants she is so fond of speak in the fetid gutters of Covent Garden, but it has no place in a Mayfair drawing room.'

Incensed, Hattie stood before her mother could respond. 'You are right, Your Grace. Therefore, I shall bid you a good day and take my language and myself to those fetid gutters forthwith.'

'Hattie…' She instantly rebelled at the note of caution in her mother's tone, no matter how well meant it was. *'We agreed* that you are better off staying at home today.'

'Even if I felt inclined to hide here as if I have committed a crime, which I very much haven't, there is a lost and lonely little boy expecting me at the infirmary who is struggling to recover from the hideous operation I advised him to have.' Then she turned to the Duchess of Warminster and briskly wiped the smug smile from the woman's face. 'As a *filthy miscreant,* poor Jim has no one who cares except me, and it will be a cold day in hell before I desert him today just to keep my seemingly good reputation clean!'

While the Duchess of Warminster's eyes bulged, her

own mother sat serenely while she digested Hattie's words. After a short pause she nodded. 'Of course you must go, Hattie, because that is the *decent* thing to do. Make sure the carriage waits for you outside the infirmary dear, for propriety's sake. But before you go...'

As imperious as Queen Charlotte herself, she skewered Felicity and her mother with her best Duchess of Avondale glare. More fearsome than any glare in society because her charming mother rarely used it. 'You will stay long enough to listen to the sincere apologies of our guests, who are likely mortified that their criticisms sounded quite so insulting to our entire family when they appreciate that you, among all of us present, are the most genuine, kind of heart and, as Jasper stated in *The Times*, the one whose behaviour has always been beyond reproach.'

Chapter Twenty-Four

With nothing else to do except ignore the constant stream of journalists who knocked on his front door, Jasper wandered into the temporary classroom Mrs Mimms had made in his never-used morning room to see how the children's lessons were going. At dawn, as the newspaper had come out, he had considered cancelling the daily appointment with Jim and the new governess before he realised that wouldn't be fair to the lad.

Jim had undergone the most painful procedure imaginable on the promise of an apprenticeship and despite the obvious discomfort of the tight splints on his rebroken leg, had worked hard on his lessons since they had started three weeks ago. Then worked even harder by helping Izzy with them too. The boy had done nothing wrong whatsoever, so it felt churlish to take away the one bright light at the end of his tunnel simply because Jasper's world had imploded after he himself had lit the fuse.

A promise was a promise after all and the one he had made to Jim had nothing really to do with Hattie beyond the fact he had embarked on it for her. That he was gaining a potential loyal and valuable employee in a few years on the back of this was its own reward. And Izzy already adored Jim, so that was that, he supposed.

Besides, it wasn't as if the dust from the scandal was likely to settle overnight, or even by the end of the year, so he reasoned it was probably the best for all concerned to carry on as much as they could as usual while he bided his time in purgatory. Therefore, these lessons would continue and the club would open tonight as usual with Jasper brazenly welcoming the guests at the door.

This was his choice.

His decision and he would make no apologies for who he was or what he did. That had always been his philosophy since the day he had first been disowned and, so far, it had always worked in his favour. He hoped the fact that he was doing right by both Cora and Izzy made the necessary absence of Hattie in his life easier to swallow, and he consoled himself that at least the ordeal he had been dreading since she first came back into his life had finally started. It couldn't end until it started and now that it had, he had to let fate's cards fall how they may.

Perhaps, in a few months, when the *ton* remembered he was destined to be a duke, included him in invitations again and he gradually ceased to be *persona non grata*, and if she felt the same, he and Hattie could pick up where they left off? If they could, he would do things properly this time, out in the open and above board. In the meantime, he would do the decent thing and give her a wide berth. Give her all the time, distance and space she needed to decide whether or not he was worth all the effort in the long run.

It niggled that he hadn't been able to tell her all that in person, or alert her to the fact that he had gone to *The Times*. But with Freddie rightly ready to turn his guts into garters, he hadn't dared send her a note at home in case her suspicious brother intercepted it and realised all his worst suspicions were completely correct.

Jasper had, however, sent a letter to her via the infirmary. A letter in which he had, rightly or wrongly, poured out his entire heart because it did not feel right to have done something as drastic as he had without letting her know why. Drastic times called for drastic measures and he loved her too much to watch her be eviscerated by the gossips simply because she had the deepest well of compassion of anyone he had ever known and wanted to rescue him.

But he already missed her. Mourned them as a partnership. Felt lost without her by his side.

'Where is he?' Hattie's distant shout snapped him out of his melancholy. 'I know the coward is in here, Mrs Mimms!' Whatever his housekeeper answered, he had a feeling it wasn't the polite but decisive 'Lord Beaufort is unavailable' which he had instructed her to tell everyone for the foreseeable future, as seconds later, Hattie's uneven stomping gait could be heard coming down the hallway from the direction of the back kitchen. 'I am going to wring his stupid neck.'

While both the new governess and Izzy stared at him wide-eyed, Jim pulled a face. 'As I don't think I've done anything wrong of late, I'm hoping it's not my neck she intends wringing.'

'It'll be Papa's,' offered Izzy in reassurance as she patted Jim's arm. 'Because Mrs Mimms told Cook she thought he had handled things all wrong.'

'Handled what?'

Jim's question went unanswered because Hattie had arrived, with his traitor of a housekeeper hot on her heels. 'You sent me a letter!' She sliced his missive in the air like a blade. 'A letter!'

'You really cannot be here Hattie. Especially today.' He gestured towards the front of the house. 'There are reporters outside. If they see you then...'

'How dare you send me a letter!' She jabbed it in the air again. 'After everything—you didn't have the courage or the decency to tell me about this yourself?'

'Have you read it?' Because if she had and she was this angry, then he had very definitely chosen the wrong words to pour out his entire heart.

'If you have something to say to me Jasper Beaufort, then you should at least have the decency to say it to my face!' She folded her arms, the offending missive dangling from her fingers, the seal glaringly intact. 'Especially as, thanks to you, the whole of Mayfair is gossiping about me this morning. Casting me as the eternal victim again. The Limping Lady scorned because not even the lowest reprobate of the *ton* with precious little other choice wanted her. A little warning would have been nice.'

'After Freddie—'

'I knew my interfering brother had a hand in this!' She cut him off to wave her arms and pace. 'I am going to wring his wretched neck the second I have finished wringing yours! How dare you make a decision about me and my life without consulting me!'

'Hattie...it wasn't like that.' Jasper raked a hand through his hair. 'And it wasn't really Freddie's fault because...' While the new governess was trying to look as if she wasn't listening, Mrs Mimms was stood with her foot impatiently tapping as if she too deserved an explanation. 'Why don't we discuss this in the drawing room?'

As he caught Hattie's rigid arm, the front door knocked again and he glared at Mrs Mimms. 'Get rid of them and then arrange for my carriage to be readied so we can smuggle Hattie out of the mews without the pack of wolves outside seeing her!'

Jasper hurried her down the hallway, tugged her inside the drawing room then closed the door. Arms folded again, Hattie walked stiffly to the window, her back resolutely to him as she faced the garden.

'Speak.'

Well, that set the tone nicely. 'I didn't want to have to hide any more.'

'I see.' Although by the clipped tone of her voice she clearly didn't.

'I realised that I have been handling everything wrong. Doing everything in the wrong order. Running before I could walk.' There were a lot of 'I's in the sentence when this wasn't about him, it was ultimately about them. 'We had to pass this milestone, Hattie, don't you see? We—I—was racing ahead to the one in the future and ignoring the one staring me straight in the face and blocking the path.'

'So you decided the best way to pass it was without me?' The catch in her voice undid him, but when he turned her around the tears in her eyes completely destroyed him.

'I am trying to protect you, Hattie.'

'If I had wanted protecting, Jasper, I wouldn't have

given you my heart, thrown all caution to the wind and handed myself to you on a plate.'

'You bastard!' Freddie flew through the door and a split second later Jasper was rammed up against the wall. 'You lying bastard!'

While every instinct told him to fight back, pragmatism warned him not to. 'It's not what you think, Freddie.'

'She offered herself to you on a plate!' His head cracked against the plaster as Freddie shook him. 'You filthy, lying, despicable bastard!' Another shake. Another painful thud to his cranium. 'You've ruined my sister!'

'Not completely.'

The next shove was so violent it knocked all the wind out of Jasper's lungs, and he gulped for air as Hattie dragged her brother off. 'Stop it!' With impressive strength Hattie then grabbed Freddie's shoulders and shook him. 'Stop interfering in my life!'

Freddie shrugged off her hands and lunged again, but this time Jasper held him back while her brother snarled in his face, 'I'll stop when that lying bastard does what's right and marries you!'

Sheer frustration made Jasper shout back, 'If I have to!'

This wasn't how Jasper wanted it to happen. Not at all part of his plan to do things properly. To give her all the choice. A plan which he hoped could still be salvaged if he could calm both furious Fitzroys down along with himself. 'But...'

Behind her brother Hattie baulked as if she had been slapped.

'But, Jasper?' She steeled her chin despite her bottom lip trembling. 'But?' The pain in her lovely eyes was more visceral than he had ever seen it. 'I should have known there would be a *but*.' And with that she dashed from the room.

If I have to.

If I have to!

If ever a proposal was so lacklustre and damning?

With tears streaming down her cheeks, Hattie stumbled down the hallway unseeing. She fumbled with the lock until the door gave way and staggered down the steps to the pavement beyond.

'Are you all right, miss?' The stranger's touch brought the world into sharp, overwhelming focus.

Broad daylight.

Russell Square. Unusually busy with people, most of whom had stopped to gawp at her. In a panic, she scanned for the best route to escape it all and her gaze instantly latched on to Freddie's horse, Hades. Always the most fearsome in the Fitzroy stable and famously cantankerous. The big, brooding brown stallion stared back at her, daring her to give him some wind and she shook her head, daunted. Afraid. Even when she could ride she had never dared ride him when even Freddie struggled.

'Miss…' The stranger touched her shoulder again, his deep voice kind and concerned. 'Is there anything I can do to help?' Then another elbowed his way close.

'Lady Harriet Fitzroy?' She blinked at him in confusion, wondering why he had a notebook and a pencil poised. 'Henry Fellows—from the *Bugle*.' A wave of queasiness swamped her as she realised she had exited through the wrong door and stupidly flung herself straight into the vipers' pit in her hurry to get away. 'Can I ask what you are doing here, my lady?'

Several more men shuffled forward, alert and clearly here to dig in the dirt. 'Give the lady some space!' Her good Samaritan corralled them back. 'Can't you see she is distressed?'

'Hattie, wait!' Jasper's shout from the steps galvanised her into doing the unthinkable.

As he ran towards her, jostling past the gathering crowd, she turned to the stranger, taking in his height and burly workman's arms. 'Can you lift me on to this horse?' Riding a horse suddenly seemed less daunting than what she would have to face if she stayed here.

Humiliation.

Shame.

Pity.

The stranger nodded and her feet immediately flew from the floor. A moment later, she flung her good leg over her brother's saddle, kicked the horse into a gallop and raced away.

Chapter Twenty-Five

'Hattie!' Freddie skidded to a stop behind him in time to witness her disappear around the corner. He gripped Jasper's sleeve, all the colour suddenly drained from his face. 'She can't handle Hades! She isn't strong enough! She's going to damned well kill herself!'

Jasper lunged for Freddie's cravat and pulled it tight, undecided whether or not to smash the overbearing idiot's teeth in or simply throw him to the ground.

'Lord Beaufort...' The same oily reporter who had just bothered Hattie sidled up to them, and because they had all already caused enough of a scene, he instead dragged Freddie back up his steps and slammed the door closed behind them.

Only then did he fling his friend backwards with a growl. 'What the hell, Freddie!' Incensed and reeling, Jasper began to pace. 'I wanted her to have a choice, God damn it! A choice! After fate has taken so much of that away from her, I wanted her to have all the say in the most important decision in her life. Wanted her to want me as much as I want her for all the right reasons! But now—' he jabbed his finger in the fool's face

'—thanks to your overbearing interference she has to marry me whether she wants to or not!'

'Only if she doesn't kill herself first.' Freddie was screaming in his face again. Irrational and panicked. 'That horse is…' Jasper did not give him time to finish, instead gripping him by the shoulders and pushing him against the wall this time.

'That horse is no match for your sister! Nothing is! Not me. Not you. Not even the last bloody rites! When Hattie puts her mind to something, nothing fazes her. Nothing beats her. When are you going to get it through your thick head that she's stronger than all of us put together?'

He let go of Freddie and stepped back, trying to calm his breathing while searching his mind for a solution which might fix this mess—but he already knew there wasn't one. There was no way to limit the damage which had just been done when Freddie had come through the front door and all three of them had left it, the most tenacious one probably already tearing down the length of Long Acre like one of the four horsemen of the apocalypse.

Realisation of that truth, and perhaps all of the others, slowly dawned on Freddie's face. 'What do we do now then?'

'There is no *we* in this situation, Freddie, as *you've* done quite enough. So have I.' He should have found a way to explain all his reasoning and his plan to Hattie before he took the decision out of her hands. In that, he was no better than her idiot brother. 'What happens next is for Hattie to decide, not us. As it always should have been.'

It took no convincing at all to send Freddie home

to deal with the aftermath there. Once he had been reminded that he had a wife, a mother and another sister at home about to be knocked sideways by the latest twist to the scandal, his friend had practically sprinted out of the back door. Jasper waited only as long as he assumed it would take for him to hail a hackney before he departed via the back entrance too, hoping he knew Hattie well enough to know exactly where she would head to find some solace and calm herself.

The relief was palpable when he saw her sitting on their little bench by the duck pond, staring out at nothing while the fearsome horse she had stolen stood nearby munching on the daisies.

'I thought I'd find you here.' Her eyes lifted to his, unsure this time rather than tear-stained.

'I read your letter.' She raised the crumpled open sheets a few inches before they dropped listlessly back into her lap. 'It was so long it took me half an hour.'

'I suppose it was a bit of a long ramble, but in my defence, I wrote it in the middle of the night.'

'If you were up anyway, you should have delivered it. Softened the ground before you pulled it out from under me.' She sighed as she stared at his handwriting. 'How much of it is the truth?'

'All of it.' He shrugged and sat beside her. 'I love you and the only way that I could see that we had a future was to confront the past. Start that big cumbersome destructive boulder rolling and get it out of our way.'

'When you say it like that, it seems almost noble that you abandoned me.' She still could not look at him and fiddled with a curled corner of his missive which looked like it had already been fiddled with a lot.

'If you read my letter then you know that I wasn't quite noble and selfless enough to abandon you completely. While Saint Jasper was adamant he was going to step aside and give all those much worthier beaus a chance to woo you for the rest of the Season, the sinner couldn't stand to give them free rein.' That was why, in his letter, he had begged her to meet him here. Twice a week. To do his own bit of subtle wooing to make sure she couldn't forget him. 'I couldn't stand not to see you, Hattie. I love you.' He reached over to take her hand which remained limp under his.

'In what way do you love me?'

'Way?'

She shrugged; her gaze fixed in her lap. 'Like a friend or a sister or…'

Jasper lifted her chin with his index finger so that she could see into his soul. 'Like a man loves a woman. The all-consuming, need every part of you, hearts and flowers for ever kind.'

'You do not have to say that just because I have been ruined and you feel sorry for me.'

'I am pretty sure I said it in that letter before you were ruined and, for the record, I have never felt sorry for you.' She scoffed at that, and he huffed. 'Well, all right… I'll confess I feel sorry for you now—as now that you are ruined you are stuck with me when I wanted you to have a choice. I wanted you to want me irrespective of everything that has happened—not because of it. I am pretty sure I said as much in that damn letter too.' He snatched the top sheet from her fingers to check. 'Are you sure that you've read it? All of it?'

She nodded.

'Then why do you doubt me still, Hattie? Why?

When I've told you that I love you and that the second
the dust from my stupid moot scandal settled I was
going to do everything that I could until I had convinced you to shackle yourself to me for all eternity?'
He pointed to the relevant paragraph in the middle of
the page.

'Because everyone seems to think you can do better. Because you blow hot and cold. Because...' One
fat tear dropped on the page still resting in her lap, the
salty droplet mixing with the ink on the paper and all
the letters began to merge in the smudge. 'I think, in
those dark moments when doubt is at its most fertile,
that you can do better too and because I cannot find it
in me to ever resist you, but you constantly resist me.'

That would have been laughable if he could not see
that she believed it. 'I have done such a good job of that,
haven't I? I've spent the last month in a haze of lust for
you, Hattie. Ever since that afternoon in my office I
cannot think straight for wanting you half of the time.
I almost had you then. Came so close to ripping all of
your clothes off before I came to my senses.' Her eyes
closed as she winced. 'I've been trying to be a gentleman and limit myself but...'

Jasper paused to run all her words back through his
head and then recall every moment of that afternoon
again then groaned aloud when he recalled exactly when
he had come to his senses. How she had reacted. Her
speed to cover herself and hide her lower body. He had
put that down to other parts of her being exposed, not
the one which he always forgot about because to him
it had never mattered. 'This is about your leg, isn't it?
You think that I stopped ripping your clothes off like a
madman possessed because it disgusted me.'

'You did freeze in shock when you felt it.'

'Oh, hell!' He was furious at himself for being so blind and deaf to it all. So clumsy at such a poignant and defining moment to have chosen that exact second to remember that he had a conscience. Furious at all the newspapers and idiots in society who judged her or pitied her for it.

Incandescent with rage at the blasted *Bugle* for calling her the Limping Lady and for every idiot man in each and every ballroom for discounting her because of it, including her own ham-fisted brother. As they had systematically whittled away all her confidence in her own overwhelming and glorious femininity. He was also annoyed at her for even thinking it. For thinking him, the man who loved her more than life itself, that shallow.

Enough was enough and frankly, it was time for her to stop hiding too!

'How do you feel about me, Hattie?'

She blinked at him, startled at the abrupt change of topic and the clipped, impatient edge to his question. He folded his arms and glared at her. 'It is a simple enough question which demands a proper answer. After all, you have not only my long and convoluted letter as proof of the strength of my feelings for you, but you also made me tell you to your face and that door should swing both ways. So before we sort all this nonsense out once and for all, I need to know exactly where I stand. Do you love me?'

She nodded but that wasn't enough.

'In what way? And I shall need actual words this time, Hattie Fitzroy, and not a half-hearted, nondescript nod. I am sick and tired of having to read between the lines with proud, independent women who hate to make others feel beholden when, frankly, where the heart is concerned, feeling beholden is surely par for the course. And I would rather wave you goodbye than ever suspect for one moment that you only think you love me when really it is just your natural compassion and overwhelming need to rescue which draws you to me.'

'You are the last man in the world I feel sorry for, Jasper Beaufort.' She lifted her chin, proud, vulnerable but resolute. The indomitable Hattie he loved the most. 'I love you like a woman loves a man.' She nudged him with her elbow. 'To quote a fool that I know who thinks he knows best when he plainly doesn't, I harbour no doubts that it is the all-consuming, need every part of you, hearts and flowers for ever kind.'

'Good.' Jasper stood then hauled her up. 'Then let us stop shilly-shallying, grab life by the lapels, go climb a mountain and pass another milestone together.'

Chapter Twenty-Six

Jasper practically frogmarched her back to Russell Square in determined silence, one hand gripping hers and the other pulling the stubborn Hades to follow. When they arrived at his house, he tied the horse to his railings and they entered via the front door in full view of everyone. Mrs Mimms met them in the hallway and was promptly dismissed when he instructed her to take Izzy and the governess with her so that they could all wheel Jim back to the infirmary. He even helped both of those ladies on with their coats and opened the door for them, then locked it behind them while Hattie stood by completely baffled by what was going on.

'Right then.' He held out his hand. 'Let's go.'

'Where?'

'Upstairs. One might as well be hanged for a sheep as a lamb.'

'I don't follow…' Yet exactly like a sheep she was already following him up the staircase. Which was why when he stopped dead and simultaneously swivelled she walked straight into the cage of his arms.

'I am going to ruin us.' The heat in his eyes was

intense. 'Once and for all and irrevocably. Because frankly, despite all my noble and apparently futile and misguided efforts to the contrary, I have already succeeded in ruining you without all the joy which usually comes from the ruining, and that is the real travesty here. I am sick and tired of trying to be a gentleman, of doing the right thing by you and denying myself when all I really want to do is rip all of your clothes off and have my wicked way with you.' He kissed her. Long, deep and slow.

'In short, in case you are still in any doubt as to where I stand, I am sick to the back teeth of being noble. Of not taking what I want. Of not prioritising my needs over those of others and to hell with the consequences. I want it all, Hattie Fitzroy. All of you—and I want it now.'

While the wayward and much too wanton part of her was thrilled to hear that, the niggling voice of doubt she wanted to ignore wasn't. 'But it is the middle of the afternoon!'

And daylight was so unforgiving.

'It is and we finally have the house to ourselves.' He kissed her again, his hands possessively cupping her bottom and tugging her close so that she could feel the strength of his desire. 'Have you any idea how rare a treat that will be once we are married? What with Izzy and Mrs Mimms—neither of whom are capable of giving me any peace—and Jim, who I am convinced will also be moving in if our daughter gets her way. Because she has her sights set on a brother and wants one immediately. And then there will hopefully, after a decent honeymoon period, be more children. If we can ever snatch another moment alone to make them in between your saintly pursuits at the infirmary and my sinful work at my club. Then before you know it every single one of my empty bedrooms will have someone in them.' He peppered his words with more distracting kisses. Distracting enough that she did not realise her gown was unlaced until he eased it from her shoulders. 'Then the only place we shall ever be able to do this will be in our room.'

Our room. She liked the sound of that.

'I do not recall agreeing to marry you.' It was impossible to say that without smiling. 'Or for that matter, you asking.'

'Are you sure you read my letter? Because I stated my intention to have you for ever in that.' His lips found her neck and she arched against them. 'Never mind that if you don't marry me then you have as good as sealed my death warrant as there will be pistols at dawn tomorrow. If your interfering brother doesn't shoot me for the liberties I am about to take with your person, I suspect your father, mother or sister will.'

He smoothed his hands down her arms and her dress puddled around her feet. Before she tripped on it, he held her hand as she stepped out of it, then flung the garment over the banister while he looked at her. 'Good grief you are beautiful.' And before she could argue that point he took her hand and pressed it flat against his hardness. 'Look what you do to me.'

As there was no denying that she did seem to have a profound effect on him, Hattie kissed him some more while she learned his shape, and when that wasn't enough attacked the buttons on his falls.

He trapped her fingers in his, his green eyes smouldering with so much desire it took her breath away. 'Are you going to marry me?'

'If I have to.' She couldn't resist quoting that back to him and he laughed, then kissed her so thoroughly she had to cling to him or fall backwards down the stairs.

Within seconds there were clothes flying everywhere. He undid her stays, but it was she who tore them off. She removed his waistcoat, but it was Jasper who tugged his shirt over his head. Then he did the same to her chemise as he twisted their positions so that she stood almost naked on the stair above him—only her stockings remained. The final barrier between them and total, brutal honesty.

She assumed he would be all over her, filling his hands with her breasts as he had so many times before when passion erupted between them. Except this time, he didn't. He moved down several steps, his gaze raking her as he savoured the moment. When he finally did touch her again, it was to lovingly trace his fingertip over her hip until he slowly climbed to bring his face level with hers. Even then, he only snaked his arm around her waist as he sighed against her mouth. 'You have no idea how many times I have fantasied about this moment.'

Gently, he lowered her to sit on the stair, and while he kissed her he quickly peeled the silk stocking from her good leg. She would have preferred that he did the same with the remaining stocking, or even better left it on, but of course he didn't. For that he sat too, so that he half faced her, hooked a finger into the top and began to edge it slowly down.

'I sincerely doubt that you are ready to believe this, but I shall say it anyway. Your dratted leg is my favourite leg, Hattie. In fact…' the silk whispered across her knee and she instinctively stiffened '…it is probably one of the things I love most about you because it epitomises all that you are.'

As he revealed her shin, she turned her head away and closed her eyes as he stripped it from her body, not wanting to witness his veiled disappointment. Wanting to believe the kind lies he was telling because he loved her. 'It is a testament to your strength and your character. Your absolute refusal to give up.' His fingers traced her scars before they explored her misshapen bone and wasted muscles. 'If it wasn't for this tenacious and wonky leg, you wouldn't be here and then where would I be?'

His lips replaced his fingers as he kissed a lazy path from her ankle to her knee, then further still up the inside of her thigh. She sucked in a surprised breath when his mouth found the most sensitive part of her, releasing it on a ragged exhale as he tortured that aching bud with his tongue.

Powerless to do anything other than enjoy what he was doing, Hattie gripped one of the spindles on the staircase and moaned her appreciation. Once again, her need hurried her to the edge, and exactly as it had the first time he had touched her so intimately, it refused to wait. Again, too soon but far too late, her body pulsed and shattered as she cried out her pleasure and those shameless cries of ecstasy echoed in the stairwell, reminding her where they were.

In full view of the front door if anyone came through it. Exposed to the entire house if another servant happened past. Only a few yards from the nosy reporters still waiting for gossip outside.

As if he read her mind the smug wretch smiled up at her from between her legs as he pressed a key into her hand. 'I dead bolted the door, the maid doesn't live in and it's Cook's afternoon off. We have the house to ourselves for at least the next half an hour.'

He stood then, the bulge in the half-unbuttoned breeches which hung dangerously low on his hips conclusive evidence that he was as undone by her as she was by him, and with a cocky, sinful smile he slid them off as slowly as he had her stocking.

His aroused body fascinated and intimidated her in equal measure, and she stared at it, drinking every muscle, plane, ridge and thick, solid inch. Fully clothed, Jasper had always been impressive. Naked he was dangerous. Her body thrummed with fresh desire, the ache in her womb returning despite it only just being relieved.

Nerves made her babble. 'Perhaps we should go upstairs?'

He shook his dark head as his big body covered hers. 'I can't wait, Hattie. I need all of you now.'

So she nodded, oddly calm all of a sudden, and ready for the next milestone. 'Then you had best have me as I need all of you too.'

His kisses were tender and reverent as he eased inside her even though she was too ready for there to be any pain. Only at the last moment was there a little discomfort, and even that was so fleeting it was insignificant, because her body blossomed as he filled it. Welcomed the sublime invasion of their joining. Needed it as much as she needed him.

They watched one another as he began to move, slowly at first because he would rather die than hurt her, until her hips developed a mind of their own and rose to meet each stroke. As the passion built within her, she felt it in him too. The muscles of his back bunched beneath her fingers while his heartbeat quickened beneath his ribs.

His kisses became more fevered. His breathing more laboured.

And as the walls of her body tightened around him and she called his name, he told her that he loved her, that he would always love her as stars exploded behind her eyes and he came apart inside her.

'I suppose I could either apply for a special licence or steal you away to Gretna Green like Freddie did Dorothea.' Reluctantly, Jasper was helping her dress, taking more care over how her bosoms were arranged within her bodice than the task warranted. Not that Hattie minded in the slightest. Especially as he had done the same with her stockings, then ripped them off again to make love to her on his dining table. Not that they had the time for another repeat performance. Even if Mrs Mimms had walked Izzy back from the infirmary in Covent Garden via the most long-winded and convoluted route possible, which the unfussy clock on the drawing room fireplace confirmed she had, they would be home at any moment.

'In fact, if I saddle a couple of fast horses, I could have you at the first coaching inn before nightfall.' He raised his dark eyebrows. 'Both literally and figuratively.'

'As tempting as that is…' Hattie lifted her hair so that he could lace up her gown. 'There's a part of me that doesn't want to give the *ton* the satisfaction of us running away or scurrying off to marry behind their backs.' She turned to button his waistcoat. 'It makes it all seem forced and dirty somehow, as if we have done something wrong when the only thing we are guilty of is falling in love, which we did after we became friends.'

'Speak for yourself.' He feigned insult. 'For you it might have happened after we became friends, but I fear my heart was lost the moment I abandoned my carriage on Long Acre and you smiled at me out of the Avondale carriage window.'

'Liar.' She snatched up his coat and snapped it open, then smoothed it over his shoulders as a feeble excuse to touch them again. She had a particular soft spot for those broad shoulders. 'You did not fall in love with me then.'

He turned, holding out a palm full of hairpins and then watched her hastily poke them in her rumpled hair in the best approximation of a style that she could manage under the circumstances. 'I didn't realise it perhaps, but I definitely had an odd moment. I have a clear recollection of you smiling at me and something strange happening in the vicinity of my heart. It did not take me long to be certain of it. In fact...' He rolled his eyes as she bent the last pin as she wrestled it into the scruffy bun, then took it from her to straighten it so she could attempt the manoeuvre again. 'I was a lost cause before you seduced me at the infirmary.'

'I kissed you, I didn't seduce you, Jasper.'

'Au contraire, mademoiselle, I can assure you that they were one and the same thing.'

To prove it he kissed her and thoroughly seduced them both for a few moments before he tore his lips away. 'But I digress...we were discussing wedding plans and the limited, scandalous options available for the ruined.'

'Well after my spectacular steeplechase earlier in front of that odious reporter from the *Bugle*, it will hardly come as a shock to anyone that we have to get married, so we might as well do it in style.'

His dark brows furrowed with interest. 'Go on...'

'If we are ruined anyway, then I say we be proud of it. Make no apologies for who we are or what we do.'

He pondered it for a second then shrugged. 'It is certainly a philosophy which has served me well.'

'Then why don't we surprise the lot of them by doing things properly? Announce our engagement. Have the banns read at St George's in front of all the good *ton* who worship at that church, then marry there with all the pomp and circumstance one would expect from the daughter of a duke and the heir to a dukedom.'

'With Izzy as a bridesmaid, I presume, and Jim as what? An usher? The best man?'

'Oh, that honour should definitely go to my idiot brother. His seal of approval for our match after all the nonsense trying to prevent it. But yes, Jim would make a fine usher and in a couple more weeks he'll be out of his splints.'

Jasper sat on the arm of the sofa and dragged her to sit on his lap. 'While I am all for it, what you are proposing is going to ruffle feathers as that is not the way things are traditionally done. We would be thumbing our noses at convention when misdeeds in Mayfair are supposed to be swept under the carpet and then whispered about for evermore in scathing tones at functions, they are never openly celebrated. Such a thing would be considered grossly improper.'

'When have we ever abided by the laws of propriety, Jasper? And I am not sure if you've noticed, but we both get whispered about anyway whether together or apart. You have been a shocking scandal for years, I have become everyone's favourite object of pity, and all eyes have been on us on the wallflower chairs for weeks.'

Hattie kissed his nose. 'Besides, you are forgetting our secret weapon.' When he blinked baffled, she pressed her lips to his mouth. 'My mother! Nobody throws a party like the Duchess of Avondale and it would be a brave soul in society who turned down one of her invitations. If anyone can pull off the most scandalous wedding of the Season, it is her.

'And talking of my mother...' Hattie dragged him to stand and then led him by the hand out of the drawing room and into the hallway. 'She will be worried about me and so will the rest of the family, so we should probably go and face the music.'

'I suppose we must.' He moaned this as if it was the greatest chore in the world. But as Hattie tried to tug him towards the kitchens and the back door beyond it, he planted his feet.

'If we are going to do things your way, we are going to do it properly.' He jerked his head towards the front door. 'No more hiding. No more skulking around. And absolutely no more pretending that there is nothing going on between us. We are a pair, you and I, and I want the world to know it.'

Hattie sucked in a deep breath then slipped her arm through his. 'Am I to presume we are walking all the way to Mayfair?'

'That shouldn't be a problem for a woman who claims to walk at least a mile a day.' He slanted her a glance filled with mischief and love—and challenge. Because Jasper never, ever felt sorry for her.

'I dare say the fresh air will do us both good.' She marched to the door then held out her hand, smiling. 'I only hope you have the stamina to keep up.'

He took it and laced his fingers in hers before he unlocked the heavy door and flung it wide to the world. 'So do I, Hattie Fitzroy.' Then in case any of the gossips outside were in any doubt about what exactly had been going on between them for the past month, he spun her into his arms and kissed her in front of everyone. 'So do I.'

* * * * *

*If you enjoyed this story,
look out for the next installments in
the Society's Most Scandalous collection*

How to Cheat the Marriage Mart
by Millie Adams
How to Survive a Scandal
by Christine Merrill

*And whilst you're waiting for the next books,
why not check out Virginia Heath's
The Talk of the Beau Monde miniseries*

The Viscount's Unconventional Lady
The Marquess Next Door
How Not to Chaperon a Lady

Read on for a teaser of the next installment of
      Society's Most Scandalous series
      How to Cheat the Marriage Mart
            by Millie Adams

'I do wish to know in truth what you're knitting.'

'Socks,' she said. 'For the children.'

'Oh. *The children.* A worthy cause, no matter who the children are, or where they might be. Worthy cause indeed for a lady of any stripe. The children.'

And it was his mockery that she could not stand. He possessed in his power the ability to ease the woes of many, and yet he mocked her. She might find the Duchess and her efforts to be insufficient, but at least she tried. At least she acted as if she cared a wit for the children. He would mock even the merest scrap of charity when he could not evince any of his own.

'Someone must care for them, do you not think, Lord Curran?' she asked.

'As long as it isn't me.'

'Well no. Why would anyone count on you for such things?'

The corner of his mouth flattened. 'You would speak to me that way?'

'And why not? You spoke to me in similar fashion. You mock me, Lord Curran, as if I am an object of scorn. Or perhaps it is simply that I'm an object beneath your notice. But I see no reason to treat you with deference simply because you have appeared and demanded that I do so with the fit of your boots and breeches and title that means naught to me. I do not want anything from you. I do not wish to marry you, and I do not need a favour from you.'

'But you do need to marry someone,' he said. 'And do you not think that perhaps my good favour might assist you in finding such a match?'

'If the man in question esteems your opinions, I am not certain I wish to know the gentleman at all.'

'But most people at least pretend to esteem my opinions.' He dropped the yarn into her upturned palm. 'You had better return to your knitting.' He looked her over with a brutal efficiency that made her feel stripped bare. 'For the children.'

She tilted her chin up yet higher. 'I should like nothing more. You had better return to… I am not clear what exactly it is you do.'

He smiled. And the impact of it was as a blow to the stomach. 'Why Kitty Fitzroy, surely you know. My one and only function in this life is to create scandal.'